CROSSCURRENTS / MODERN FICTION

HARRY T. MOORE, *General Editor*
MATTHEW J. BRUCCOLI, *Textual Editor*

PREFACE BY

HARRY T. MOORE

EDITED, WITH AN INTRODUCTION BY

HARRIS WILSON

H. G. Wells

THE WEALTH
OF MR. WADDY
A Novel

❧ ❧
❧

SOUTHERN ILLINOIS UNIVERSITY PRESS
CARBONDALE AND EDWARDSVILLE

FEFFER & SIMONS, INC.
LONDON AND AMSTERDAM

CONTENTS

Preface

By Harry T. Moore

It is an exciting adventure to be publishing a hitherto unknown novel by H. G. Wells.

It is also an unfinished novel. Like several other books which fall into that category, however, we have notes and outlines pointing to the completion of *The Wealth of Mr. Waddy*.

Unfinished novels provide an absorbing chapter of literary history. The most famous of them is *The Mystery of Edwin Drood*, which Charles Dickens worked on until the day before his death. The book was apparently only half-finished, but we have some idea of its direction from what Dickens had given away in conversation with several persons, including his younger daughter Kate Perugini and one of his sons-in-law, Charles Collins. Another uncompleted novel is Robert Louis Stevenson's *The Weir of Hermiston*. As far as this book went, it was its author's masterpiece; some critics have doubted whether Stevenson could have sustained the tone. We at least have an idea as to how Stevenson intended to carry on the story, for he explained part of his plan to his daughter-in-law, Mrs. Isobel Strong, who in turn told it to Sir Sidney Colvin; and Colvin wrote a summary of it. There is also F. Scott Fitzgerald's *The Last Tycoon*; like the books of Dickens and Stevenson, it remains incomplete because the author died while working on it. He left a diagram and some notes which were carefully edited by Edmund Wilson to show how Fitzgerald planned to end the story.

That paragraph may have seemed to swing away from Wells and *The Wealth of Mr. Waddy*, but actually it helps to place the book in perspective, although there is the difference that Wells did not die while writing it. In the cases of Dickens, Stevenson, and Fitzgerald, their last novels when finished might have turned out quite differently from the proposed ending; and Wells himself made changes in his *Mr. Waddy* material, for he took parts of it for his notably successful novel, *Kipps* (1905), and made some of them quite different in the process.

Wells himself told the story of the transformation of the *Mr. Waddy* material into Kipps:

> Kipps was written nearly forty years ago. It was planned as a very long abundant book indeed, but in those days, alas, both public and publishers set very definite limits on the length of the novel. My plan had to be reduced and shortened. But out of it walked Kipps with a life of his own.

In short, the novel *Kipps* was only part of the longer book, *The Wealth of Mr. Waddy,* changed (as noted) in the shortening. *Mr. Waddy* is the story of an eccentric invalid, the benefactor of young Kipps. Waddy and Wells's book about him are ably discussed, in detail, in the Introduction that follows, which was written by Professor Harris Wilson of the University of Illinois. Indeed, it was Professor Wilson who put the present book together, from various Wells manuscripts, and made it into a full novel.

His work was done at the Wells Archive, which itself deserves a few words. Located on the University of Illinois campus at Urbana, the Archive was largely the achievement of Gordon N. Ray, who was chairman of the English Department and then Vice President and Provost of the University, before he left to take an executive position with the John Simon Guggenheim Memorial Foundation, of which he is now President and Chairman of the Board. Dr. Ray built the Wells Archive with the enthusiastic help of the late London bookseller Bertram Rota. Harris Wilson was also on hand; from the Archive he has also edited the Wells-Bennett correspondence, *Arnold Bennett and H. G. Wells: A Record of a Personal and a Literary Friendship* (1960).

He has in his Introduction to the present book not only dealt with its background thoroughly, but has provided a full critique of it, so that there is little further left to say about *The Wealth of Mr. Waddy;* I can only agree that it is a work which Wells wrote when he was at his best.

And that is a very good best. We don't rate Wells at the top of the modern novel, yet he has his place, and at this point it

is a good one. In my Foreword to the New American Library
edition of his *Tono-Bungay*, I said, "There are three aspects of
Herbert George Wells as a writer: the educational reformer, the
science fictionist, and the traditional novelist somewhat in the
vein of Dickens." This last aspect is the dominant one in both
Mr. Waddy and *Kipps*. The latter book, incidentally, earned
great praise from Henry James, who thought it was Wells's
masterpiece. James, with whom Wells was later to have a tremendous quarrel over the technique of novel writing, said much
in praise of Kipps in 1905, such as, "But of course you know
yourself how immitigably the thing is done—it is of such a
brilliancy of *true* truth."

Wells years later looked back over the 1915 controversy
with James, in *Experiment in Autobiography* (1934). Wells
felt that some of his own work, whether or not up to James's
standards, would last: "A lot of *Kipps* may pass, some of *Tono-
Bungay*, *Mr. Britling Sees it Through* and *Joan and Peter* and
let me add, I have a weakness for Lady Harmon and for Theo-
dore Bulpington and—. But I will not run on." He admitted that
he often was crude in sketching out scenes and characters, but
"the important point which I tried to argue with Henry James
was that the novel of completely consistent characterization arranged beautifully in a story and painted deep and round and
solid, no more exhausts the possibilities of the novel than the
art of Velásquez exhausts the possibilities of the painted picture."

Fortunately, some of us can enjoy both James and Wells.
And those who like Wells, or who like any excellent modern
novel, now have a chance to read what can rightly be called a
new Wells book, with the added pleasure of a look into the author's workshop. I can only repeat that this is an exciting adventure.

Southern Illinois University
May 1, 1969

Introduction

By Harris Wilson

In the Preface written in 1925 to *Kipps* for the Atlantic Edition of his works, H. G. Wells recalls: *"Kipps* was written in 1903–4. It is only a fragment of a much larger and more ambitious design. The original title was *The Wealth of Mr. Waddy* . . . it was put aside, and I'm afraid destroyed. I seem to remember it as a quite amusing story, but my utmost efforts have failed to unearth the manuscript of those abandoned chapters." Contrary to Wells's recollection, however, those abandoned chapters were not destroyed; they are in the Wells Archive at the University of Illinois, included in the seven years' accumulation of outlines, drafts, and revisions from which *Kipps* finally evolved in 1905.

My chief purpose in this edition is to bring to print that unpublished novel, *The Wealth of Mr. Waddy.* The publication of this extended segment of Wells's early work is justified in itself. It was written as Wells approached the peak of his career as a novelist and gives its own testimony that he was writing at top form. In addition to its intrinsic high quality, *The Wealth of Mr. Waddy* throws important light on a crucial period in Wells's literary development.

The Wealth of Mr. Waddy consists of fifteen chapters (about 35,000 words), which are, with the subsequent revisions I have incorporated, largely finished copy; and twenty chapters (about 15,000 words) which are mainly outlines of projected characters and action, with an occasional fully-developed scene. I have reproduced these outline chapters in order to show how the novel would finally have developed if Wells had completed it. Also, these chapters afford an interesting and extended example of the kind of preliminary scaffolding that Wells would erect for later drafts of his novels. In these chapters, I have indicated the spaces left for subsequent composition by three spaced asterisks.

My text is based on a typescript that Wells sent in January, 1899, to J. B. Pinker, his literary agent, for circulation among publishers, and the subsequent surviving revisions Wells made in that typescript until he abandoned his original conception of the novel, apparently in the latter part of 1899. The holograph sections and inserts in the typescript are, as far as I can determine, revisions of the Pinker typescript intended by Wells to be included in the final version of the novel, but they either never reached his secretary's hands, or, if so, the typed versions have been lost. I have enclosed extended sections of holograph manuscript in pointed brackets and have indicated shorter inserts in the typescript by small caps. I have made no attempt to indicate revisions in the sections of holograph manuscript.

Beginning with Chapter 7, "A Full Account of This Mr. Kipps, His Parentage and Upbringing," in *The Wealth of Mr. Waddy*, there are large segments which Wells used later in *Kipps*. Portions of these segments are quite scantily developed, but since I intend *Mr. Waddy* to be read as a book in itself, not as a supplement to *Kipps*, I have reprinted the *Mr. Waddy* versions. These segments are annotated to enable the reader to identify them and, if he wishes, to compare them with the finished versions in *Kipps*.

In the summer of 1898, H. G. Wells and his wife returned from their first visit to the Continent. Wells set to work finishing *Love and Mr. Lewisham*, but was troubled by "a general sense of malaise"[1] which he attributed to lack of exercise. He set out, accordingly, with his wife on a cycling trip through the south of England, but increasing discomfort and a cold forced him to take lodgings, in the last week of July, in Seaford. His condition worsened, however, and his wife took him by train, "a peevish bundle of suffering," to New Romney where he put himself under the care of Dr. Henry Hick, whom he had met through George Gissing. Dr. Hick diagnosed his illness as degeneration of the kidney, a complication of an injury incurred by Wells ten years before, and advised its removal.

[1] H. G. Wells, *Experiment in Autobiography* (London, 1934), II, 582.

Wells must have been in despair. The operation was to be a risky one with the quite possible result that he would remain a permanent invalid. Since 1887 he had been an apparent consumptive, dreading in every cough "the peculiar tang of blood." A promising academic career had been ended in 1893 by a near fatal hemorrhage. Forced to turn to writing as a full-time career, he had written in the subsequent five years six novels, at least forty short stories, and scores of popular articles. These had brought him the reputation in publishing circles of a "coming man," and he was making his first bid as a serious novelist in *Love and Mr. Lewisham.* Once again, or so he must have thought, his keen ambition and demonstrated talent were to be thwarted by his body's weakness.

His luck still held, however. The London surgeon who was to perform the operation decided that the offending kidney, in Wells's words, "had practically taken itself off" and canceled the operation. Wells's recovery was rapid, and he felt himself again reprieved. His sense of relief and consequent high spirits during his convalescence are illustrated by a series of "picshuas" in *Experiment in Autobiography.*[2] One panel dated October 8, 1898, and entitled "Reminiscences of August" portrays the various stages of his illness and convalescence in New Romney, ending with a picture of Wells in a cotton hat over the caption "Noo 'at—not a 'alo this time after all." More relevant to my purpose here, however, is another sketch, dated October 5, showing Wells sitting on an egg with the caption, "This egg was laid at New Romney in September." The egg hatches, a small figure is revealed, and upon being addressed by Wells, "Hullo. What's your name?" answers, "Kipps, sir."

The Wealth of Mr. Waddy, then, in which Kipps is the central character, was conceived and for the most part written when Wells was in a euphoric state after a brush with, at the worst, death or, at the best, a prolonged invalidism. That he transferred his high spirits to the writing of the novel is obvious in his letters to J. B. Pinker.[3] In early October he writes of "plans for the great novel on the Dickens' plan." In a letter of October 27, he writes: "But the new novel, *The Wealth of Mr. Waddy,* will be

[2] *Experiment in Autobiography,* II, 586–95.
[3] Photocopies of the manuscript letters of Wells to Pinker, his literary agent, are on file in the Wells Archive at the University of Illinois.

—I say it sincerely and hope you will avoid unnecessary levity— the finest thing I ever wrote. I don't like leaving it." On December 4, his enthusiasm is still strong, but somewhat alloyed: "It is quite unlike any other stuff I have done and I'm writing at times with loud guffaws. Whether other people will find it amusing is another matter. The attempt to get comic relief into *Love and Mr. Lewisham* certainly failed. This book so far is solid comic relief."

Wells's effervescent state was, as such states always are, transient. His health was still precarious, and he had been told by his doctors that he must live in a dry climate on sand or gravel. He decided to build a house on the southern coast of England specially designed for easy access to all rooms by wheel chair. On December 10 we find him writing to Pinker in dejection. He is having difficulty obtaining a site for his house, and his financial affairs are worrying him. He has had some stories rejected by *Strand Magazine* and *Pearson's*; he is especially bitter toward the *Strand*: "They want stories about comic human beings—The Wall-Eyed Grocer and so forth. . . . I shall have to do the bloody things, but it will cripple my reputation with educated people. . . . I shall have to set aside *The Wealth of Mr. Waddy* to do it. And about that—what confidence can I feel that when it's done it will be any good to me? *Love and Mr. Lewisham* is a drug. It's not like Jacobs and it's not like Jules Verne, and I must be dead and stinking according to the rules before anyone will find any merit in its being like me. Nobody seems to have been got ready for it. It may hang about and block the way for the W. of Mr. W. for months."

Five days later, however, Wells writes to Pinker matter-of-factly that *The Wealth of Mr. Waddy* will be "in a state to negotiate" after January, 1899. As it turns out, he is able to send the manuscript to Pinker on January 16: "By this post the stuff of *The Wealth of Mr. Waddy*. I will be glad if you will read it over and if it impresses you as too incomplete to give a hopeful impression, return it to me. But if you think it will look promising to an Editor Beast, then I shall be glad if it can be arranged serially . . . I think it is stuff *They*[4] may like." Wells conceives of *The Wealth of Mr. Waddy* as being about one hundred thousand words in length in finished form and would like £1000 for the serial rights.

[4] Wells is referring here to the reading public.

Wells makes two more references to *The Wealth of Mr. Waddy* in his correspondence with Pinker in January, 1899. On the twenty-second he is willing to accept £800 for serial rights to the novel. On the twenty-sixth, he disagrees with Pinker on the matter of illustrations: "I think you're wrong about Waddy not standing illustrations. It has a number of strongly marked characters and a good character artist might do marvels." The last reference to *The Wealth of Mr. Waddy* comes on March 22: "Can you get £750 out of McClure for *The W. of Mr. W.* for American book and serial rights? Delivery Jan 1st. If so, I think I'd close. But for more prosaic prices I don't think there's need to jump." Then, after more than a year's silence concerning either *The Wealth of Mr. Waddy* or *Kipps* in the existing correspondence, Wells writes cryptically to Pinker on April 23, 1900, "I dunno. Just at present *Kipps* turns out well," and from this point onward, Wells refers to the novel as *Kipps,* never *The Wealth of Mr. Waddy. The Wealth of Mr. Waddy,* in title and, as we know from the published version of Kipps, in major substance, has been discarded.

Wells gives the reason for that decision in 1925. "A whole introductory book was written before Kipps himself came upon the scene. . . . But it became clear to the writer by the time he had brought Kipps and Chitterlow together that he had planned his task upon too colossal a scale. There was no way of serializing so vast a book as he had in hand and no way of publishing it that held out any hope of fair payment for the work that remained for him to do. Now books are meant to be read, and there is no interest in writing them unless you believe they will get to readers. So *Kipps* was clipped off short to the dimensions of a practicable book."[5]

Wells's point is a good one. *Kipps,* as it stands now, comes to approximately one hundred and ten thousand words. If Wells had developed *The Wealth of Mr. Waddy* according to his original plan, the novel would have reached a length of well over two

[5] *Works,* Atlantic Edition (28 vols., London, 1924–27), VIII, ix. When Wells recalls that a "whole introductory book was written before Kipps himself came upon the scene," his memory is at fault. Kipps plays an important role in the opening chapter of *The Wealth of Mr. Waddy* as observer and commentator. He appears again in Chapter 4, "Mr. Chitterlow," before virtually taking over the novel in Chapter 7, "A Full Account of This Mr. Kipps, His Parentage and Upbringing."

hundred thousand words and would have been unmarketable in 1900. In this instance, at least, one can regret the disappearance of part issues and three-decker novels before Wells could take advantage of them. There is good evidence in *Kipps*, and most of Wells's best novels, that he would have found that Victorian method of composition quite congenial.

It is worthwhile at this point to consider the differences between the story of Kipps as Wells first conceived it in 1898 and the novel as it was finally published in 1905. In both versions of the Kipps story, the central fact is Kipps's inheritance of a fortune from Mr. Waddy. In *Kipps*, Mr. Waddy is Kipps's paternal grandfather. Kipps, an illegitimate child because of Mr. Waddy's opposition to his son's marriage to Kipps's mother, has been given by his mother in his infancy to her brother and his wife, Old Kipps and Mrs. Kipps. His mother dies, and Kipps is reared by his uncle and aunt. On his death bed, Mr. Waddy repents of his ill treatment of his son, Kipps's father, who has, in the meantime, died in Australia. This melodramatic state of affairs (redolent of one of Muriel's romantic novels in *Mr. Waddy*) results in Kipps's receiving his rightful inheritance at the propitious moment when he has been "swapped" at the Folkestone Drapery Emporium. Mr. Waddy never appears in *Kipps*. Kipps first hears of him from Mr. Bean, Waddy's lawyer, when he tells Kipps of his inheritance. The only remnant, aside from his wealth, of the Waddy of *Mr. Waddy* in *Kipps* is a scrapbook of his letters to the *Times*.

Kipps's relationship with his benefactor in *Mr. Waddy*, on the other hand, is purely fortuitous. His inheritance results from the chance of his walking up a path on the cliff face of the Folkestone Leas at the moment a runaway bath chair careens with Mr. Waddy down that path toward disaster. Kipps saves Mr. Waddy's life, and Mr. Waddy, because Kipps is "the only person to do him a disinterested service in the last twenty years," makes him his heir.

The most important difference between the two versions, however, is the development in *Mr. Waddy* of the characters of Mr. Waddy, Chitterlow, and Muriel. In *Kipps*, as we have noted, Mr. Waddy is merely an off-stage convenience. In *Mr. Waddy*, he dominates eight out of the first eleven chapters of the novel. We are told in detail of his volatile (to understate it) disposition, his way of living, the accident that crippled him for life, the source of his wealth, and his death. Muriel, the shadowy wife of Chitterlow in *Kipps*, known to the reader mainly through Chitterlow's frequent assertion that she possesses "the finest completely untrained contralto voice in England," emerges fully developed in *Mr. Waddy*. Shaped by an omnivorous reading of sentimental novels, she inserts herself into Mr. Waddy's household and becomes a kind of pseudo niece to him, only to alienate herself from him permanently by her elopement with Chitterlow, whom Mr. Waddy despises. Chitterlow himself is a major character in *Kipps*, but in *Mr. Waddy*, Wells gives him another full dimension. At least a part of Chitterlow's motive for courting and marrying Muriel is his expectation that she, and in turn he, will benefit from the wealth of Mr. Waddy. When, in spite of all efforts, Chitterlow is consistently disappointed in that expectation during Waddy's lifetime, he attempts to gain it by a manipulation of Waddy's various wills after his death.

From the point at which Kipps learns of his inheritance, the two versions of Kipps follow the same broad lines of development.[6] Kipps, with Mr. Waddy's fortune, is freed from his life as a draper's assistant and aspires to a life in "society," mainly through his acquaintance with Chester Coote and his engagement to Miss Helen Walshingham. He eventually finds himself temperamentally and intellectually unable to cope with their world and incontinently elopes with a childhood sweetheart, now a domestic servant, Ann Pornick. Their plans for a new house and an existence of comparatively genteel leisure, however, are shattered when it comes to light that Miss Walshingham's brother, whom Kipps has entrusted with the management of his money, has embezzled it. A small residue remains, however, and that, with the rather gratuitous returns from Kipps's share in

---

[6] There are three major exceptions in *Mr. Waddy*. One, rather fully developed, is the pursuit of Kipps by Daisy Dorcas, also a draper's assistant, to whom he has written a letter containing a facetious proposal of marriage before he learns of his inheritance. The other two, merely sketched, concern Chitterlow's collaboration with "the anaemic Binyon" on a successful play, and Kipps's engagement of Mrs. Chudleigh Mornington to instruct him and Ann in social manners. The major exception in *Kipps* is the introduction of Masterman, the socialist. In 1925 (*Works*, VIII, ix) Wells states that "after Kipps had been ruined by young Mr. Walshingham, there were to have been the adventures of young Mr. Walshingham as a fugitive in France," but there is no evidence that Wells ever actually launched the story.

Chitterlow's successful play, allows them to buy a book shop and revert contentedly to the lower middle-class life of their origins.

The Wealth of Mr. Waddy, had it been completed, would have been what J. D. Beresford in his study of Wells calls a novel of "sheer exuberance."[7] Wells himself, as we have seen, feels as he is writing it that it is "solid comic relief." Yet it is curious and significant to note that the characters common to *Mr. Waddy* and *Kipps*, aside from Kipps himself and Ann Pornick, undergo an unmistakable lightening as they pass from the early version to the later. Chitterlow in *Kipps* is little more than a well-intentioned buffoon; in *Mr. Waddy* he approaches the sinister at times, as witness the scene in Chapter 11, "Postmortem," in which he attempts to manipulate Mr. Waddy's will to his advantage with Waddy's corpse lying in the next room. Old Kipps and Mrs. Kipps in the final version are very lightly drawn, except for their enmity toward the Pornicks; in *Mr. Waddy* they are portrayed in caustic detail as examples of middle-class snobbery. Chester Coote, a rather simple-minded social climber in *Kipps*, is given a lascivious leer in the sketch Wells makes of him for *Mr. Waddy*. The reader is inclined to like and sympathize with, to pity rather than censure, Helen Walshingham in *Kipps*; Wells intends to preclude any such feelings in *Mr. Waddy* when in a preliminary sketch of her character he writes ". . . putting it crudely, she is an overeducated aesthetic prig."

The most interesting character, however, in a comparison of the two versions is Mr. Waddy himself, who does not make an appearance in *Kipps*. It is apparent from Wells's letters to Pinker that he intended to create in Mr. Waddy a purely comic figure; it is just as apparent to the reader of the novel that he does not succeed. Mr. Waddy, it is true, does amuse at times. His denunciations of the behavior of his fellow-creatures and his splenetic correspondence with tradesmen and organizations make entertaining reading. Wells's account of Waddy's conduct under the determined blandishments of Muriel is on the whole hilarious. But we see him as essentially a lonely, embittered old man railing against his "Luck" and a "Perfect Ass of a World." There is nothing funny about his death. In this connection it is of interest that in the series of "picshuas" of October 8, 1898, depict-

[7] J. D. Beresford, *H. G. Wells* (London, 1915).

ing Wells's convalescence from his serious kidney ailment, one portrays him being pushed in a bath chair, Waddy's mode of conveyance, by his wife.[8] The best explanation of the failure of Mr. Waddy to "come off" as a completely successful comic figure might well be that in Waddy Wells is projecting himself as he would be if permanently crippled, and the possibility of just that eventuality in his own life at the time he was writing prevented him subconsciously from creating the comic character that he avowedly intended to create. Wells himself was adept at invective, as many people during his lifetime learned to their cost, and his writing gives ample evidence of his eye for mankind's absurdities and pretensions. Waddy's attitude toward Muriel and her sentimental novels, as we shall see, is Wells's own. In Mr. Waddy, he was "exploring that cell of Being called Wells,"[9] an exploration that was a major preoccupation with him throughout his life.

The lightening of tone between *Mr. Waddy* and *Kipps* should not be pressed too hard, of course. The character of Kipps remains constant in the two, and if Wells had finished *Mr. Waddy* according to his original conception, it would still have been a comic novel—more a comic novel, in fact, in the Dickensian sense, than *Kipps*. But the juxtaposition of the two versions does offer further evidence to support the contention of some critics that the early Wells was much "darker" than the later. Wells, more than most writers, drew his materials from his own personal reactions and experiences, and the world could not have seemed a very happy place to him in his adolescence and early manhood. The clearing up of his health after 1899, his increasing stature as a literary man and especially as a social analyst, his improved financial standing—all these brought changes in his attitude toward life and consequently in his work. As his social criticism widened and became more authoritative, objective and outspoken, his critical tone became less pessimistic; his characters tended to lose their depth and become abstractions. *The Wealth of Mr. Waddy*, 1898, and *Kipps*, 1905, reflect this tendency.

Another significant element in *Mr. Waddy* that disappears

---

[8] *Experiment in Autobiography*, II, 589.
[9] *Arnold Bennett and H. G. Wells*, ed. Harris Wilson (London, 1960) p. 47. Wells used the phrase in a letter to Bennett dated July 5, 1900.

entirely in the transition to *Kipps* is the satirical reflection of
Wells's views on contemporary fiction developed during his ten-
ure as fiction critic of the *Saturday Review* from 1895 to 1897.[10]
We see this reflection in Muriel, in her addiction to popular
novels and her determination to see life in the distorted image
she derives from them. Wells's general attitude toward the popular novel and its readers can be illustrated by his statement in an
article concerning the extreme popularity of Marie Corelli: "For-
merly the illiterate could not read. But lately [through the Education Act of 1870] we . . . have taught them to do so. In our
simplicity, we had thought that English Literature would be
enough for them to go on with, and with English Literature we
stocked our public libraries. We were quite astonished when recent statistics showed us that the thing was a failure, for we had
supposed that being able to spell out pages of type must surely
create good taste. 'What, then,' we cried, '*do* the illiterate read?'
Other statistics make answer. In the sale lists of the booksellers
we read the names of Hocking, Caine, Du Maurier, Maclaren,
Crockett and Corelli; after each name, certain appalling numer-
als. As we read them, we bow our heads."[11]

In a sense, *The Wealth of Mr. Waddy* is Wells's *Joseph
Andrews* or *Northanger Abbey*. Superficially, all the essential
trappings of the sentimental novel are there: the rich, misan-
thropic old "uncle"; the artless, girlishly endearing "niece"; the
dashing, impecunious lover; the sympathetic housekeeper; and,
if all else fails to bring about a satisfactorily romantic conclusion,
a charming little "grandnephew" to brighten and soften the old
man's declining years. But Wells throws all askew by making
reality, not sentimentalism, dictate the plot. Mr. Waddy sees
Muriel quite clearly as the artificial, empty-headed young woman
she is, and his misanthropy is quite impervious to her persistent
overtures; the romantic elopement of Muriel and Chitterlow
arouses in him only rage and disgust; Mrs. Satsuma is a complete
failure as a go-between; and young Master Chitterlow, who is

---

[10] For a general discussion of Wells's contributions to the *Saturday Review*, see Gordon N. Ray's "H. G. Wells Tries to Be a Novelist," *English Institute Essays*, 1959 (New York, 1960), pp. 109–
12. Mr. Ray also provides a provisional list of Wells's contributions
in "H. G. Wells's Contributions to the *Saturday Review*," *The
Library* (March, 1961), pp. 29–36.

[11] "Our Lady of Pars.," *Saturday Review*, September 26, 1896,
p. 337.

actually a very horrid little boy, instead of restoring "family" unity shatters it irretrievably.

Wells portrays Muriel as a victim of the popular novelists she reads so voraciously, one of those "millions of readers who are so ignorant of life that they are contemptuous of its probabilities."[12] Mr. Waddy judges her accurately when he exclaims, "Girl! She's no girl, she's the Frankenstein monster of all the women scribblers in the world, she's a circulating library on the bust!" And Muriel is beyond redemption. When, after the fiasco of little Harry's meeting with Mr. Waddy, she still persists in her attempts at a reconciliation, and Mr. Waddy asks her, "Why . . . *don't* you chuck it?" she replies, uncomprehending, "I've nothing to chuck."

Finally, a comparison of *Mr. Waddy* and *Kipps* provides a concrete explanation of the general dissatisfaction critics have expressed with *Kipps* as it finally appeared. Arnold Bennett complains about a lack of "artistic righteousness."[13] In Vincent Brome's judgment, "*Kipps* was good, very good indeed, but it wasn't great and it might have been,"[14] and Gordon N. Ray, speaking of *Love and Mr. Lewisham* and *Tono-Bungay* as well, concludes "it cannot be claimed that they are harmonious and consistent works of art."[15] In comparison with the inventive and skillfully executed opening of *Mr. Waddy*, the beginning of *Kipps* must be accounted relatively drab and unimaginative. Old Kipps and Mrs. Kipps lose a great deal of vividness, and I would place Chitterlow's loss of effectiveness between *Mr. Waddy* and *Kipps* as high as 50 per cent. A serious flaw in *Kipps* is the incredibility of Chitterlow's becoming, as Wells presents him, a successful playwright; the sudden success of *The Pestered Butterfly* strikes the reader, to say the least, as unconvincing and, in even the most superficial terms, gratuitous, since Kipps has no need of the money which the play brings him. The whole of Book III in *Kipps,* in fact, seems designed to give Wells a chance to exploit his own experiences in building Spade House at Sand-

[12] "Popular Writers and Press Critics," *Saturday Review,* February 8, 1896, p. 145.
[13] *Arnold Bennett and H. G. Wells,* p. 127.
[14] Vincent Brome, *H. G. Wells* (London, 1951), p. 101.
[15] Ray, "H. G. Wells Tries to Be a Novelist," p. 125. Mr. Ray's discussion of Wells's pattern of "hurried overproduction" in his major early novels to their artistic detriment applies with special force to *Kipps.*

gate and to provide a commonplace happy ending for the novel. Wells admits that Book III was "scamped" in a letter to Pinker in June of 1904: "*Kipps* is quite done now. . . . Book III is a thing of shreds and patches, but it is quite handsomely brought off."

There is a more basic reason for dissatisfaction with *Kipps*, however. After all if the novel were "sheer comic relief" according to Wells's first conception of *Mr. Waddy*, criticism of structural defects in *Kipps* would be as pointless as in *Tristam Shandy*. But in March 1903, writing again to Pinker, Wells describes *Kipps* solemnly as "the complete study of a life in relation to England's social conditions." The fact that the sheer exuberance of *Mr. Waddy* underwent a sea change to the social purposiveness of *Kipps* does not, of course, in itself condemn *Kipps*. Indeed, Masterman's strictures on society have the poetic sting that made Wells's social commentary so compelling to his young contemporaries, and when Wells himself takes the stage to comment directly on the "clipped and limited lives" of Kipps and Ann, the reader is reminded of the absurdity of applying too rigidly our own contemporary convention of the "silent" author. The idea of using little Artie Kipps's vicissitudes as an indirect commentary on injustice and cruelty in English social life is a very good one. The trouble with *Kipps* is that Wells attempted to superimpose one kind of novel on another kind, and did not entirely succeed. We are left with a rich and brilliant picture of Kipps in a frame legitimate enough in itself, but somewhat awry.

As I indicated earlier, however, the principal interest of *The Wealth of Mr. Waddy* is the extensive, previously unpublished sample it gives of Wells's humorous writing as he approached the height of his career as a novelist. The picture of Kipps himself, as he observes Mr. Waddy for the first time on the Folkestone Leas, is as appealing as any in *Kipps*. In spite of my reservations concerning Mr. Waddy as a purely comic figure, he deserves an honorable place in the gallery of Wells's characters. Muriel, laying siege, "pure *Imitatio Pippae*," to an obstreperous Mr. Waddy is memorable. And Chitterlow writing his play, shouting "Oh Damn Construction!" must, it seems to me, have a place among the more delightful moments in English comic fiction. *The Wealth of Mr. Waddy* provides further abundant confirmation of Henry James's opinion in his statement to Wells, "Mind you that the restriction that I lay on your work, still leaves

that work more convulsed with life and brimming with blood
than any it is given me nowadays to meet."[16]

My principal resource in this study has been the H. G. Wells
Archive at the University of Illinois. I am indebted to the John
Simon Guggenheim Memorial Foundation for the grant that allowed me time from administration and teaching to launch this
edition and other projects, and to the University of Illinois Research Board for grants supporting my research in the H. G.
Wells Archive. Mrs. Charles H. Shattuck, former custodian of
the H. G. Wells Archive, gave invaluable aid in isolating unpublished material from the *Kipps* manuscript and identifying successive revisions. Dr. Gordon N. Ray, Sir Rupert Hart-Davis,
and Professor Gwynne Evans have been kind enough to read the
manuscript in its various stages and give me the benefits of their
comments and suggestions. I am greatly indebted to Professor
Matthew Bruccoli for his advice on handling the numerous textual problems involved. I am, of course, finally responsible for
all aspects of this edition. Only Catherine Wells and Wells's later
secretaries could fully appreciate the services my wife has given
as typist in preparing this manuscript for publication.

University of Illinois
April 22, 1969

[16] *Henry James and H. G. Wells,* ed. Leon Edel and Gordon
N. Ray (London, 1958), p. 168.

THE WEALTH OF MR. WADDY

❧ I ❧

Prelude

THE very first time that Mr. Kipps saw Mr. Waddy was on one Sunday afternoon A WEEK OR SO BEFORE WHIT-SUNTIDE scarcely THREE WEEKS before Mr. Waddy died. It was upon the Leas at Folkestone; THE SEASON WAS BUDDING HANDSOMELY; Mr. Kipps was wearing his new tail coat for the first time, and Mr. Waddy was in a violent rage and using shocking language.

It was A BRILLIANT AFTERNOON and that broad spread of grass along the cliff edge, which is Folkestone's especial glory, was crowded with admirably dressed people. Some of them were clearly the very best sort of people indeed and very rare, for Folkestone is so fashionable that before all other watering places it claims the adjective; and others were at least of the second best sort, and others again of the third best sort, and so on; few were really common ordinary people in all that brilliant multitude. The band was playing Sacred Music and the sun and the sea and the cliffs of France and the clothes of all the people shone resplendent. The air was full of the rustle of costly and correct costumes, full of subdued murmurs, and everybody was behaving with that furtive hauteur that becomes the English better quality so well. And through it all, I say, regardless of it all, smote Mr. Waddy blaspheming.

The impression received by Mr. Kipps was brief and vivid. His private concern with the shadow of his LEFT coat tail—he was uncertain whether his handkerchief did not make IT stick out in an unbecoming manner—prevented his observing the little wave of sensation that rippled through this multitude towards him and marked the coming bath chair for a remarkable thing. UNTIL suddenly his ears were smitten . . .

He looked up amazed at the indecorum, and beheld an elderly black-coated man with a singularly peaceful face and expressionless blue eyes, pulling the chair, and therein—! A mouthing face, a sort of MALE Gorgon in a silk hat, a face distorted and awful, framed in a Medusoid halo of spiky dingy hair. The crooked fingers clutched forward in strenuous unavailing appeal. And from the convulsive mouth came an enormous torrent of hoarse voice in which there floated, distended and horrible, the abused and writhing semblance of words . . .

Such words!

They filled Mr. Kipps with a vision of imminent thunderbolts, and the police. They roared to a climax and passed and sank, and Mr. Kipps stood aghast regarding the back of a receding bath chair.

"Crimes!" he whispered slowly, recovering. "And 'im a invalid!"

He caught the eye of a young man dressed in striped flannels. It seemed a sympathetic eye.

"He's a corker!" said Mr. Kipps. "I'm *blowed* if he ain't!"

He laughed, to express amused disgust, and then he perceived the young man inclining to "distance" and recollected that it was Sunday afternoon and a fashionable occasion, and that "crimes" and "corker" consorted ill with such a get-up as his. His cheeks and ears glowed instantly at the thought but he did his best to sustain an appearance of *sang-froid*. His gape became a well-bred stare, his limp left hand posed itself upon his thigh, and avoiding any further address to the young man in flannels he turned about and proceeded on his way, whistling faintly and whirling his brand new cane . . .

He wished heartily that he had not spoken in quite that way. It was "low"—nothing more nor less. But he had been surprised out of himself, out of his Sunday self, that is, INTO WEEKDAY DEMEANOR. As indeed anyone might have been surprised.

"††††††," said Mr. Waddy in something between a hoarse whisper and a roar. " x x x x x . You - - - - - - fool. You § § § fool! You (Printer three blacks [Wells's note.]) fool! Do you hear? I want to go home! *I want to go home.*"

"Of all the ††††††!" cried Mr. Waddy appealing to circumambient being. "This comes of finding jobs for a deaf man! This comes of doing kind deeds. # # # # # #."

"If ever I do a kind deed again MAY I BE - - - - # * / / ' ' ' ' ' ! ! ."

(PRINTER, SPACE THESE WORDS [Wells's note.])

"Ugh! you *old* fool! You—"

The deaf old man trudged along regardless of these things. His face was very beautiful and peaceful, his mild blue eyes were fixed on the remote white cliffs of Dover. He was thinking of the sudden comfort that had come upon him. He had found a situation at last that he could fill.

For a week he had given satisfaction. Mr. Waddy had told him as much only the day before. He was a good old man, he knew, and he had always kept himself very respectable and so things were coming right for him; and he trudged along resolved to go to the very end of the Leas and give good value for his money. Mr. Waddy was really the kindest old gentleman, and the living—never had the good old man eaten such stunning meals before. Up to your neck so to speak—every time. This very afternoon fruit pie with cream—real cream! Yes, indeed, things were coming right at last. And how it showed one that in spite of temporary trials—

He was aroused from these pleasant reflections by the impact of Mr. Waddy's hat brim. It struck his own hat and knocked that forward. He caught them both with his hand. Mr. Waddy's dropped and he stooped to pick it up. But the bath chair had not stopped and the way was a little downhill.

So it ran him down and turned his stoop into a complicated stagger.

He came into something between kneeling and sitting on the two hats, and his face expressed extreme surprise.

"Yah!" said Mr. Waddy, still in that awful hoarse voice. "*Now* do you hear? ! $x^x x^{x\,x}$ ؍."

(Printer, print these as irregularly as possible as in copy. [Wells's note.])

(Arrange blacks in a second line with inverted commas at each end. [Wells's note.])

The good old man had expected nothing but sympathy for his misfortune. The only aspect of Mr. Waddy he had permitted himself to perceive hitherto was a sympathetic one. There had been transient doubts of course, but he had dismissed them. He tried not to think that Mr. Waddy's inaudible lips could say such things as they seemed to be saying.

He struggled to his feet with a shaky alacrity, replaced his own hat—it was battered now and in his agitation he gave it a rakish curve unsuited to his years—and brushed the other against the nap with his sleeve as he approached Mr. Waddy.

"Jest a minute, Sir," quavered the old man, still clinging bravely to his optimism and accompanying his words with a mild smile of self-depreciation THAT SLANTED ATHWART HIS FACE. "Jest a minute. It ain't no good your talking, you know, till my trumpet's out. Nary *bit* o' good, it ain't."

And having put Mr. Waddy's hat on with a little confirmatory pat, he fumbled for his ear trumpet.

"Now," he said in the bright cheerful tone that is so good for invalids. "Now I can hear you nicely. Go on, Sir. *I* can hear . . ."

Mr. Kipps saw them going back home just as he was hesitating whether it would be fooling away money to take a chair. If he took a chair the projection of his LEFT coat tail (if so be that it did project) would not show. But he forgot that question at the sight of Mr. Waddy's return.

The bath chair clove its way through the promenaders about the bandstand; a silence went before it and followed after it, and people drew aside from it as from some infectious thing . . .

Mr. Waddy's exhausted wrath scowled from beneath a rakish obliquity of brim, and the old man's hat was still jauntily cocked over one eye. But the old man's face had the solemnity of one who has come upon terrible things. It was a striking effect to watch their approach, to see that jovial outline grow nearer, grow distincter, reveal at last these faces of wrath and terror. Disillusionment! A person with a turn of mind for things symbolical might have made this, as Hawthorne says in those charming notes of his, "symbolical of something." It struck even Mr. Kipps as a significant and memorable vision, though his bias for symbolism was slight. It gave him an anecdote for the supper table that night.

"I do *not* think," he said, "that I ever 'eard worse language than I 'eard a old gen'man using up on the Leas thisarf'noon. *Never*! AND I'VE 'EARD SOME TIDY LANGUAGE TOO—ONE TIME'N NOTHER."

✤ 2 ✤

The Habits of Mr. Waddy

MR. Waddy had not deliberately acquired this habit of low and violent language. It had come to him in the days of his poverty when he had been an engineer, and most of it had come to him east of Suez. It had indeed been forced upon him. There, as people in this country are regretfully discovering, it has been so long the custom for Englishmen to address their native subordinates in ELIZABETHAN language, that a gentler vocabulary is not understood by them. You say to this one, Go, and he goeth not, but if you speak with a vigour that would be regarded as objectionable in England he does your bidding with cheerful acquiescence.

Even in his early days Mr. Waddy had been an irascible man, and the complications ensuing upon the assault of a native stoker had seriously imperilled his professional prospects. He returned to England with an alleged invention—a thing with which an irascible man should not have dealings. (Better far to throw the thing away and keep your peace of mind.) The patent fizzled out and there was an epoch of technical journalism <precarious, and the electric light. This liaison with journalism did him no good; it is a raging calling and offers no such inducements to restraint as the control of

machinery and native stokers, both in their several ways frag-
ile and explainable things. He let himself go. So his natural
dis>position to choler was ENHANCED as the years went by.
He inclined to a theory of luck, a scornful pessimism. PUT-
TING IT CRUDELY THE Luck was against him and this was a
Perfect Ass of a World. THEREFORE, WHAT WAS THE GOOD?
Yet he kept A QUARRELSOME face to things nevertheless,
SPENDING MUCH OF HIS CHOLER QUITE USEFULLY UPON
THE ADMIRALITY, THE WRITERS OF BOOKS FOR REVIEW, AND
SUCHLIKE ENEMIES OF MAN UNTIL HIS TRICYCLE ACCI-
DENT OCCURRED.

His tricycle accident happened when he was forty-five
AND GAVE THE FINISHING TOUCH TO HIS CONSTITUTION.
The brake would not work on Putney Hill. He had known it
was out of order but he had been too impatient to dismount.
"Just my Luck," he said with a savage satisfaction as the
people shouted and the machine went faster and faster. For
awhile he swept downward, accelerating rather than attempting to retard his whirling pedals; and then grimly resolving to
snatch a share in his own destruction, he gripped his handles
tighter, deflected his machine abruptly and charged resolutely
at an unfortunate BUT NO DOUBT OBNOXIOUS 'bus horse.
"*Now* then," were the last words between his clenched teeth
before he was knocked insensible . . .

He found that some of his luck still remained to be
worked out when he came to his senses again three weeks
after. He was bandaged from head to foot and a log from his
waist downwards, and very gently they broke it to him that he
was now not only crippled for life but—a rich man.

They explained more fully. Death had fallen in with the
whim of an old schoolfellow who had made him residuary
legatee, and had removed four intervening expectants. He was
suddenly endowed with land and houses near Folkestone, a
share in a steam laundry at Surbiton and nearly forty thousand pounds'-worth of stock and shares. As the story proceeded he became silent. At the end he remained silent under
their eyes . . .

He became aware of attention. He perceived he had a duty
to himself in the matter. "It's just my xxx luck," he said at
last. "What good can it do me now?"

Having adopted this attitude he felt bound to adhere to it.

He would not go to see what was visible of his property for some years, and he accepted his income under protest. "Chuck it out of the x window," he said hoarsely. "What good can it do me now?"

But it was not chucked out of the x window. Perceiving every one else disposed to overlook this renunciation, he finally overlooked it himself. <He admitted, with needless curses, that he must adapt himself to his new conditions. He took counsel with the doctors and his own tastes. His paper, already moribund, had died with his accident. He determined upon a life henceforth of luxurious ease.> He organized a peripatetic household under A GODSEND, one Mrs. Satsuma, who professed a CONVENIENT selective deafness, <could cook admirably, and was otherwise energetic and capable. He was introduced to the bath chair. He took furnished houses by the year, moving> from one place of resort to another. <In the course of a year or so he had so settled down to this manner of life that he could wonder how it felt not to be an invalid and rich. His able-bodied poverty became an almost incredible reminiscence.

The last palpable vestiges of Mr. Waddy's self-control seems to have vanished when he killed the horse. (I should have mentioned that he killed that horse.) Thereafter the pursuit of his days, the solace of his leisure, was rage. It is not sufficiently recognized, it is a fact that one of the most sedulously respected conventions in literature conceals, that to have a good, hearty towering rage is a natural and healthy craving of the ordinary human being. The convention is to find some exciting cause, to call it righteous indignation or unreasonable conduct, as though it had anything to do with reason and was not a perfectly straightforward organic desire. Certainly for a modern, Mr. Waddy carried this pleasure of raging to excess.>

Commonly he began over the details of his morning toilet. He was an ill man to shave, and his collar stud boggled its buttonhole at the peril of its life. AND THEN the monotony, or some such feature, of his breakfast WOULD GIVE him AN opportunity. HE WOULD LIFT OFF HIS COVER, AND STARE, AND THEN IN THE TONE OF ONE WHO PROTESTS AGAINST INTOLERABLE INJUSTICE HE WOULD BEGIN—

"D——nation! is there no other meat in the world but EGGS AND kidneys?—Kidneys and eggs—kidneys and eggs! On an everlasting background of bacon. ˣ ˣ ˣ ₓ ˣ ₓ. I'm bursting with eggs. I shall start laying. AND AS FOR KIDNEYS. One would think I was marked at the mouth 'Kidneys shot here!' It's my x perquisite. If they kill a sheep anywhere in the three kingdoms, off come the kidneys here! Off come the indescribable kidneys here! I've eaten seven and eighty kidneys this week—seven and eighty. Yes, seven and eighty, seven and eighty! I swear seven and eighty—four and forty great sheep. Half a hundred great sheep! Each cockEREd up on its own silly bit of bacon! Bacon! Bacon! Bacon! Bacon! Bacon on the brain! Bacon and Kidney. Bacon and eggs. I swear if I see any more bacon for breakfast for a week I'll turn Jew. I'll turn a x x x x Jew, a floridly decorated and elaborately qualified Jew! I'll . . . Yah! Here! Help! Here's the damned coffee machine upsetting again!"

And amidst such tumults came the post and newspaper. THESE IRRUPTIONS WERE USUALLY SUFFICIENT TO withdraw his attention from the wreckage of the breakfast table, and he would rend open envelopes and wrappers with trembling fingers, grunting ominously. Sometimes he would get a letter card, a modern novelty that he detested with extraordinary vehemence, and this after a brief but savage struggle he would tear to fragments unopened, and sometimes a foolishly involved wrapper and its contents suffered the same fate. AFTER THAT HIS BREAKFAST WOULD GET EATEN, AS IF BY INADVERTENCE. A sound of castors FOLLOWED; the rustle of the unfolding newspaper and a heavy breathing mingled with LOW noises of execration. MR. WADDY WAS LEARNING ALL THAT THIS LARGE AND BUSY PLANET OF OURS HAD DONE TO ANNOY HIM DURING THE PRECEDING DAY.

HIS CHOICE OF A newspaper varied. He transferred his allegiance on an average once a week and if the newsvendor by any chance sent the wrong one he was for the first offence called out to Mr. Waddy's bath chair and publicly expostulated with, and for the second "changed." On the whole he favoured the *Times*. He liked it because it ignored SUCH MATTERS AS Jaggers and never faked its correspondence, but it exasperated him by being in two parts, one of which invariably got into the butter, and by occasionally failing to print the letters he addressed it, while on the other hand it printed the letters of people quite obviously unfit to live.[1]

The newspaper disposed of, Mr. Waddy would read prayers to his household, all burrowing devoutly into the seats of chairs, and then he would have an interview with Mrs. Satsuma. He arranged with her every possible and impossible contingency for the day.[2] It was not a large household, consisting in addition to Mrs. Satsuma and an abject page boy frightened long ago out of the carelessness proper to his age, of an unstable series of girls. For the most part—unless they got dismissed summarily for creaking shoes or "breathing"— these young women no sooner learnt to cook potatoes than they married local tradesmen, securing handsome dowries and elaborate anathemas from Mr. Waddy. There was furthermore a fluctuating ingredient in the household called the "man." The duties of the man were to assist at Mr. Waddy's toilet, to wheel his bath chair, to clean the windows, carry coals, and display an intelligent alacrity and forebearance that for sixteen years Mr. Waddy failed to discover in any mortal breast. He would have nothing to do with valets, butlers, men nurses or any qualified attendants, "flunkeys, mamelukes and scoundrels" were his mildest terms for all such as have trained themselves elegantly for the personal service of man, and the succession of honest rather than amiable and ingenious rather than capable old sailors, promoted bath chair men, retired and unsuccessful tradesmen, ex-national schoolmasters and heartbroken clerks, that Mrs. Satsuma saw come respectfully and retire in truculent revolt, damned if they would stand the old gent any longer, would have restocked a good-sized monastery on the old-fashioned lines.

The day's arrangements decided—they were usually altered later—Mr. Waddy would attend to his correspondence. He would clutch the collected envelopes and letters from his breakfast table in a hairy hand and be wheeled to his bureau, breathing resolution. His correspondence was extensive and peculiar, and it was his proud boast that he never failed to answer a letter. <There were correspondents who found this a doubtful virtue. He derived an enormous satisfaction from expressing his disinterested objections upon a number of topics.> His position in the world was known to that large and prosperous class of persons who sell righteous self-applause, the exploiters of orphans, convalescents, and institutions of all sorts; and against these he waged honourable war. To their circulars he replied with warmth and colour. He would then attend to any more personal communication, and thereafter to any controversy that chanced to be on hand. He was a severe and outspoken critic of the tradesmen who served him, of the Folkestone local authorities and his neighbours on either hand. You imagine him beginning in a tall old-fashioned handwriting.

Sirs,
I am returning you herewith, less one bottle which I retain for analysis, the wine you sent me invoiced as port. You surely must be aware—

Or restraining his epithets to the requirements of print in the matter of the Amusements Association (*Sic*)—of which sarcastic particle he was inordinately fond.

Beyond these more immediate provocations he had others of a more public sort. There was a touch of the reformer's fire about Mr. Waddy, as we have noted. He believed strongly in mending this disorderly world of ours, if possible by violent means. He had been fitfully a member, until the mismanagement of the various secretaries led to an acrimonious withdrawal, of quite a number of societies for the checking of this or the prevention of that, and his pen did yeoman service to these causes before it came round to the secretarIAL DEFECTS.

Refreshed and calmed by these epistolary exercises, Mr. Waddy, with echoes of his rhetoric still running through his mind, would if the day was fine, be taken abroad in his bath chair to mark new matter for castigation and gain an appetite for lunch. Lunch HE TREATED, PERHAPS UNWISELY, AS a serious matter. So soon as he was abroad, Mrs. Satsuma would repair to his bureau to blot up scattered ink, put out fresh blotting paper and collect the smashed and rejected quills, the vehemently torn paper and other debris incident to literary exertion. <One met him chiefly on that sheltered path, that pleasant wrinkle in the very brow of the Leas. Many an inane self-complacent trifler glancing at the passing chair would meet an Eye of singular intensity and be smitten into distress.> He returnED to his lunch about two.

After his lunch came slumber. From this he would awake in a mood of poignant bitterness, only to be alleviated by copious draughts of very hot and strong tea. The noises and concussions that signalised his awakening were the signal for an instant scampering and calling downstairs. The entire household set itself with amazing singleness of purpose to secure the instant making and service of the tea. Even "the man" would stir himself in an eager, scared, aimless manner, and come into the kitchen and get run against and jostled about during that period of panic suspense. All conversation was carried on in hasty whispers. And upstairs, a mighty bellowing:

"*Why* isn't my tea ready? Why in the name of [such and such a thing] can't I have my tea? Clammy taste in my mouth, head fit to split—and every blessed servant in the house gone and hidden. Might as well be in a desert, a damned sandy desiccated desert, as in this Christian home. No tea for hours —not for hours. Fire raked out and water turned out of the house! Every possible precaution taken, every possible precaution against tea! *Tea*! TEA! Do you hear? *TEA*!!" Until the tea things had jingled their way to him, and a breakfast-cupful or so had vanished with mighty gulps and blowings and ejaculatory "Ahs!"

And then for a space Mr. Waddy was equal to a book or a visitor or whatever other demand life made on him.

He dined at half past seven, and thereafter came a book perhaps, which might or might not exasperate ("Latter-day trash"), and at times the current doctor would call in or a reckless young curate who found, he said, something refreshing in Mr. Waddy's vocabulary after the austerities of his day's duty. These after-dinner hours, unless they were ruffled by a humorous novel or some such intolerable provocation, were the serenest of Mr. Waddy's day. He would harangue his visitors on various insupportable aspects of life. To the curate he would denounce the various charitable enterprises that had appealed to him since their last meeting.

"Here's a big scoundrel been to see me—a great distended, oily, swaggering thing, perfect bladderful of inflated charity —cadging for some infernal convalescent Home or other. Convalescent Homes indeed! Lethal chambers are what we want. The way we encourage people who are miserable themselves and a perfect nuisance, burthen and eyesore to other people to go on living—living! Ugh! Why in Heaven's name should they live? What we want is a Mission—the Elder Brothers of the Better Dead—to give them a finer self-respect. We want tracts handed about in public places to probable looking people. 'What is your duty to the World?' 'Cui Bono?' and things like that. And an Institution for putting them away."

He got through his income chiefly however in the costly sort of travel his condition necessitated. He organised a peripatetic household under Mrs. Satsuma, and he carried his powers of criticism, his futile good impulses and his intermittent volcano of burning eloquence from one place of resort to another. He did not confine his indisputable gift for vehement indignation to ink and paper. He was the gentleman in a bath chair—some reader may remember him—who was at last requested to leave Dieppe because of his expressed indignation at English gentlemen—"Gentlemen forsooth!"—participating in mixed bathing. And he it was who, being suddenly angry at the levity of the headgear about him and by way of example, stopped C——e R——k[3] one Sunday morning on the Hove Parade, and, callous to the pleasantness of that gentleman's smile, asked him if he was not *ashamed* to be seen out on a place and day like that with a ninepenny ha'penny cotton hat.

❧ 3 ❧

Muriel

DURING THE FIRST DECADE OF MR. WADDY'S INFIRMITY and while he was at Eastbourne—NINE YEARS IT WAS AND MORE before THAT lamentable outbreak on the Folkestone Leas—there WAS FOR A TIME AN ADDITION TO THIS PERIPATETIC household, NAMED MURIEL. She was a girl of one and twenty and she had a romantic turn of mind, nourished to excess on an exclusive dietary of novels. She had been brought up in genteel poverty by a similarly addicted mother, who had christened her Muriel out of a well-known book;[1] she was an orphan and she had spent two or three years as an unsuccessful governess. She had formed a rather pathetic picture of Waddy before she saw him—she was one of those people who imagine you before they see you and persist in their preconception in spite of all your efforts—and it seemed to her almost a duty that her fresh young brightness should ameliorate the painful days of this helpless, rich and quite conceivably dying invalid. She was remotely related to Waddy's benefactor and her frequent meditations upon this score led at last to a letter.

It caught Mr. Waddy in a softened mood, fresh from a brilliantly successful—too successful—reproof of a lady cyclist in knickerbockers. This person had looked a hardened hussy, but perhaps she had met with a fall or some other outspoken friends of refinement that day. She was neither young nor tidy nor good-looking, and yet instead of some stimulating retort she had at a mere passing touch of opprobrium burst into tears. "Go on," said Mr. Waddy to his chairman, "Go home," and returned with a vague feeling that this woman had spoilt his afternoon.

He read Muriel's letter in the presence of Mrs. Satsuma and the knickerbocker controversy rankled in his mind. He perceived Muriel's standpoint clearly.

"I suppose they think they ought to have a share."

"It's reasonable."

"I'm not a cad, you know. I'm always ready to consider people who deserve consideration. No one more considerate than I—"

"What I always say," said Mrs. Satsuma.

"Of course, if people put themselves out of court . . . Then they must be prepared to take what comes.

"I am—always . . ." He reflected. "Always.

"It's not much of a home for her, poor girl; but she will have to be put up somewhere until she can find another situation. Poor girls may work to death minding the children of hussies who do nothing but half undress themselves and fly about the world on wheels. And as for these confounded people who have dismissed her," he continued, with his mind running into a more congenial tone, "turning her out into the world as she says, I think such xxx CONDUCT ought to be xxxx shown up. Confounded xxx . . ."

So Muriel, ENORMOUSLY ASTONISHED AND EXPECTANT AT THE SUCCESS OF HER LETTER, came. She was a tall and slender girl, with a whitish complexion, hazel eyes, a full throat, a SLIGHT natural lisp, and remarkable imaginative powers. On the journey she read a novel by Mrs. Piper Petersen,[2] which novel in a strangely ominous way turned on a will and much short-sighted scoundrelism. There was an uncle in it, SUCH AS Mr. Waddy might be, even to the armchair infirmities. In the story the uncle took quite a fancy to his niece in spite of HER NOBLE REFUSAL TO FLATTER HIM AND the dreadful cunning of a machinatory nephew. Incidentally the niece was bound hand and foot and nearly

drowned, locked for three weeks in a room, and forced in
self-defence to stab the nephew. Nothing seemed to ruffle her
as the illustration shewed, and in the end her equanimity was
fully rewarded; she married the nephew (reformed) and had
every penny of the old gentleman's money left her in her own
right—every penny.

<When she had finished the book, she leant back in the
carriage in a pleasant dream. The heroine of the book had
won her uncle's heart by her native goodness and the natural
charm of feminine refinement, and Muriel resolved that she
also would not fail in these particulars. She thought out the
little scene of her arrival at Eastbourne and all the things she
would say, things about his goodness and how she would try
to make him happy. And most of these things she did say, in
spite of a certain nervousness on her own part that marred the
accent and a certain unexpectedness in the responses of Mr.
Waddy.

She would not take her hat off before she saw him,
because it was a new hat and suited her, and it was necessary
to make a good impression. So she sat with it on against the
light on the desk and its bows and feathers worried him
extremely. He was in a mood of considerable amiability. He
interrupted Muriel's gratitude to make her assure him that she
did not ride a bicycle nor confess. Muriel was innocent of
these crimes and reverted to her protestations. They quite
embarrassed Mr. Waddy.

"I'm sure," said Muriel, "if there is anything I can do—
anything. One thing I am resolved to do—I will read to you
every day."

. She would take no denial, though his eyes were as good as
his voice and he read abundantly.> She read him selected
passages from *John Halifax Gentleman*[3]—a very nice book
for nice people, but one scarcely adapted to his profoundly
vitiated tastes. Her brief years of teaching had imparted a
certain didactic accent to her sustained voice—it was the only
governess trait about her—and her sense of punctuation was
defective. <After a time Mr. Waddy became fidgety and
whispered to himself.

"Aren't you comfortable?" said Muriel, stopping consider-
ately. "Shall I get you a pillow?"

Mr. Waddy suppressed some remark about pillows. He decided to be open.

"Look here," he said. "I wish you wouldn't read to me."

"It's no trouble—"

"It *is*. It's a trouble to me. I don't like that book, and you don't mind your stops."

Muriel stared. She had a moment of illumination.

"Oh! *Have* I been *boring* you?" she said in sudden horror. She understood Mr. Waddy to say that she had.

A reaction toward good behaviour followed promptly. "At least not bored—you meant well, my girl, you meant well. But I'm an old man you know and a bit irritable—just a bit irritable."

"I'm *so* sorry," she said in beautiful contrition. "I *didn't* understand."

"Of course not," said Mr. Waddy. "Of course not."

"I am so very, very sorry. I did so want to do something, something to show—"

"Of course," said Mr. Waddy. "Of course."

"If I had known."

"We won't argue about it," said Mr. Waddy.

"Of course not," said Muriel brightly. "Well—I won't read to you again—anyhow. And now you must tell me something that *will* please you. Something that I *can* do for you—"

Mr. Waddy meditated. "You go—somewhere—and enjoy yourself. *I* shall be all right."

Muriel looked at him with a face full of emotion. "Oh!" she said. "You *are* kind."

He did not look it.

Her face lit up. "*I* know," she said. "I know! Yes." She clapped her hands together and stood up with her eyes wide and bright. "Yes—I know what I can do. *Now*. And—if I go, you won't be lonely?"

"Not a bit," said Mr. Waddy.

And Muriel full of some bright purpose flitted lightly from the room.

Mr. Waddy watched her from the room, then he distended his cheeks and blew the air out slowly. "Good Lord!" said Mr. Waddy. "Good Lord!" Then he reached a vast hairy hand for the novel which was lying on the table. "By?" he said. The author's name was not apparent and after an unsuccessful search for it, Mr. Waddy hurled the offending work across the room. He gave a grunt of relief, and rang his hand bell for Mrs. Satsuma.

"Make it perfectly clear to that young woman, Mrs. Satsuma, that in this room—when I am in this room—I like to be alone."

Muriel's secret intention did not come to fruition for a couple of days. Then came a tapping and her clear bright, "May I come in?" Silence seemed assent, and she entered to a strictly defensive Waddy. In her hand she held a moderate size something in tissue paper. She stopped midway across the room, in pleasing perturbation.

"You won't be cross?" she said.

"What about?" asked Mr. Waddy.

"I've done something for you."

"Ah! It's here?"

Mr. Waddy screwed down a hostile eye to the tissue package.

"Promise me something."

"What about?"

"If I give this to you, you won't open it till I'm out of the room?"

The condition seemed promising. "All right," said Mr. Waddy with a conscientious amiability. "What have you done me?"

"You promise?" she said—pink forefinger out.

"All right," said Mr. Waddy.

She came forward quickly and placed the parcel on the table. "I don't think I will *now*," she said in pretty coyness and withdrew it again. Then, impulsively, "Yes I will. *There*." She put it in his hand. "If you don't like it," she said, "you must tell me. No!" Her quick hands restrained his trembling fingers. "Not till I'm out of the room. Your promise Sir!"

In an instant she had flitted away from him. She stood for a moment, with a half face at the door, and vanished. Mr. Waddy, breathing heavily, attacked the tissue paper tearing it into strips that fell right and left. The object revealed itself as something circular, became patent as a small round cap of purple velvet, cleverly but unsoundly decorated with loops of gold lace. For a moment, one precious moment Mr. Waddy was speechless. There follows a decorous break in the narrative.

Afterwards he saw the thing in a more charitable light. The girl meant to please him. He rang for Mrs. Satsuma and asked her to pick the cap out of the corner where it had "fallen," dust it and put it on his table. "That girl," he said, "made it." He meditated over its uncongenial colorings. "It shows a kind disposition," he remarked. "Will you please tell her I am much obliged."

Muriel was delighted at this. She perceived the thing she could do and embarked at once upon an elaborate scheme that should at last revolutionize> the dullness of his room by the importation of bright little knicknacks and ornaments. Many of these she would make with her own hands from the instructions that are occasionally to be met with in the ladies' papers. SHE BEGAN AT ONCE. She bought with some of the money he had given her a versatile three-legged table for him to have near him when he sat at the window. She began a fringe in Macramé work for this, but that she never finished because by some accident the table got broken one day when she was out. AND NEXT SHE made him LEAN AND LUMPY cushions for his excellently stuffed chair.

HER SUCCESS WITH THESE THINGS LED TO OTHERS. She took up her long neglected piano practice so that she might play to him WHEN HE DESIRED IT. He hated music. THE PIANO was the piano of a furnished house and no PEDANTIC tuner had ever marred its picturesque decay. It was part of her idea of fresh girlishness that she should vary HER MORE mechanical exercises by little snatches of melody, sometimes remembered, sometimes half remembered, sometimes quaintly improvised. And sometimes she would sing queer little airs; "la la, la la—lar!" letting her ample untrained voice swell more and more towards a sustained culmination. And upstairs Mr. Waddy would also exercise his voice, in A deeper richer flow.

<By miraculous efforts Mr. Waddy concealed his appreciation of her gifts, and they multiplied, growing cleverer and sketchier and more unsound each time. But at last came a crisis that gave her a glimpse of his heart. On occasion she would rap and ask "May I come in?" before entering his room but at times she would enter artlessly>—like Pippa. She had

heard of Pippa first in a novel, and had found the poem at last after a resolute search. When she got the book home she was dreadfully disappointed to find it verse, but she read the poem nevertheless and appreciated it. She loved Pippa. <To be something tripping, singing and sunny became her ideal. She sought to be a Pippa herself, a heavier Pippa with a contralto voice.> There were days in her life of pure *Imitatio Pippae*. Until <that memorable day when she came bounding in upon him with a tobacco bag while he was involved with a dependent sentence. After hurling his pen, ink and papers in diverse directions among the furniture, he spoke.> He asked her WITH QUITE UNNECESSARY WARMTH NOT TO ENTER HIS ROOM WITHOUT RAPPING AGAIN.

For THE moment she allowed herself to be annoyed and left the room AT ONCE—IN OFFENDED DIGNITY. She was reading "The Sorrows of Satan" just then, and she really could not help comparing Mr. Waddy's manners very unfavourably with those of the arch-enemy.[4] But she soon got over that, and made him a hasty untrustworthy but bright and pleasing shaving-tidy to show that she forgave him. <He eyed it distrustfully but accepted it. "Ask Mrs. Satsuma—to put it somewhere—for me," he said. "With the others."> And so they were friends again.

She and Mrs. Satsuma speedily became intimate friends; she trimmed Mrs. Satsuma's bonnets, and went to church and shops with her. They read their favourite novelists turn and turn about, and until they agreed to use differently coloured papers as bookmarks they would often go on each from the other's marked "place" and miss out important things, marriages and engagements, in an extremely confusing way.

They invented little names for the people who came within their ken and wove little romances about them, and if the curate coughed or looked up during the lessons they got to the bottom of the matter. They found analogies between the people they saw and the people they read about, and a sort of secret language sprang up.[5]

They told each other little secrets about themselves, and Mrs. Satsuma late one evening told Muriel all about a disappointment which she was clearly under the impression she had suffered in her youth. She showed a faded photograph of a young man in a misfit, with his hair brushed up on one side, standing beside her seated incipient self. "That was 'im, my dear," said plump little Mrs. Satsuma with a sigh, "and that's all"; and the sympathetic Muriel cried a little because it was all so sad. And Mrs. Satsuma folded her fingers before her apron and watched Muriel weep with great satisfaction.

Mrs. Satsuma, while thus engaged in the display of her heart, could not conceal a certain preoccupation about legacies. She told quite a number of stories of other housekeepers to old people who had been "left" quite considerable sums; one old friend of hers was "quite the lady" on a hundred pounds a year. And when faint criticisms of Mr. Waddy's irritability passed like little cloud shadows across the warmth of their confidences, she sustained a doctrine of his essential goodness.

"Short he may be," she said, "and given to saying things— There!—I could tell you things he's said to me, no one would believe. But a more generous and kindly man, my dear, never breathed. That I am sure of. That I would say now, if this was my last dying breath."

Quite a number of things Mrs. Satsuma was prepared to say with her last dying breath, when at last that solemn moment should come. Indeed her last hour promised to be a most extraordinary miscellany of asseverations, testimonials to the character of various people and particularly of herself and Mr. Waddy, views of domestic management, maxims in practical medicine, loyal, moral and patriotic sentiments, disapproval of flowers in the hats of under servants, and SO ON.

Apart from her more immediate concern, Mrs. Satsuma could not but glance in a speculative way ever and again at the possible destinies of the rest of Mr. Waddy's wealth. "Much of it, my dear, lying idle and accumulating. Now, if it belonged to somebody young—they'd circulate it."

"Neither chick nor child nor relatives he has," said Mrs. Satsuma, looking pensively into the fire and smoothing her dress with her hands—they were "warming their toes" before retiring for the night—"neither chick nor child." For some dark reason she evidently found great satisfaction in the thought that Mr. Waddy did not keep poultry.

"Now, *I* know somebody," she resumed, "a young lady, it

is, beautiful, charming, well educated. Plays her music, she does, and arranges her flowers. *My*! If she had it—*what* a catch she'd be!"

"And who is that?" asked Muriel innocently.

"*Ah*!" said Mrs. Satsuma, very archly. "Who is that?" She looked at Muriel, laughed a funny little laugh and made an eyeglass at her with her fingers. "Who can *I* see blushing?" said Mrs. Satsuma.

Muriel hesitated whether to confess her knowledge. She had coloured, she knew, and so she decided to be open.

"Don't you put silly ideas into my head, Mrs. Satsuma," she said. "Things like that don't happen to me."

"We shall see," said Mrs. Satsuma. "We shall see."

Muriel tried to conceal her blushing satisfaction. "What's the good of talking nonsense?" she said. "Why! he's sure to leave it all to a Charity."

"I've heard him say things about charities," said Mrs. Satsuma. "There!—you wouldn't believe, even if I could bring myself to repeat. No, my dear, depend upon it he won't leave it to a Charity, whatever else he does."

"But what did he say?" asked Muriel eagerly.

"My *dear*!"

"But one would like to know rather."

"My dear I couldn't even spell it. I couldn't bring myself even to write it down. ONE OF HIS WORST—HIS VERY WORST. But he won't leave his money to Charities, you take my word."

One night Mrs. Satsuma, AFTER AN ELABORATE PREFACE, PROPOSED THEY SHOULD carry her curiosity about legacies to a higher power—"JUST FOR FUN"—and they spent several perplexed evenings over a pack of cards and a stimulatingly indistinct article in a ladies' paper. They adopted the modern liberal attitude about the matter, they were NOT SUPERSTITIOUSLY credulous in the ancient fashion nor YET intolerantly sceptical. They thought there was probably "something in it": they determined to give it a trial. It was of course rather difficult; the fact that quite different cards turned up each time they repeated a question was particularly puzzling. So far as they could gather Mrs. Satsuma was destined to marry young, have much feasting, be betrayed in love, have another early marriage (or perhaps the same one—they could not tell), and they learnt also that she would marry three times, each time to a wealthy person, that she would have many children, a letter, and be a flirt and fond of company. Reading between the lines of these cryptic portents AND ELIMINATING THE IMPOSSIBLE, Muriel felt convinced that the old lady might be reasonably sure of a handsome bequest. But she admitted that the thing did not amount of course to an absolute proof. That would have been superstition.

As for her own fortune, she felt a queer disinclination to have it told. But at last she consented, saying that there was nothing in it of course, and anyhow it could not matter whether she did it or no. So they began to cut and shuffle again.

This time the SORTES pointed to marriage, romance, and trouble and journeys—each time they told that tale. And each time—they tried three times—there was something about a bad RED man—A FAIR MAN THEY INTERPRETED IT—who was to be Muriel's lover (twice) and husband (once).

She said he was a horrid man and would not try again. She held Him—he was the King of HEARTS—in her hand as though she had His photograph. Then she said "Ugh" suddenly and stuck him into the middle of the pack. And then Mrs. Satsuma said, "Eh dear! what nonsense it all is!" and got up for her copper kettle.

Muriel also said it was all nonsense of course, but SHE did not forget the King of HEARTS. From that time she took no further interest in DARK men—they were as women to her. But to enter an omnibus suddenly and find a FAIR OR AUBURN-HEADED man in the opposite corner, even to pass TEUTONIC SHOCKS upon the parade stirred her emotions. What if this were he and this VERY moment THE FIRST LINE OF Chapter I of her own unwritten novel!

After a time it became evident EVEN to her that if her stay with her adopted uncle was to be prolonged she must mitigate the ardour of her attentions to him. Apart from the defensive hostility her attentions aroused, his attitude to her was not unfriendly. SHE REFLECTED UPON CERTAIN EXPRESSIONS AND IN A FLASH OF UNWONTED INSIGHT decided that he really *liked* to be uncomfortable, and discontinued the supply of cushions and suchlike kickshaws. The piano practising she discontinued because it was her way to discontinue things. She kept away from HIM more and more, associating more and more with Mrs. Satsuma, and at last he understood that if he wanted to see her he must ask for her. He did not ask for her for a long time, and then in a softened mood he let her new-born tact have its reward, and hoped through Mrs. Satsuma that she was STILL comfortable AND FOUND THINGS TO AMUSE HER. Her reply was full of gratitude.

And when at last the time came to move she found her opportunity. She displayed wild enthusiasm to help. She could run after porters, run into them if they ignored her, she could leap from trains, manipulate luggage and control cabs. Mr. Waddy admitted with a sort of reluctant astonishment that she had been of use to them, and his eyes showed an unwonted respect for her powers of locomotion . . .

In two years' time she was still a tolerated member of Mr. Waddy's peripatetic household, and the question of her next situation had vanished from the earth. It is doubtful if at any time Waddy can be said to have liked her. But until THE catastrophe it is doubtful if he can be said to have disliked her AND NO DOUBT HE HAD GOT SOME WAY TOWARDS THAT SENSE OF USAGE WHICH IS THE BASIS OF MOST AFFECTION. It is the common fallacy of our INTERPRETATION OF HUMAN RELATIONSHIPS to require that A. should be either a friend of B. or his enemy. As a matter of fact we are much more analytical than that. It may be taken that at last Mr. Waddy liked her a good deal in an habitual sort of way, and at the same time detested her pretty cordially. They went from Eastbourne to Torquay and thence to Tunbridge Wells. There her position was so stable that she could tell him casually she was going to join the Art classes for the entire winter session. "That's right," he said. "It'll give you something to do."

And such is the moral effect of a quiet persistence, that not only she and Mrs. Satsuma, but the lower servants and even Mr. Waddy were by that time completely inoculated with the idea that she was—albeit in some occult and unusual way— Mr. Waddy's niece and entitled to all the natural expectations of that position.

And then came passion, that foe of all ORDERLY human ambitions, and whirled her suddenly away. Scarcely was her adoption of Mr. Waddy complete when, according to all the prescriptions of romance and against all the dictates of reason, she must needs marry an impecunious actor, in flat opposition to Mr. Waddy's expressed wish. She eloped, and there were scenes and weeping and terrible goings on.

But this episode surely merits more than the fag end of a chapter . . .

❧ 4 ❧

Mr. Chitterlow

WHEN I say that Mr. Chitterlow was an actor, I mean he had been one. Yet after all acting is not so much a profession as a temperament. He had left the stage on the score of some professional pique and had taken to that most fascinating of all vices, the writing of unacceptable plays.

While his play was germinating he wandered about the country in an adventurous and inexpensive manner, lodging in cottages and making many friends. His finances speedily became tortuous and secret. He was certainly hay-making at one time in Berkshire, and at another billiard marking at Brighton. For some months he appears to have had an unstable position on the yacht of the Honourable Thomas Norgate. These things were no doubt by way of accumulating material FOR THE PLAY.

His memory he kept green in the Strand and Waterloo Road by periodical excursions of diffusive amiability, meeting more "dear boys" and men of the right sort in a day than a common man does in a life's journey. In the matter of treating such congenial hearts he was prone to pursue the difficult question whether it is more blessed to give than to receive, to uproarious conclusions. To THEM he conversed of the play in

26

hand and of the Honourable Thomas Norgate, "very firm chap," he said, "good old friend of mine." HE ALSO EXPA-TIATED UPON ALL THAT HE HAD "IN HIM," ALL THAT WAS PRESENTLY TO COME OUT.

It was universally admitted to his face that he had a Lot in him, a tremendous Lot in fact, but about the precise nature of that Lot there was, except on his own part, A DISCREET SUSPENSE. He held that the Lot was genius of the Shake-spearian type—only "up to date" of course. He was fully resolved to prove this to all the world—in due time—and *pendente lite*, he insisted, even vociferously, that his friends should recognise his claim. Admit that, and you were free of his pockets and reminiscences—if the former were empty, the latter were not, and indeed he grudged his company to no man or woman. His play, which was still in a fluctuating state, was to present his own nature, certain tremendous conceptions of passion he entertained, and an absolutely novel staging of a railway accident which he had come to believe was his own invention.

HE WAS A RED-HAIRED YOUNG MAN WITH A HANDSOME PROFILE, EFFECTIVE REDDISH-BROWN EYES, AND A RICH IMPRESSIVE VOICE AND MANNER that an ample mouth and a walk of cork-like buoyancy did much to contradict. He had a childlike faith in his personal charm, a faith that was particularly effective in his intercourse with the opposite sex. His conquest of Mr. Waddy's niece was indeed only the culmination and end of a long series, a fact perhaps unduly prominent in his domestic conversation, and a cause it appeared of considerable virtuous pride in her.

He met her at that TUNBRIDGE WELLS Art Class. He had joined it during a temporary hesitation whether the lot that was in him might not after all lie in that direction. He had drifted down to TUNBRIDGE WELLS from Essex in the first place to escape an importunate creditor—a map of England SHADED WITH THE SPHERES OF INFLUENCE OF his VARIOUS creditors would have been black, for he had spent some years in the smalls[1]—AND partly because he had a sort of unformed idea of a scene that might be just as well laid there as anywhere else, and at that time he entertained strong views of the importance of local colour; and partly also no doubt by reason of a genuine fondness for GOOD LANDSCAPE.

He had fallen into conversation with the art school master, while that gentleman was painting the Toad Rock in the most atrocious fashion and for the seventh time, ostensibly with a view to gain but really from a sincere fondness for the unintelligent use of oil colours, and in addition to an unanticipated and very grateful warmth of appreciation, Mr. Chitterlow chanced to mention the large number of actor managers he knew personally who were eager to patronise the sister arts. The art school master's natural hospitality was quickened by a vision, among others, of his picture "slap in the centre of the stage" during a run of "perhaps five hundred nights," and he invited Chitterlow diffidently to his modest home.

Chitterlow, it was speedily evident, had nothing better to do. They had tea, and Mr. Chitterlow forgot to leave before supper. Chitterlow's conversation dealt freely with his reminiscences and his extraordinarily favourable first impressions of the art school master, and he developed a doubt as he proceeded whether his own indisputable genius might not after all lie in the direction of painting. He asked abundant questions.

The art master explained how it was done with ease and fluency—FOR when he was deprived of the brush, art had no better exponent. At any rate the thing presented itself to Chitterlow as an incidental diversion from his dramatic invention, and he was one of those people who make the pursuit of incidental diversions their CHIEF occupation IN LIFE. The art master was already profoundly impressed by the undefined but indisputable lot there was in this man and saw nothing absurd in the suggestion. FUSELI learnt to paint after five and twenty, and Rossetti never learnt to draw at all. It was decided therefore in the small hours that without definitely abandoning his dramatic authorship, Chitterlow should give the thing a trial under the art master's instruction. He would also, he privately resolved, make a study of the art master's character for the purpose of the play.

Nothing passed between them, then or subsequently, in the matter of fees, for the art master was a diffident delicate-minded man as Chitterlow MANIFESTLY perceived.

The début at the art class was extremely successful. With the fine sense of make-up that characterises your true actor,

Chitterlow wore A SEA-GREEN tie that harmonised admirably
with the flowing hair and effective profile—he was one of that
fortunate minority of actors who escape a blue-joweled fat-
ness. There was a sort of static flutter throughout the class, of
which he presented himself as entirely unconscious. Mr. Waddy's niece was next BUT ONE to him, and her stippled drawing
from the antique made no progress. Instead she secretly did a
sketch (and hers was not the only one) of a leonine head.

Mr. Chitterlow marked her girlish freshness but he did not
know of the sketch. Indeed he could not determine to his own
satisfaction all through the evening whether she was looking
at him all the time or whether she never looked at all. But
then his mind was distracted by his effect on the others. His
doubt about her piqued him on reflection. His impression of
her dress and bearing was that she was real upper class. He
resolved to note her behaviour with greater attention on the
next occasion.

She had recently been reading the Life of Lady Burton,[2]
and possibly on that account, she went straight home and
wrote in her diary these cryptic words: "*I have met my fate.*"
It was a true prevision, as indeed such feminine previsions
usually are. She would have told Mrs. Satsuma all about it,
had there been anything to tell. But for some reason she could
not bring herself to exhibit the picture . . .

She raised no obstacles to predestinate things. At the next
meeting of the class she tipped a box of charcoal stumps
towards her Destiny, and there ensued a blushing scene. He
knelt at her feet to pick up her scattered material, and she
blushed all the better for the evident comprehension in the
eyes of the other girls.

<When the chalks had been collected Chitterlow ven-
tured upon a few appreciative criticisms of her work. At the
next meeting they talked like old friends.>

Chitterlow HAD NEVER DISGUISED THE FACT THAT HE
knew an extraordinary lot about WOMEN but he was a little
afraid of Young Ladies. He held perhaps exaggerated ideas of
non-professional refinement, and this may have exerted a
beneficial restraint on his natural exuberance <in the earlier
stages of their intercourse. He professed himself a beginner at
art, a beginner at everything, a stark, storm-tossed genius, who

counted her conversation the greatest privilege there was left to him in life. And the third night he overtook her and walked with her.

It was a moonlight night, and Muriel's face was transfigured. Chitterlow told himself he was violently in love and gave his emotions play. His limbs trembled as they walked and his voice took on new cadences. He talked of himself, of his loneliness, and so drew near to her, and presently they came upon a silence more eloquent than all. "Goodbye," she said, at the door waiting until he had gone before she rang. He made no sound, but he took her hand and she did not withdraw it. Suddenly he bent forward and kissed her lips. Then abruptly he broke from her and fled into the night . . .

The next day he waylaid her, and his passion was no longer dumb. He was splendid; well might the cards present him as the King of Hearts. He could not live without her, she was his "from all eternity," she must come to him, whatever the obstacles between them. She tried a maidenly reticence but her emotions were too genuine for that. She ended with tumultuous confessions. And Chitterlow walked down the Pantiles as though he was lord of the earth.

There was a painful attempt to introduce Chitterlow to Mr. Waddy—so much will this madness essay—quasi-explanations, a tumult, a blasphemous prohibition and then they fled and married in spite of him, in accordance with all the formulae proper to their case. For a time they vanished from Tunbridge Wells altogether, and then they returned, still flushed and glorious, to be forgiven. >

(Printer, a white line. [Wells's note.])

It is worthy of incidental note that in this same ART class Chitterlow met Mr. Kipps. His effect upon Kipps was also a very powerful one. Kipps had joined the class in a gust of educational zeal, but of that more hereafter. Chitterlow impressed Kipps as one of the most extraordinary looking persons he had ever met. At the third meeting of the class which Chitterlow attended Kipps confided to a fellow student that "that chap's a regular actor—you mark my words."

Chitterlow in some occult way was aware of the comment and marked Kipps as a suitably docile subject for self revelation. It was a proud day for Kipps when that began. ON THE NIGHT WHEN MURIEL WAS ABSENT CHITTERLOW POSI-

TIVELY WALKED HOME WITH HIM. When at last the elopement convulsed the art class Kipps shone with reflected glory
and could speak even of a certain vague foreknowledge.

"He was a tremendous dashing chap," said Kipps. "I could
see that all along. There was a thing or two between him and
me—"

He lifted his eyebrows, looked meaningly at his interlocu-
tor and said no more, concealing by this simple expedient the
natural poverty of his invention.

"No," said Kipps, "I'd be glad to tell you. Only I'm not
free to tell."

(Printer, a white line. [Wells's note.])

The ROMANTIC elopement OF MR. CHITTERLOW WITH
WHAT TO THE END OF HIS DAYS HE IMAGINED TO BE THE
NIECE OF A WEALTHY MAN, was financed to a large extent
with Muriel's pocket money—<an almost symbolical circum-
stance. Muriel had been reading a little book with a key on
the cover and she knew that under the circumstances she
could not fail to be "transfigured in the glory of her love."
Overnight she had trimmed a special hat for her flight and she
knew it was a success. In the train she and Chitterlow talked
about what they were doing with immense pride, so that the
two common everyday people in the compartment could not
but share the knowledge of their splendid guilt. A lady with a
bundle indisputably admired them, but a fat red-haired little
man with spectacles was doubtful. He fidgeted greatly, glared
at the young people over and through his spectacles, and made
a number of inaudible remarks to himself. He appeared to
have some unpleasant taste in his mouth. Chitterlow not in
the least abashed by these dubious symptoms continued his
amorous discourse, gave swift impressions of a wild but credit-
able past and displayed what a brilliant daredevil adventurous
blade he was to the very best advantage. Muriel glowed with
pride. To the end, however, the effect on the little man was
uncertain. He got out before the tram had stopped at Seven-
oaks, publicly thanking Goodness for some reason or other
and entered another compartment.

Something set Mr. Chitterlow talking about Puritans. He
was always very severe against Puritans—it is the way in the
Profession. He declared his intention of satirising these hum-
bugs, the spoil sports and refusers of credit, scoundrels secretly

addicted to all sorts of inelegant wickedness, in that compendious play. The lady with the bundle was evidently fluttered afresh to be travelling with a man who wrote plays. Her face was intoxicating flattery. Relieved of that ambiguous little man, Chitterlow could let himself go. He had a beautiful time.

At Cairns[?] Street where the lady with the bundle alighted, there was a touching little scene. She hesitated. "I'm sure I wish you, sir, and the pretty lady, every happiness," she said.

Chitterlow deeply moved was waving his hat out of the window long after the lady with the bundle had vanished into the past.

(Printer, a white line. [Wells's note.])

And just at that time Waddy banged his little table that carried the wreckage of his breakfast and discoursed to Mrs. Satsuma. In his trembling left hand he held out a little pink note, and that was his text. As usual his staple was denunciation, denunciation of > "this (indescribable) business of pinning notes on her dressing table and all the rest of it."

< "It's the acting. I can't stand this idiotic incapacity to say anything, do anything, think anything, that she hasn't got out of a book. Girl! She's no girl, she's the Frankenstein monster of all the women scribblers in the world, she's a circulating library on the bust!" >

"*I* don't care who she marries," he REITERATED. "It's no business of mine. But it's confoundedly uncivil to go off from a house she was free to leave at any time, as if it was a prison. EH?"

MRS. SATSUMA HAD RELUCTANTLY TO ADMIT THAT WAS SO.

"SHE wants to make an ass of me, as though my infernal Luck hadn't done that for me already. THAT'S WHAT SHE WANTS TO DO!"

"She may want to play the beautiful niece with me, but I'm hanged if I play the cross old uncle. EH? She MUST think I'M an adjective doll. <An adjective doll. I've never been so infernally larked about with before in all my born days! Heaven send that I never set eyes on her again!" >

✤ 5 ✤

Cut Adrift

IN relation to Mr. Chitterlow there were three classes of people—people who understood him perfectly, people who had understood him perfectly but now understood him better, and people who declined at any price to understand him at all. Mrs. Chitterlow remained the only professing member of the first class and even in her there was a PERCEPTIBLE change, all others who entered it graduated sooner or later into the second, the art school master for example. And unhappily quite typical of the third was Mr. Waddy.

He asked questions, questions that were criticisms and which Muriel, in the tearful interview that followed the elopement, answered in vain. "Where does he come from?" demanded Waddy. "What does he do for a living? Not that it's *my* business, you know."

"I *told* you," said Muriel. "I told you long ago when I wanted you to see him again. He writes plays."

"I said, what does he do for a living? Writing plays isn't a living—it's a game."

"It isn't a game."

"What does he get by it?"

33

"He's going to get enormous sums—royalties. He told you."

"Never mind what he's going to get, what is he getting now?"

"He isn't appreciated yet. He's not an imitator, you know, he's a man of genius, LIKE IBSEN, and he has to conquer the public."

"Lord!—and meanwhile?"

"You ought to see him—you ought to hear him explain—"

"No, I won't. I *have* seen him. I'VE HEARD HIM EXPLAIN. FOR TWO HOURS—Why doesn't he cut his hair like other people? GINGER-HEADED BEAST! Why does he let his tie ends blow over his shoulder? IT ISN'T A FLAG. Why does he walk about as though he was being photographed? How does he get a living? You can't get a living by writing plays, you have to sell them."

"He *will* sell them."

"Yes, yes—and meanwhile? MEANWHILE?"

"Oh, you *are* unkind!" said Muriel. "You *are* unkind."

"Unkind! I think you one of *the*—But there! Why have you come back to me?"

"To implore you to forgive me."

"*Yeah*!" said Mr. Waddy, and was speechless for some seconds.

"Look here!" he burst out. "I never asked you to come here. If you don't stop this play-acting I'll—I'll smash this window. I never asked you to come here. For two years—"

"How *little* you understand!" she cried, "how little you understand!"

"For two years you've imposed upon me—"

"Uncle," she cried warningly. "*Uncle*!"

"Yes—imposed upon me. You have played such antics at me as no man in his senses ever endured before. Now I think of it—I'm astonished at myself. Astonished. You've wrapped me about with lies and nonsense, and finally you insult me, you use me as a sort of diving board—an x diving board—for this infernal elopement foolery. And you have the brazen impudence . . ."

"Oh!" she cried and her eyes were swimming with tears. "*Uncle*!"

"You have the brazen impudence . . ."

"Oh! it isn't you," she sobbed; "it can't be you. Not your better self! It's some evil spirit, uncle . . ."

For some moments it was doubtful whether Mr. Waddy would not have a fit. When at last he spoke it was in simple English unadorned. His voice was almost weak. "I'm *not* your uncle," he said. "And this has got to end. Go away. I'll send for a policeman if you don't."

When Mrs. Chitterlow returned to their modest apartments Chitterlow received her with elaborate indifference. His was an independent spirit, he would accept but he would not ask, and this pilgrimage for pardon had been entirely at Muriel's initiative. But her news when it came staggered him a little. He regarded her tear-stained face with an eye that was not entirely free from criticism and a natural emotion found vent.

"Why don't you let *me* see him?" said Chitterlow, WARMING HIS FINGERS IN HIS HAIR. "He's all right if you rub him the right way. He seems to be a spirited old chap. He listened to me all right that time I saw him. If I could only get at him a bit more and tell him a story or so . . .

"Not of course that *I* want to run after him. Only it's hard on you to be separated . . ."

He meditated on Mr. Waddy and his own personal charm. "I hate misunderstanding," he said.

"If only he saw you," said Muriel the loyal. "That's what I told him."

And as this seemed the most hopeful course to both of them, Mrs. Satsuma in a state of fluttered adventure, took soundings.

In vain. "I won't have that FLAMING ass in my house again, and that's flat. He's talked Bosh about art and himself at me for TWO mortal hours, and more I cannot and will not stand," said Mr. Waddy going on to add quite needless emphasis.

His subsequent conduct was spirited and consistent. "He's a good old chap," said the indomitable Chitterlow, after inconceivable rebuffs. "A very firm old boy. And I know he likes me really. I know he does. I only wish I could see him. I *know* we should get on together."

But he could not see him, and when Mr. Waddy presently left Tunbridge Wells, and Muriel's little accumulation of pocket money ran short, our young couple realised they were in for bad weather.

But Chitterlow was a man of resource. He had lived for all his life, with immense variety of interest and comfort, on nothing, and he was not the sort of man to be crushed by the delicate addition of Muriel. It is true that at the outset he made the suggestion that she should return to Mr. Waddy. But he presented it in far too harrowing a light for her. They had made an informal balance sheet. And he sat in an attitude of profound depression, with one leg over the arm of the dingy lodging-house chair. "I cannot bear that you should suffer hardship," he said musingly. "A girl like you should walk in silken wrappings . . . I would rather—yes—I would rather—face the world alone."

"Then," he added with a sigh of anticipatory relief, "I shouldn't care what became of me."

But he had aroused a passion that was to be the cardinal fact of his life henceforth. Muriel grasped his hand.

"I will never leave you," said Muriel through a cascade of tears.[1]

Mr. Chitterlow, I say, was a born actor, compact of emotions, and so far he had never failed to play up to an emotion. He did not fail now.

"It's noble of you," said Chitterlow. "The women I have known—! I did not expect it of you, Muriel. You give me new ideas—new ideals. Do you know, I HAD never known a pure brave woman before I met you."

HE PUT IT AS SOMETHING UNSPEAKABLY PATHETIC.

Muriel had no phrase ready. She flung herself upon him and there was an interval. Presently they were sitting side by side on the sofa with the broken springs, she with her head nestling to his lapel and his arm about her waist.

"He doesn't respect me," said Chitterlow, clenching a dramatic fist. "He shall."

"Yes—he shall."

"He shall see my play—the play I am writing. Already—Already much of it is IN A STATE to be written. He shall see that play triumphant. It is no ordinary play. I have compared it with the work of other men, Jones, Grundy, Sims, Parker.[2] Well—Their work is—Tzit!" He grimaced and snapped his fingers.

"Yes," said Muriel. "Yes!"

"Tzit!" repeated Mr. Chitterlow.

"Our honeymoon—such as it was—is over. I am going—" He paused before the tremendous announcement, and his voice sank to that hissing whisper that is so important an element in every great actor's outfit. "*To work*! . . . *Work*."

"We will both work," said Muriel.

"We will both work," (Printer, space. [Wells's note.]) he repeated in an impressive staccato, and thought ostentatiously while she feasted on his profile.

"Yes," he said, "the thing to do is to hold out as well as we can until the play can be done. After that I have no fear."

"I daresay I could get some work OF SOME SORT," said Muriel. <"Sewing or something like that. Anything would do to tide over—until the play is done."

"Anything," he agreed, and thought.

"I have never shown you the play," he said. "I will. You must see it. That has been one of the things—one of my dearest hopes."

He sprang up, and went into the bedroom. She heard him open his box and drop things carelessly on the floor. He shouted to her as he did so but only fragments reached her. "It will surprise you . . . things in it . . . work . . . but you must hear . . . rubbish . . . you must tell me. *I* think it tremendous of course . . . naturally would."\>

HE returned flourishing a small quarto exercise book, enriched with the sporadic meditations of his last three years of wandering. "It is all here," he said, talking even AS he REAPPEARED in the doorway, "all here. But you won't understand it a bit. It is—compressed. But the things I have—things that have never been done before—never. Situations, passions —psychology. That is where we moderns score. Psychology. Shakespear? Didn't *know* the word. And the situations! Jones never thought of them—Grundy—none of them. If they *had* thought of 'em, wouldn't know how to treat 'em. None of them have had my experience, really. In their way of course Jones and Grundy are big men, probably bigger than me ("No, no," from Mrs. Chitterlow)—but in this way, in *my* way, and it's the right way, that I'll swear, they can't touch me, can't come near me . . ."

He continued in this strain for some time. It was dark

before he had told her all about the railway accident, the
<aspects of his own nature, and the tremendous conception
of passion that was to be introduced. The aspects of his own
nature he proposed to introduce were other than those he had
originally designed to work upon, and his conception of passion had altered materially since he met Muriel.>

He described a scene originally designed to bring in a
picture by the master of the school of art. <He had perceived
certain "business" possible with this, and as he had developed
the idea of this "business" into definite action, he had forgotten the master of the school of art altogether.> The picture
had been replaced FIRST BY A PAINTED TAMBOURINE, AND
THAT BY A REAL ONE AND THAT AGAIN by what Chitterlow
called a "Strad"—a sort of fiddle—on which the leading character, a person not unlike Chitterlow, was NOW to play (or-
chestra) up to an effective curtain. Instinctively he thrust
himself into the foreground AS HE DETAILED THESE THINGS,
changing the play as he went on, until it had but one single
superb figure. He knew his hearer. And at last he made an
end—ACTING HIS PART. "He comes very slowly into the
middle of the stage and stands—so—WITH FOLDED ARMS—
THOUGHTFUL. And then—very slowly and quietly mind—so
—comes the curtain . . . down."

Her eyes shone at him out of the dark. "It will be splendid," she said, "splendid. I would DO ANYTHING—ANYONE
OUGHT TO BE WILLING TO DO ANYTHING, rather than you
should be prevented from writing a play like that."

"He shall see us," said Chitterlow. "All the world shall see
us. Boxes, stalls, circle, pit, gallery, all—packed. We'll have
him. In a box. You can get invalid carriages. I'll arrange all
that. Pay for it out of my own pocket. I don't want his money.
Grundy, Jones, Sims, Rose—all in the stalls—I'll see to that.
Up goes the curtain. Tzit! Act one, knocks 'em. Act two,
knocks 'em. Act three, KNOCKS 'EM!" Chitterlow was
shouting now and his arm waving wildly. "Bif!—Bang!
Who's first playwright now? Grundy?—no! Jones?—no!
Wilde?—no! Sims! Rose? No, no, no! Who then?"

"Chitterlow!" choked Muriel, glowing with an almost
religious enthusiasm.

"And so to work," shouted Chitterlow springing to his
feet. "Ink! Pens!" He rushed up and down the little room.

"I'll go out and get some sermon paper," he bawled as if he was on a hurricane deck. "Five quires for sixpence. Here's sixpence! *You* get table, pens, ink!"

He rushed from the room and it was as if a RED Bengal light had ceased to burn THERE.

Muriel was immediately active. Pens, ink, and table in order, she had a brilliant idea. She rushed into the bedroom, and after headlong ransacking re-emerged—in time.

It was a vermilion coloured flannel penwiper surmounted by a monkey of elaborate design worked in beads, the flannel was pinked irregularly and was of the proper sort, with lovely interwoven long red hairs to get into the pen nib, and the whole thing had already been blessed, collectively and in detail, by Mr. Waddy with all his heart and strength.

"*There!*" she said with tears of pride in her voice as Chitterlow reappeared.

Chitterlow worked with fury for four days, HE TORTURED HIS UNSHORN MANE UNTIL HE LOOKED LIKE A CAMEL'S-HAIR PAINTBRUSH WORN OUT IN THE SERVICE OF SCARLET, and his landlady, after one slip, went carefully among the sheets of sermon paper with which he strewed the little room. Mrs. Chitterlow flung herself at a hostile world with equal resolution, and it immediately gave her some children's garments to cut out and make. They spent several hours each day holding hands and telling each other how desperately they were toiling FOR EACH OTHER. BUT on the fourth afternoon Chitterlow broke up the harmony of things by howling aloud, tearing up four sheets of paper, and only desisting from tearing up all he had written at Muriel's violent intervention. "I can't," he shouted. "I can't. It's bosh I have written—bosh!" He tore AMIDST THE TUMULT OF his hair and got up and paced, until he trod upon a little heap of sheets in the corner and was calmed by the consequent wild stagger across the room.

Then, talking more consecutively from the sofa, he made it clear that the trouble was "construction." The play could not work on its present lines because it would involve <killing somebody, and there was nobody could be spared from the big dénouement that came just before the hero was left alone with the Strad. On the other hand the public would not stand, no one could stand, Chitterlow could not stand, a costly and

complex railway accident without killing somebody material
to the play. But if the railway accident was omitted then the
Third Act could not possibly happen in the Alpine snows
where at present it did happen, because the only thing that
could possibly bring people there together was a St. Fithian
train de luxe. Besides which, if the railway accident were done
"offstage" the Third Act would not be long enough—could
not last five minutes. "Oh Damn Construction!" said Chitterlow. "Damn it!">

They talked it over GRAVELY, but got no further with the
problem. <Incidentally they discovered that he had inadvert-
ently so arranged things that the spiteful governess whose
betrayal of the heroine precipitates the big dénouement must
—on account of her possession of the secret—be at least fifty
years old, while on the other hand, she has been thrown over
in love by the hero, who is three and twenty, in favour of the
heroine.>

"No," said Chitterlow with emphasis. "I must rest. I must
clear my mind of it for a bit. That's what I must do."

Muriel suggested a walk. He asked her to come too, but
after a struggle with contending duties she decided she must
keep her promise to finish the garments in hand. They parted
in a glow of devotion, and Chitterlow made his way to the
seafront. There he presently fell into conversation with three
young holiday keepers from London. They were "flats," knew
nothing of the stage and fancied, he gathered, that they could
sing comic songs of the shady type. He was speedily relaxing
his mind by telling them all about the old life he had re-
nounced when he married, and after a few feeble attempts to
brag back at him they listened with gratifying awe. Somebody,
it may have been Chitterlow, suggested that he should go to
their apartments with them and do some choice recitations he
knew. He went home with them to supper, and they had a
glorious evening, recitations, songs, Chitterlow's reminiscences
and so forth, and he got back to Muriel about two.

She had finished all the little garments and was reading
Donovan.[3] At first she seemed a little inclined to resent his late
appearance, but when he explained how much his mind had
been relaxed and stirred up and particularly what a splendid
solution of the difficulty had occurred to him during the
evening, she rejoiced with him. The solution had been greatly

helped by the acquaintance of one of the three young men, whom he proposed to study for the play.

＜He proposed to so interweave this young man, that he could be killed in the railway accident. Instead of the governess betraying the secret, it was to be found in the pocket of the dead young man—it would be quite easy to invent how it got there, in the morning—when they sought his address and read out by a comic Swiss official with an imperfect knowledge of English, as the curtain incident for act three. "That's the sort of thing I like," said Chitterlow. "Funny! Grim! See? Laugh one minute. Funny. Then—what's he reading? *He* doesn't know. Doesn't understand."＞

He felt a little "chippy" the next morning, but a nip of brandy in an egg cup put that all right. He soon declared himself "tremendously keen" on his new arrangement. In fact he now proposed to carry it further and ＜to increase the importance of the young man, so as to make him a principal character, if not the principal character. He was to be treated in an ironical manner, and the play would no longer be tragic. The young man was to be in love with the governess, who was also to be promoted to a more important position, and the incident of the comic Swiss officia¹ was to be greatly enlarged —in fact made the chief incident.

Chitterlow＞ went out in the afternoon to find the young flat again and study him further. As he learnt that they were returning to London in three days' time he devoted the whole time to his and their edification.

These festive enquiries completed, Chitterlow after a day of gloom, interior disorder and brandy nipping, arose in his might and proceeded to recast the play. Muriel already had some more work to do, and albeit her industry was rather less feverish than at first, she still felt herself a most exemplary heroine. She read by chance a paper on Great Men's Wives in a threepenny-half-penny popular periodical, that interested her very much. A number of Great Men, for the most part previously unknown to her, had been circularised by the editor, and advantageously posed photographs of their wives adorned the page. ＜It certainly was prettier than the Great Men would have been—Great Men wind up appearing so remarkably plain. Several of the Great Men ingenuously confessed how much their wives had helped and inspired them, and the paper stirred her to emulation. She even elaborated and threw out a number of suggestions for the development of the play. But Chitterlow displayed a curious disinclination for that sort of assistance.>

They stopped quite a long time at Tunbridge Wells. The Chitterlow credit had never been so good, for many of the tradesmen had seen Muriel with Mrs. Satsuma and her purchasing power was lit by the refulgence of Mr. Waddy's wealth. The art school master MOREOVER had a touch of romance in his nature, albeit a timid man himself, and he sympathised deeply with their emotions. (It cost him five and twenty pounds in the end, besides the minor charges for entertainment.) His wife did not like Muriel very much. When at last the Chitterlows' financial position became so austere that a departure from Tunbridge Wells seemed advisable, the play had progressed considerably. It was still of course unwritten, but great things had been done in clearing the ground.

Chitterlow was eloquent on the amount he had learnt in those few brief months of profitable labour. He could now see quite plainly that the railway accident had no legitimate place in the play. NEITHER HAD THE ALPS. THESE INGREDIENTS WERE essentially melodrama and he reserved THEM for a subsequent triumph. In THE place OF THESE MERETRICIOUS ORNAMENTS was to be more of what he called "psychology" —the thing that Shakespear did not know the name of. <The detailed specification of that psychology was not as yet arranged. The original hero and heroine and certain successors had long since vanished, and an ingenious four o'clock tea opening had been reluctantly abandoned.> The character of the young man visitor was also PERCEIVED AS an excrescence. That too was rejected and the play now stood, SAVE FOR THIS PSYCHOLOGY, an extremely hopeful void—"DE-JONAH'D" SO TO SPEAK.

All this was satisfactory progress. Their search for winter quarters came as an appropriate relief and rest after these achievements. That over, he had a conviction amounting almost to a certainty, that he would sit down and without intermission write off the completed play.

✤ 6 ✤

Little Lord Fauntleroy

FOR six years that great estrangement continued. It was certainly not for want of forgiveness on Muriel's part. SHE KEPT ON FORGIVING. She went from postal address to postal address during those years—lapsing at times to the *Era* letter-box—and obviously leading a life of remarkable and interesting adventure unhappily outside the limits of this novel. No doubt her life was full and vivid, for to marry a genius of the Chitterlow stamp is simply to hook the creature —to MAKE SURE OF him takes years. <For all those years Mrs. Satsuma kept up a correspondence with the dispossessed heiress. At times the letters flew hurtling to and fro, intimate and frequent; at others the thread was stretched to an extreme tenuity. A series of pictures of variable intensity were left on the mind of Mrs. Satsuma; some were essentially impressionistic performances, others minute in detail, others were blankness veiled.

There was a season of very tender sentiment indeed and Muriel became a mother. In that long correspondence Chitterlow interpolated a letter of pride and thanksgiving and anxiety and their immediate stresses were alleviated at the expense of Mrs. Satsuma's post office account.

The Honourable Thomas Norgate appeared for a time in the capacity of host, contemporaneously with a marked improvement in the quality of Muriel's note paper. Then one livid gleam and darkness. "Harry has had a dreadful fight with Mr. Norgate, blacked both his eyes he says, and please dear never mention that horrid man's name again." And Mrs. Satsuma never did in spite of a painful gnawing in her mind. From certain phrases Mrs. Satsuma gathered that Chitterlow was now away from home sometimes for weeks together. At certain seasons she had a feeling, instinctive rather than reasoned, that Muriel must be in some sort of situation.

Through all their vicissitudes loomed the figure of the great play that would not get itself done, labouring like a ship in a hurricane. Now it was on its beam ends, "he is doubtful whether to throw it out altogether and start upon a new idea he has," and it lit up gloriously in an unexpected ray of sunshine, "quite by accident we have found out some things that will really help us over all the difficult places—for there *have* been difficult places dear." Presently it would appear, keeling perilously before the wind, "he is writing very fast now." Anon, it pitched up again, jury-masted and changed almost beyond recognition. "Did I tell you he is making his play into a comic opera?" And soon the flying scud of necessity drove so thick and fast that it vanished out of sight altogether. There were clearly times when the sordid distrust of tradesmen could even drive Chitterlow to uncongenial toil. "Lessons in elocution," "Harry's pupils," "Harry is busy with a little job," gleamed in the letters ever and again. And once it seemed they had fallen to a hired cinematograph on tour. But from that they were happily delivered by a seizure of debt.>

But through it all she maintained a close correspondence with Mrs. Satsuma, and never once did she flinch from her attitude of the disinherited niece. Mr. Waddy too went from place to place, quarrelling with air and soil and aspect as poor invalids will, and ever Mrs. Satsuma, faithful to Muriel, watched his moods and counselled and advised.

At first his anger was hot against Muriel. He said the most painful things about her, called her an impostor and an Arthur Orton-ess[1] and the like, in great variety. He made nine different wills in the three months immediately following her departure, and over each there was trouble with Grimflack, his solicitor, BECAUSE OF the allusions made to her. Not that he left her anything. And throughout those early days Mrs. Satsuma found it wise to dissemble her love for Muriel. Then for a year and more came a period of "never mention her name again," from which he emerged apropos of two Christmas cards—one from Muriel and one from "my little Harry to his uncle." "Who in grace is little Harry?" he asked Mrs. Satsuma, and that led to general enquiries.

"And they drag the wretched child about the country with an x cinematograph show, do they!" he said, flaming into the familiar mood.

That marked an epoch in this relationship. Waddy's quarrel with Mr. and Mrs. Chitterlow rested no longer on a purely personal basis. He took up the cause of that unhappy infant with hot indignation. Insensibly too the burthen of his animosity shifted on to Chitterlow's shoulders. And as the years passed and the great play failed to emerge, the vigour of his denunciation increased.

"That poor little chap," he said. "That poor little fellow. Where are they now? What are they doing with him?"

< "Been so fortunate as to have the cinematograph seized for debt. Cinematograph people owing the debt. Well, they're quit of that anyhow. But what'll they do next—and how about the boy?"

"Stopping with the Honourable Thomas Norgate. How long will *that* last? Nice company for a little boy, *he* is."

"Any more news of that poor little boy. The holiest of responsibilities. Ought to devote their lives to him. Try and make him a better human being than *they* are. Instead of which they x . . ."

"Muriel wasn't so bad. It's that x red-haired xx. Oh! if I could only get about . . ." >

Now while Mr. Waddy thumped and raged in the pitiful little tragi-comedy of his exterior being, there was another quite unexpected drama going on within him; as hidden from HIM and from all, save perhaps two doctors, as though it was a life in another planet. It was the silent inevitable development of his cycling disaster, the slow downward change of unhealed tissues. There came a time when his energies ebbed and he tired of controversies and world-mending. He became reflective for hours together, he surveyed his life and THE vision of a generous active nature in a mean, exasperating and inadequate environment. (An x environment.) He was guilty of self-pity and self-condolence. He pictured himself weather beaten and not ignobly sad. And one day, *apropos* of the Chitterlows, he had a sudden vision of this worn, sad, ill-used old man grouped with a little boy, a nice, clean, sensibly dressed, sympathetic, agreeable, respectful little boy, a little boy who at that very instant was being neglected and possibly ill-treated by two—well! *Magna est veritas et prevalebit*—x vagabonds . . .

That dream became a motive. There came first incidental remarks to Mrs. Satsuma, vague nothings that yet conveyed an unwonted promise of reconciliation. She reported these hopeful enigmas to Muriel. < "He's dreadful set against your dear husband," wrote Mrs. Satsuma. "It seems as though he *must* be cross with one of you. And yet about your little Harry he says the *kindest* things."

And one day Mr. Waddy showed his mind to Mrs. Satsuma. "Wouldn't it be possible to save that youngster—to adopt him. I mean. Surely if *she*, poor girl, must drag about the world after that scoundrel, the child needn't . . ."

Mrs. Satsuma had the hardest work in the world to conceal her surging delight until she had left the room.

So it was that> suddenly the Chitterlow family—Chitterlow breaking an engagement to coach a municipal ornament of Liverpool in a speech—hurled itself across England to Folkestone. Muriel's face was radiant with hope. <Master Harry was to be adopted; there was to be a week on approval first, but who could doubt the little fellow's success? And then? The title of a novel kept running through Muriel's head —the story she could not recall—and the title was *At His Gates*.[2] It conjured up pictures of a meritorious siege. At any rate the Chitterlows meant to camp conveniently in Folkestone, ready to follow up this opening. Muriel knew that it was only necessary they should be understood. And now at last was an opportunity of getting themselves interpreted.>

Some years ago, as the reader will remember, there was published a charming story called *Little Lord Fauntleroy*.[3] It had what novelists, I AM TOLD, are accustomed to speak of as a Boom. It was about a beautiful little boy who was brought up in the poorer circles of a simple American town, and chiefly by virtue of innate tendency emerged an extremely frank and refined little gentleman. In due course his exclusive, cross and irritable grandfather—he was an English nobleman AND THE BOOK WAS WRITTEN BEFORE SANTIAGO[4]—sent from England for him. The TRANSATLANTIC freshness and gentleness of this little man acted like a charm upon that morose ARISTOCRAT, developed long unsuspected seeds of goodness in his withered heart, and led to a small local Millennium. The little boy was dressed in beautiful velveteen and had long golden hair down his little back, and as the boom boomed an epidemic of little boys in velveteen and with long AND AS golden AS POSSIBLE hair marked its spreading triumph. Little boys in velveteen and with long MORE OR LESS FLAXEN or golden hair swarmed first throughout the United States of America, then they broke out abundantly and almost simultaneously in Canada and England. They sprang next, from the seed of the Tauchnitz Edition, in every continental resort, and slowly permeated the colonies and dependencies, until at last Mrs. Hodgson Burnett had a visible empire, unshorn and velveteen clad, that girdled the earth. And even nowadays the book is to be got in any circulating library not too violently up to date, and belated votaries hasten to the purchase of Vandyke collars. Among these Muriel was numbered. The book so fascinated her that, in spite of considerable pressure from unpaid tradesmen, she bought it.

<Master Harry's upbringing had developed a certain severance of sympathy between his parents.[5] So far as it affected herself she had never resented Chitterlow's tumultuous manifestations of virility, but she developed altogether new traits in relation to her child. Fiction had acquainted her with "wild Irish girls"[6] in great abundance, and the essentially refined freedoms of the delightful young people in Mrs. Rhoda Broughton's *Cometh Up as a Flower*.[7] But these things did not affect little boys. From Mrs. Henry Wood in particular she had acquired ideals of maternity that were perhaps on a higher level than any other part of her mental equipment.[8] She insisted that Master Harry was to be a "little gentleman." Unhappily her ideas of a "gentleman" were perhaps pitiful, but she set out to realise them with a strength of purpose that astonished Chitterlow. He was one of those men who had known "all about women" quite early, and this was one of

those things that bring men into a wiser and more respectful frame. She insisted that under all circumstances Master Harry was to be picturesquely dressed, but from the outset Master Harry's treatment of his costume was contumacious, and from the earliest date, Master Harry's hair displayed a vigorous distaste for curling.[9]

Discipline varied considerably according to the character of the novel that chanced to be in the ascendant. Chitterlow, whose earliest emotion on the matter of Harry had been a sort of disgust of fatherhood, had mingled with that a considerable jealousy of his offspring. And Muriel knew how near this spirited being had been to ignominious flight from his widening responsibilities, and indeed all the eminent professional persons he had known and respected agreed in regarding a "blessed kid" as the final tragedy of love. But presently Nature suborned rather than subjugated his extraordinary egotism, by insisting on the amazing resemblance between Master Harry and himself. Master Harry showed spirit before he showed a tooth, and Chitterlow feeling into the remote past found a marvellous memory of his own parallel precocity. His expressed opinion that his son was a "goggling bubbly little beast" was heard for the last time when Master Harry walked a yard. He began to feel a growing pride in his son, a returning interest in Muriel,[10] but the passionate romance of the elopement had gone forevermore. He was no longer her fate and her lover, he was the man she had reformed, to a certain extent that is, and a person open to criticism. The men with whom she identified him now, in her still voracious novel reading, were conveniently married when the book began.

His influence on his son was gusty and spasmodic . . .[11] taught him to recite with all the airs of an infant prodigy[12] . . . do imitations of Irving.

And emerging from this rapidly sketched tangle of circumstances appears Master Harry, six years old, thin legged, small and hard with something of his father's profile, his mother's eyes, and eccentric wavy hair, apparently altogether his own. >

And now as they flew southward she re-read *Little Lord Fauntleroy*, in such times as she was not checking Master Harry in his attempts to clean the window with his velveteen sleeve, or wiping his face and knees after the consumption of

an orange, or attending to the thousand and one little duties
her maternal responsibility demanded. As their custom was,
Chitterlow travelled by a different train.

Every now and then she would cease her reading and
regard little Harry with an optimistic eye. <He too would say
frank winning unexpected things, she felt sure—she had tried
to coach him in a few impromptus. Before the frank eyes, the
unblemished thought, the artless wisdom and loyalty of childhood, Waddy's distrust and suspicion would fade like the
mists of the morning before the rising of the sun. And so forth
—pleasant, gold-tipped dreams.>

And meanwhile Mr. Waddy was in a mood of unprecedented amiability, he radiated an egotistical and untrustworthy benevolence. He BEGAN TO read Hugo's *L'Art de 'être
Grandpère*, and found it not incredible. But he was an Englishman and he felt instinctively that the kindliness to be dealt
out to Master Harry must be of an austere sort. The great
thing was to get the lad away from these parents of his, give
him elementary notions of self-respect, in which he was
conceivably lacking, and an idea of the proper way to do
things. Proper notions—that is to say a hearty dislike of actors,
Jesuits, atheists and radicals, solicitors, town AND (MORE
PARTICULARLY) COUNTY councillors of all sorts, AND OF
ALL PEOPLE INIMICAL TO MARINE ENGINEERS—were to be
carefully instilled. NO PAINS WERE TO BE SPARED TO MAKE
HARRY A BRAVE, HEALTHY, HAPPY, ENGLISH BOY.

PRACTICALLY MR. WADDY WAS STILL OF the same way of
thinking when Master Harry arrived. The *Times* had been a
trifle irritating, it is true, that morning, but he had exercised
self-control. On the table beside him WERE GRAPES, a
draughtboard and <*L'Art d'être Grandpère* was in his hand.
Mr. Waddy was reading of that gift of the special strawberries
to the children. "Oh you dear little birds, you gourmands from
Paradise, it belongs to you," read Mr. Waddy.>¹³

He heard Mrs. Satsuma coming upstairs with an unfamiliar light footfall, AND PUT THE BOOK DOWN. He experienced
a transitory nervousness. He recalled that he must be prepared
with a smile, and he prepared one.

"Leave go my shoulder, will you," said a small voice as the
door opened. Then Mrs. Satsuma appeared, and round the
contour of her person about one half of Master Harry.

"Here's our young gentleman, Sir," she said, smiling pleasantly, and dexterously brought the young gentleman in question into full view.

He was a small pinched little boy with thin legs and large eyes. His hands were deep in his trouser pockets and a suspicious scowl rested on remarkably expressive features. Except for a shoe buckle he had already removed, he wore the regulation Fauntleroy costume, but his HOT CHESTNUT hair was of an eccentric wiry sort that had defied even Muriel's vigorous ideality. From his pocket projected the end of a tin whistle.

For a moment neither spoke, and then Mr. Waddy roused himself to an amateurish amiability. "And so you're Harry Chitterlow," he said. "Eh?"

Master Harry answered nothing but his scowl seemed to deepen.

"Aren't you going to shake hands with me?" asked Mr. Waddy.

Mrs. Satsuma enforced the suggestion with a vigorous thrust and Master Harry advanced with obvious reluctance. He placed a small but grubby hand in Mr. Waddy's palm, and withdrew it promptly to his knickerbocker pocket. His BRIGHT BROWN eyes were almost disconcerting. He breathed heavily.

"Won't you sit down in that chair?" said Mr. Waddy. "And talk to me?"

Master Harry assisted by Mrs. Satsuma acceded. He folded his arms on the table. There was a pause. Mrs. Satsuma smiled steadily between the antagonists.

< "So you've come to see your sick old uncle?" said Mr. Waddy.

Silence. "Say 'yes' dear," said Mrs. Satsuma gently.

"Leave the boy alone," said Mr. Waddy with a flare of irritability. "Let him speak for himself. He's just a bit—nervous. And you needn't wait. We shall get on all right together in a minute—famously."

Master Harry turned his eyes to Mrs. Satsuma, who hesitated.

"Go on," said Mr. Waddy.

"I'll come back soon," said Mrs. Satsuma, turning to go. Before she was half way across the room Master Harry had slipped down from his chair. "Lemme come," said Master Harry, in pursuit. "Lemme come," and his face relaxed to tears.

"I don' LIKE 'im," said Master Harry. "I don' LIKE 'im."

He gripped Mrs. Satsuma's skirts. She stopped.

Mr. Waddy's face was expressive of the will to be amiable rather than of amiability pure and simple. "You've been set against me Harry," he said. "And I don't suppose you *do* like me at first. But you will."

"*I* don' LIKE 'im," cried Master Harry, growing shriller.

"But he's your kind uncle, dearest," said Mrs. Satsuma. "He's going to give you all sorts of things."

"I don' LIKE 'im," insisted Master Harry clutching tighter.

Pause.

"Harry," said Mrs. Satsuma, "d'you like sweeties?"

No reply.

"Does Harry like grapes?" asked Mr. Waddy.

"Beautiful grapes," said Mrs. Satsuma. "Look at them."

Master Harry looked. Then his expressive eyes went to Waddy, and then back to the grapes. He was obviously weighing the two.

"Come and have a grape, old chap," said Mr. Waddy.

Master Harry looked at Mrs. Satsuma.

"Go and take a nice grape, Harry," said Mrs. Satsuma impelling him gently forward.

In scarcely more than five minutes Master Harry was seated once more at the table, eating grapes with a certain lack of silent refinement and keeping a trying gaze on Mr. Waddy. Mr. Waddy affected to admire the view. Mrs. Satsuma edged away by degrees, and pretended to engage in dusting the volumes in the book case.

It was quite clear to Mr. Waddy that Master Harry's shyness was due to improper treatment—all that would have to be altered. The first thing to do would be to encourage him, to give him confidence. The grapes were disappearing rapidly. It was necessary to develop some new interest before they came to an end.>

"Beautiful view from this window," he said.

"Eh?" said Master Harry.

"Beautiful view—pleasant expanse—sea—grass—people. Interesting to watch."

"We had a winder in Sheffield 'd beat this ole winder into fits," said Master Harry.

"Oh?" said Mr. Waddy.

"Into fits. You saw our winder in Sheffield you'd never want to see outer this ole winder again. I lay."

Mr. Waddy took a moment to recover.

"We had a better winder than this a'most everywhere we've been."

Mrs. Satsuma felt called upon to intervene. "You can see *France* from this window dear."

"No, I can't," said Master Harry. "See? And besides, you could see Germany from our winder in Sheffield—easy. France ain't nuffin. Out'v our winder in Sheffield—besides Germany —you could see[14]

"Ssh," said Mrs. Satsuma.

Mr. Waddy directed his eye to her. "Leave the boy alone," he said. He hesitated. "I'll ring if I want you," he said. And Mrs. Satsuma after a doubtful look at Master Harry, withdrew.

Pause. Master Harry's eyes went about the room, he whistled contemplatively between his set teeth—after the manner of small boys who have yet to learn the nobler sort of whistling—and began a rhythmic series of kicks against the leg of his chair. Mr. Waddy sought some new conversational opening. "Is your mother well?" he asked.

"*She's* all right," said Master Harry, and slipping off his chair by an effort, went across the room to Mr. Waddy's bureau.[15]

Went round the room opening drawers. OFFERED TO RECITE "Pút a fézzer iń is moúf and cáll im mácarōni."

DEAFENING shrieks with grass held in fingers.

"I gotcher nose," violent blow on nose.

"Gotcher," blow on back with net.

There was murder in Mr. Waddy's eyes.

"Send that brat home!"[16]

"Has that boy gone?" he demanded, fixing Mrs. Satsuma with an imperative forefinger.

"Very well. Understand you are never to admit the little

beast again. Never. If you do—we part. I'd as soon live in a cage with monkeys. Understand me, Madam. *Monkeys*!"

He brought his fist down with violence upon the book that lay upon the table (*L'Art d'être Grandpère*, it chanced to be), and glared glassily to indicate the force of his will. Mrs. Satsuma, deeply moved, bowed her assent and withdrew.

He kept talking to himself in a picturesque way, about various sorts of monkey, throughout his lunch, and the subject still exercised his invention when the good old man with the bath chair called for him in the afternoon. Even along the Leas he was downcast and mumbling with indignation. He was aroused by the stopping of his bath chair.

He looked up and beheld the figure of his self-constituted niece.

It was the first time he had seen her for six years and his first impression was that maturity had not improved her. SHE WAS FULLER IN THE THROAT, RATHER WHITE IN THE COMPLEXION, AND LAXER ABOUT THE MOUTH. Her unfounded claim to the ladylike, that COMMON justification of fraud upon tradesmen, asserted itself in the style of her threadbare unseasonable clothes. Yet, looked at from a little distance, regardless of dates and with the eyes partially closed, she might have passed for one of the serene and enviable heroines of her fiction. So much at least is it given to mortals to accomplish in the pursuit of romantic ideals. Master Harry stood beside her. He had been washed recently, the velvet suit was mended and he wore a clean Vandyke collar. There were, however—though this is sordid realism—crumbs about his mouth. The interview was evidently none of his seeking, and his little white face regarded Mr. Waddy with lurid animosity.

"Oh Uncle!" she cried.

"*Uncle*!" snarled Mr. Waddy.

"He is *so* sorry, poor little fellow. He did *not* understand."

"Yah!" said Mr. Waddy. "Whaddyer want now?"

"Nothing," she cried, "nothing! Oh Uncle, how you mistake us!"

"What 'r upsetting me for now then?"

"He wants to beg your pardon, Uncle. Harry."

The antagonism of Harry's face relaxed not at all. "Want to beg your pardon," he said as though it was a curse.

Mr. Waddy regarded him pensively for a moment. Then he turned to Muriel. "Why . . . *don't* you chuck it?" he said.

"I've nothing to chuck," she said. "Oh Uncle, why are you always—"

She stopped abruptly, for Mr. Waddy had taken a deep breath and seemed on the verge of shouting. Her sudden silence averted that. There was a pause between them.

"What *have* I done?" he cried with aimless gestures of his hands. "What *have* I done? That Heaven should send lunatics from the ends of the earth to badger me in this fashion." He caught the eye of his chairman. "Go on!" he cried with a gesture of the fist suddenly clenched. "Go on."

He turned to Muriel who had taken a step forward. "If you follow me," he shouted, and his face was awful; "I'll— I'll—"

She stopped, made another step, stopped again. A rare, and almost overpowering sense of the futility of her hopes struck her. For a time her gestures and expression were almost natural; the despair and disappointment in her face came from no story but her own.

"Silly o' Beast!" said Master Harry—unreproved.

"Good Lord!" fumed Mr. Waddy receding. "What a fool I was to have that boy! How the deuce am I to end this badgering? I must settle things. Oh! I *must* settle things."

"Leave it to Charities. By God! I'll leave it to anything or anybody rather than to these antic dealers! Charities—why not? What on earth does it matter?"

He went on snarling and grumbling to himself, heedless of the passers by. He looked up and to his excited senses it seemed that Muriel and Master Harry were far away on his right and stalking him. Immediate action became imperative. He lugged with startling violence at the small piece of twine that nowadays linked his hand to the coat tails of the good old man. "Come here!" he shouted with the volume of a speaking trumpet, and the good old man was hauled rather than came to him. Mr. Waddy released the string a little so that the good old man could turn round and bring his ear down.

"Go and tell her," bawled Mr. Waddy pointing. "That it's all left to Charities. Don't you understand? Tell that lady, you xxxxxxx, that it's all left to Charities. Xxx! Xx! Charities. Go on. Tell her now. No—never mind *what—it*. See? The lady—ah! He's got it after all!"

It is doubtful if the poor man had got it after all, but anything was better than asking Mr. Waddy again, and he started off with a pathetic hobbling alacrity after Mrs. Chitterlow to tell her something—all he had clear was xxx—and neither he nor Mr. Waddy nor anyone noticed that the bath chair stood on a gentle slope. But Mr. Waddy very speedily discovered it.

He never saw his alleged niece receive that parting shaft —if ever she did receive it. He found himself running down a slanting way and already going at a good walking pace. He swore and tried to stop himself by steering into the bank. A wheel lifted in the air, and for a moment he had all the sensations of falling over. But the moment passed and he saw he was not upset. Neither had he stopped.

He shouted in alarm, and damned all such as did not hear him. He was, he saw, on one of the ways that clamber down the cliff face of the Leas. He yelled with the desperate rage that is born of sudden fear. The way fell slanting down before him and halfway down it zigzagged. He was already well on his way to the angle and moving faster and faster.

At the angle? No, he would never round that! Over he would go, roll headlong for sixty feet or more and smash, he hoped, upon one at least of those silly deaf blockheads promenading below.

He was not afraid now, only intolerably angry. An excitement that was near exaltation seized him. He gripped the guide of the front wheel tight, ready to steer at the bend. He knew he could never do it.

The wheels creaked faster. A startled ground beetle heard him coming, made a short ill-advised run and was flattened out of existence by his passage . . .

⚜ 7 ⚜

A Full Account of This Mr. Kipps, His Parentage and Upbringing

ALLUSION has been made to a Mr. Kipps during the course of this story. He has flitted in a transitory way into quite a number of scenes. At the very outset you saw him at Folkestone, aghast at Mr. Waddy's language, and in the chapter immediately following he appeared again, a younger and simpler Kipps apprenticed at Tunbridge Wells, and as a round eye and a raised eyebrow regarding the noble Chitterlow with reverent astonishment over the edge of an art class easel. Then you glimpsed him after the elopement, flushed and proud, amidst a scandalised circle . . .

The manifest intention of the author has been to arouse interest and curiosity in this person, to provoke the reader to ask, What the devil has Kipps to do with it? I don't see how Kipps comes in. Who *is* this Kipps? Dammy, here's Kipps again! and so forth. Now, manifestly while Mr. Waddy trundles with a steadily accelerated velocity down that steep place upon the Leas, there comes a pause of awful expectation. And in that pause there can be nothing more fitting than two or three intercalary chapters about this same intrusive Kipps. That mystery disposed of, the time will be ripe for us to return and look for the surviving fragments (if any) of Mr. Waddy.

It explains a great deal that will follow when it is said that Mr. Kipps was born at New Romney. The place earned its epithet of "New," by the bye, somewhen in later Saxon days. It ruined its harbour by indiscreet inning of marshes in the late Plantagenet times, and abandoned dredging and its claims to novelty in despair when such new-fangled follies as oversea trade in deep-draught vessels with Spain and such unheard of latter-day places as India and America dwarfed the good old-fashioned traffic through France . . .

It explains still more to add that his parents were quite superior people. There is the superiority that arises from birth, the superiority of wealth, the superiority of distinctly exceptional and acknowledged strength, skill, beauty or courage; but the superiority of the parents of Mr. Kipps was none of these things; it was a sort of superiority that rarely flourishes in cities or where men mingle greatly together, but which still produces abundantly the most beautiful blossoms of conduct in isolated old-world villages; it was in fact superiority pure and simple—superiority for superiority's sake, in fact blank usurpation. It was at once the delight and torment of this excellent couple. It was such a temerarious superiority, a superiority that admits of no weak concessions, a thing as insecure as the good name of a bad respectable woman, and they guarded it jealously and bitterly all their lives. The worldly position of Old Kipps was that of a "respectable" tradesman and the adjective involved a distinction. He sold the apparatus of games, guns, toys, small stationery, minor ornaments, local photographs, and gaudily bound classics. He spoke of himself as a "bookseller and stationer" and ranked himself equal with wine merchant and chemist in the hierarchy of trade. If anything the literary connexion gave him a point against them, and put him near the level of auctioneer and surveyor. Yet they would not admit it, and that made him hate them.

For Pornick the little haberdasher next door, and indeed for all "counter jumpers," he affected a profound contempt—at least until the apprenticing of his son to that calling; grocers he held were unfit for human society by reason of their "tup'ny-'apenny profit cuttin'," and because they publicly exposed themselves in white aprons and shirt sleeves to the derision of all thinking men. Butchers were rough bawling scoundrels, all such as dealt in refreshments "pot-house keepers," and as for tailors—!

For the nobility and gentry, for bankers, stockbrokers, judges, the ampler clergy and elderly acquisitive lawyers he entertained a treacherous respect, an envious obsequiousness. To such he touched his hat and held that to deal with the stores after such honour had been done them was the vilest immorality. And his secret bitterness against these was greatly alleviated by the sort of standing snub their secluded existence administered to doctors, auctioneers, unprosperous clerics, schoolmasters, artists, chemists and the like poorish stuck-up creatures who vaunted themselves above him. If he personally could not take down such creatures of pretence, it was consoling to think there was a class of persons who could. He openly claimed to be "a bit superior" to all other orders of men.

And to be a bit superior to anyone was to arrogate a salute of hat touching for that person, a right to insult unanswered. Nothing enraged him more than the latter-day democratic view of tradesmen which would make them mere servants of the lowest of the low. An unwashed sweep who once presumed to propose the purchase of a toy bat, he ignominiously ordered out of his shop without further parley.

The perfect equal had yet to be discovered. Against such as presumed on equality Old Kipps waged an incessant warfare. There was the stationmaster, for example—"Just a promoted porter chap," said Old Kipps; and the national schoolmaster whose function he alleged was "to wipe the noses of all the labourers' brats in the place." (How Old Kipps would have got on in America strains the imagination.) A certain resplendent butler came as near equality perhaps as any. Old Kipps admired him as a possible thief of choice vintages. But in secret he resented this unwilling admiration. "These here yellow-plusses get their selves made butlers and nothin' ain't too good for 'em," he remarked to Mrs. Kipps. "All very nice down here in his grey soot, and lardy da, and How are you today, Mister Kipps?—quite the gent. But see 'im up at the 'ouse with 'er liddyship's lap dog. Yes m'lady, and no m'lady, and nothing that I can do for 'im that I won't, m'lady. Only say the word."

In such wise did Old Kipps requite himself for the gift of life, bespattering all other pilgrims in this vale of tears with

ignominious epithets and a generous hate. He was at any rate
frank about his feelings, led no man to suppose him amiable.
The publican he honoured with his patronage shivered at the
sight of him.[1] To "get the laugh" of some aspiring rival, "to
take him down a peg" was meat and drink to Old Kipps. His
laugh was a loud prolonged affair, accentuated by an extended
finger and tasteful repetitions of the barbed point.[2]

In person Old Kipps was rotund, his eye steadfast and
reddish, his head thrown back, and his mouth which was large
and oblique projected its lower lip in a permanent aggression
of pride. In addition to sporadic bristles, he had a beard
between his first and second chin, and he was heavy on his feet
and aided his steps with a stout stump of cabbage. Between
each step was a massive oscillatory pause, and his eye seemed
to seek opposition. On Sundays he wore a black frock coat
dating from a slimmer past, and went to church to shew his
superiority to Dissenters; on week-days his costume was easy
to the point of negligence. In winter he increased his girth by
additional jackets and vests.[3]

Mrs. Kipps was of a less agressive superiority. She professed even a sort of charity, "pitying the ignorance" of such as
would not give her the respect she claimed. In spite of the
declared contempt of Old Kipps for the inferior clergy—he
held the officiating curate, he said, no better than a "stuck-up
haw-haw jackanapes"—she inclined to piety, finding in familiar communion with a Higher Power much private consola-
tion for the pride and "uppishness" of such as kept servants
("if you please") and "gave themselves airs" unspeakable,
regardless of the snubbing that awaited them (thank God!)
at Judgment Day.[4]

She was a sturdy-looking yellowish woman, with a cold
active eye and a twist of the mouth between contempt and a
critical disapprobation. Such relations of Kipps as he had not
estranged before his marriage had been speedily engaged and
routed by her. Only one downtrodden household at Hastings
preserved the formality of a rare brief letter. These letters
were read aloud at the breakfast table with scornful comments
in the presence of Master Kipps. Any happiness that had
happened to the "Hastings lot" aroused a spirit of malignant
deprecation; any misfortune a stern satisfaction tempered by
the thought, "they'll be spongin' on us in a bit." "That Has-

tings lot," albeit of his blood and name, shared in the mind of little Master Kipps the nadir of human contempt with the Pornicks and labouring men.

This charming old-world couple were not natives of New Romney; and on that account Old Kipps was free to speak of it as a "one-eyed place" and score a point from the aborigines. They came from the inland parts about Lewes. Certain historical particulars, inimical to his superior attitude, Old Kipps was thus enabled to suppress; for example that[5]

Neither brother nor sister mitigated the early upbringing of Young Kipps. His mother set herself from his earliest years to steer him along that narrow way between the "stuck-up" above, and the "voolgar" below. He was forbidden to associate with children "below" him, and their general detestableness had been made clear to him, and the general unworthiness of labouring people to live in the same world with respectable tradesmen, before he reached knickerbockers. All children are ready enough to learn the lessons of envy and pride, though that is one of the things people do not care to be told. It makes them feel responsible and uncomfortable; it is not optimistic. If anything the Kipps parents overdid that lesson, rendering it even unattractive by gibes and sneers and persistent rappings of the knuckles. They early instilled the undesirableness of frankness, fearing "pumping" abroad, and that circumstances of their board and household might transpire. What if it "got about New Romney" that there were no carpets upstairs, or that they had only two silver spoons, or that Master Arthur's knickerbockers were *née* Mrs. Kipps' skirt? Would they not be despised by every upstart parvenue with three silver spoons, and their social position imperilled? He was instructed in the art of dodging questions. He was told to say he "didn't know" things that he did know, to pretend not to hear and to "turn the subject." It was made clear to him that lies were of two orders differing in moral value, those told by the Pornicks for example on one hand, and "little tiddywhoppers" occasionally necessary for the defence of the Kipps' family secret on the other.

These lessons in the art of qualifying truth went some way to ameliorate his extreme social exclusiveness. An early attempt to establish his superiority over Sid Pornick by violence led to bloodshed of the usual sort and an edifying drawn battle. And that of course meant a friendship that no mere parental prohibition could shake.

Now it has already been mentioned that the Pornicks lived next door to Old Kipps and that Pornick was by way of being a haberdasher—"counter-jumping ninny" in the language of Old Kipps. He had a considerable family—"swarm," Old Kipps—and one or two had died—"pewny lot," Mrs. Kipps. He was a white-faced man with an abundant black beard and a bass voice—"blaring jackass," Old Kipps—and his wife was a small person of indifferent health—"poor helpless creature," Mrs. Kipps; "I'm sure we're all sorry for her." He wore a blue ribbon—"washed-out teetotaller," Old Kipps—and worshipped with the Primitive Methodists—"nyar yar yar hymn singing Methodis'," Old Kipps. He cultivated mushrooms—"mucker," Old Kipps. His family—"brats," "dratted snivelling crew," Old Kipps—were prone to call aloud to one another in the garden, "Sid-dee," "Arn," awakening at times startling ironical echoes over the wall. Neither of these adjacent houses had carpeted stairs and it was one of the constant lessons urged upon young Kipps, to mark how abhorrent, how worthy of sanguinary reprisals was the sound of the Pornick household "lumpety lumping"—Old Kipps—up and down stairs.

There were endless disputes chronic between the households, about the party wall, about their cats—"I won't 'ave that cat over here" followed by a missile—about the pillar between the shop windows, about sweeping the pavement, about the banging of the Pornick doormat. Old Kipps held that Pornick waited until there was a suitable wind in order that the dust disengaged in that operation might defile his shop. Certainly Old Kipps waited for that event. Then he would issue forth, and in tones of mild protest begin what Mr. Pornick on one occasion inspired by wrath and newspaper French stigmatised as a "Frackass." "Look 'ere, Muster Pornick, I shall summins you if you do that," or "At it again! *At it er-gain,* he, he!" Such were the gentle beginnings of these memorable controversies.

On Sundays Master Kipps learnt his Catechism, in the full consciousness that "them Pornicks" did nothing of the kind, and with thimble tappings and suchlike spurs he was taught to repeat:

"*My juty towards my neighbour is to love 'im as myself.*"

"Who is your neighbour?" interpolated Mrs. Kipps. "Not just next door, Artie, is it?"

"No muver, it means everybody. Everybody we've got to love. *Not* them Pornicks, muver."[6]

"Very good, dear. Go on."

"My juty towards my neighbour is to love 'im as myself, to do unto all men as I would thay should do unto me. To love honour and succour my father and mother—"

"Mind you do," said Mrs. Kipps, and Kipps mistaking her tone, hastily snatched away an exposed knuckle.

"To honour and obey the Queen and all that are put in authority under her, to submit myself to all my governors, teachers, spirishal passers'n marsers . . ."

In the early days of Mr. Kipps the educational affairs of Romney were at a low ebb, indeed they were at such a low ebb that one hesitates to describe them lest one offend the reader's sense of scientific possibility. New Romney is a borough, it has a noble old church, one survivor of the many it possessed in its Cinque Ports days, whose splendid Norman doorway has recently been repaired in accordance with modern ideas; its past is the envy of all America, it has a mayor and corporation, three doctors, numerous well-equipped inns and able, intelligent, active, public-spirited clergy of various denominations; its flourishing dependency of Littlestone-on-Sea has golf links, several stuccoed lodging houses, numerous sites to be let for building—some with lodges already erected—an hotel and two really admirable bathing machines. Yet until a little while ago it had neither the local self-respect nor the patriotism nor the necessary care for its future to get itself any sort of educational establishment beyond a national school, and that in spite of a local endowment for the purposes of education. One conceives the pious founder presently haunting the local distinguished. Recently there has been a Charity Commissioner and some vague promise of awakening, but so things were in A. D. 1898. And since the extraordinary superiority of the parents of Mr. Kipps prevented the sending him to the national school, his early education was extremely precarious. Sometimes he had special lessons from the national schoolmaster and sometimes he had not—it depended on the state of the feud—and finally he was sent away to a boarding school in Hastings to "finish" his education.[7]

This school was established in a battered private house in the part of the town remotest from the sea; it was called an Academy for Young Gentlemen and many of its young gentlemen had parents in "India" and other inaccessible places. Others were the sons of credulous widows anxious to get something a little "superior" to a board school education as cheaply as possible; and others again, like Kipps, were sent as the outcome of that universal British passion, social ambition.

Its "principal" was a lean long creature of indifferent digestion and temper, who proclaimed himself on a gilt lettered board in his front garden "George Garden Woodrow F.S.Sc.," letters indicating that he had paid certain guineas for a bogus diploma. A bleak white-washed outhouse constituted his schoolroom and the scholastic quality of its carved and worn desks and forms was enhanced by a slippery blackboard and two large yellow out-of-date maps, one of Africa and the other of Wiltshire, that he had picked up cheap at a sale. There were other maps and globes in his study where he interviewed enquiring parents, but these his pupils never saw. In a glass cupboard in the passage was several shillingsworth of test tubes and chemicals, a tripod, a glass retort, and a damaged Bunsen burner, manifesting that the "scientific laboratory" mentioned in the prospectus was no idle boast.

This prospectus, which was in dignified but incorrect English, laid particular stress on the sound preparation for a commercial career given in the Academy, but army, navy and civil service were glanced at in an ambiguous sentence. There was something vague about examination successes, and a declaration that the curriculum included art, "modern foreign languages," and "a sound technical and scientific training." There came insistence upon the "moral well-being" of the pupils and an emphatic boast of the excellence of the religious instruction, "so often neglected nowadays even in schools of wide repute." "That's bound to fetch 'em," Mr. Woodrow had remarked when he drew up the prospectus. Attention was directed to the matronly care of Mrs. Woodrow, a small partially effaced woman in a state of permanent nervous exhaustion, and the prospectus concluded with a phrase intentionally vague, "Fare unrestricted and our own milk and produce."

The memories Kipps carried from that school into afterlife were set in an atmosphere of stuffiness and mental muddle, and included countless pictures of sitting, bored and idle, on creaking forms, of blot licking and the taste of ink, torn books with covers that set one's teeth on edge, of the slimy surface of the laboured slates, of festive marble playing, whispered story-telling, and of pinches, blows, and a thousand such petty annoyances being perpetually "passed on" according to the custom of the place, of standing up in class and being hit suddenly and unreasonably for imaginary misbehaviour, of Mr. Woodrow's raving days when a scarcely sane injustice prevailed, of the cold vacuity of the hour of preparation before the bread and butter breakfast, of horrible headaches and queer unprecedented internal feelings resulting from Mrs. Woodrow's matronly cookery, of dreary walks two by two, all dressed in the mortarboard caps that so impressed the widowed mothers, of the dismal half-holidays when the weather was wet and the spirit of evil temper and evil imagination had the pent boys to work its will on, of unfair dishonourable fights and miserable defeats and victories, of bullying and being bullied, of a coward boy whom he at last goaded to revolt by incessant persecution, of sleeping three in a bed, of the dense leathery smell of the schoolroom when one returned thither after ten minutes play, of a playground of mud and incidental sharp flints.

His work varied, according to the prevailing mood of Mr. Woodrow. Sometimes that was a despondent lethargy, copy books were distributed or sums were "set," or the great mystery of book-keeping was declared in being, and beneath these superficial activities interminable guessing games with marbles and lengthy conversations went on while Mr. Woodrow sat inanimate at his desk heedless of school affairs, staring in front of him at unseen things. At times his face was utterly inane, at times it had an expression of stagnant amazement, as if he saw before his eyes with pitiless clearness the dishonour and mischief of his being . . .

At other times the F.S.Sc. roused himself into action, and would stand up a wavering class and teach, goading them with bitter mockery and blows through a chapter of Ahn's First French Course or France and the French, or a Dialogue about a traveller's washing or the parts of an opera house. His own knowledge of French had been obtained years ago in another English private school, and he had refreshed it by occasional weeks of mean adventure in Dieppe. He would sometimes in their lessons hit upon some reminiscence of these brighter days, and then he would laugh inexplicably and repeat French phrases of an unfamiliar type.

In such manner was the first stage in the education of our Kipps completed, the first stage in that process of under-feeding, dwarfing and whittling down "to that state of life unto which it had pleased God to call him," which is the average lower-class Englishman's lot in these enlightened times.

He did not call on his Hastings cousins during his first term, his parents disapproving of all unseemly alacrity towards inferiors.

What had previously been the normal life of Kipps, the glorious days of "mucking about" along the beach, THE SEIGE OF UNRESISTING Martello towers, THE INCESSANT INTEREST OF the mystery and motion of windmills, the windy excursions with boarded feet over the yielding shingle to Dungeness lighthouse—Sid Pornick and he far adrift from reality, smugglers and armed men from the moment they left Great Stone behind them, the wanderings in the hedgeless reedy marsh, the long excursions reaching even to Hythe where the Gatling guns are forever whirling and tapping, and to Rye AND WINCHELSEA, PERCHED LIKE DREAM CITIES ON THEIR LITTLE HILLS, the wintry TUMULT OF THE SKY AND SEA, THE wrecks, real wrecks—NEAR Dymchurch pitched high and blackened and rotting were the ribs of a fishing smack, flung aside like an empty basket when the sea had devoured its crew —THE LONG SERIES OF THESE EXPERIENCES, SO VARIED AND YET IN SOME INEXPLICABLE WAY AKIN, was cut up now by his school terms into memorable slices of holiday, and at last, as will be told most pathetically in its place, ceased altogether. But how much brighter now by virtue of those dull intercalations of hardship and discipline had his Romney days become. In the memory of Mr. Kipps they came at last to shine like strips of stained glass window in a dreary waste of scholastic wall.

The last of these windows was the brightest, and instead of the kaleidoscopic effects of its predecessors its glory was a single figure. For in the last of his holidays before the Moloch of Trade consumed him, Kipps made his first tentative essays at the mysterious shrine of Love. Very tentative they were, for the austerity of his home influences had made of Arthur Kipps a boy of subdued passions and potential rather than actual affectionateness. But Destiny, as regardless of feud and clan as in the days of Montague and Capulet, ruled that that central figure of that last brightest memorial window to the days of his boyhood should be none other than Ann Pornick, the daughter of that offensive mat-beater, that blaring gaby, that inglorious grower of mushrooms, that nincompoop and ninny, next door.

❧ 8 ❧

_____

Ann Pornick

NEGOTIATIONS were already on foot to make Master Kipps into a draper before he discovered the fluctuating lights in Ann Pornick's eyes. But as yet he did not realise the thing that was designed for him, it lacked the shadow of an assured reality. He was home for the holidays and it was chiefly present to him that he was never to go to school—that squalid den of confinement and ineffectual labour, again. The "breaking up" of school had been hilarious; and the excellent maxim, "Last Day's Pay Day," had been observed by him with a scrupulous attention to his honour. He had punched the heads of all his enemies, wrung wrists and kicked shins, he had distributed all his unfinished copy books, all his school books, his collection of marbles and his mortarboard cap among such as loved him, and he had secretly written in their books "remember Kipps." He had also split the anaemic Woodrow's cane, carved his own name deeply in several places about the premises, and broken the scullery window. He had told everybody so often that he was to learn to be a sea captain that he had come almost to believe the thing himself. And now he was home and school was at an end for him for evermore.

He was up before six on the day of his return, and out in

the hot sunlight of the garden. He kept continually whistling a peculiarly penetrating arrangement of three notes supposed by himself and Sid Pornick and the boys of the Hastings Academy, for no earthly reason whatever, to be the original Huron war-cry. As he did this he feigned not to be doing it, but to be admiring a new wing of the dustbin recently erected by his father, a pretence that would not have deceived a nestling tom-tit. Presently there came a fuller echo from the Pornick hunting ground. Then Kipps began to sing, "Ar pars eight tra-la, in the lane be'ind the church." To which an unseen person answered "Ar pars eight it is, in the lane be'ind the church." In order to conceal their operations still more securely, both parties to this duet then gave vent to a vocalisation of the Huron war-cry again, and after a lingering repetition of the last and shrillest note, dispersed severally to light the house fires for the day.

Half past eight found Kipps sitting on the sunlit gate at the top of the long lane that runs towards the sea, clashing his boots with a slow rhythm and whistling with great violence all that he knew of an excruciatingly pathetic air. There appeared along the churchyard wall a girl in a short frock, fair-haired and with those odd blue eyes that are sometimes very pale and sometimes very dark. She had grown so that she was a little taller than Kipps, and her colour had improved. He scarcely remembered her, so changed was she since last year. Some vague emotion arose at the sight of her. He stopped whistling and regarded her, oddly tongue-tied.

"He can't come," said Ann advancing boldly. "Not yet."

"What—not Sid?"

"No. Father's made him dust all his boxes again."

"What for?"

"*I* dunno. Father's in a stew 's morning."

* * *

"Can you run?" said Ann.

* * *

"I got a lot to see to home," said Ann.

* * *

They became aware of Sid approaching them. "You better look out, young Ann," said Sid with the irreverent want of sympathy usual in brothers. "You been out nearly an hour.

Nothing ain't been done upstairs. Father said he didn't know where you was, but when he did he'd warm y'r young ear."
* * *

"Your sister ain't a bad sort," said Kipps off-handedly, halfway to the new wreck.

"I clout her a lot," said Sidney modestly.

The new wreck was full of rotting grain and stank abominably, so that they had it all to themselves. They took possession of it in force and had speedily to defend it against enormous numbers of imaginary natives, who were at last driven off by loud shouts of *bang*, *bang*, and vigorous thrusting and shoving of sticks.
* * *

These things drove Ann out of mind for a time. But when
* * *

"It's rather nice 'aving sisters," said Kipps
* * *

"Sisters," said Sid, "is rot. That's what sisters is. What I say is, 'ave girls."

"But ain't sisters girls?"

"N-*eaow*," said Sid with unspeakable scorn, and kept Kipps waiting some time before he resumed.

"For instance," said Sid, "Ann is my sister, but my girl— *You* don't know who my girl is, Art Kipps."

"But she's a girl—Ann is."

"Ah!—but you don't know who *my* girl is, Art Kipps."
* * *

"I'd like to 'ave a girl jest to talk to sometimes," said Kipps.

So these boys talked, sitting on a blackened rotting old wreck in which men had lived and perished, and staring out to sea. They were pensive for a while, and then Sid started up. "I'm going to rig a jury-mast," said Sid, "that's what I'm going to do."

The next time Kipps saw Ann Pornick he remarked to himself more definitely how extremely pretty she had grown since his previous holidays.

❧ 9 ❧

How Mr. Kipps Became
a Draper and a Fickle Soul

THUS it was Master Kipps became Mr. Kipps and departed to Tunbridge Wells, with a mean little tin trunk, a new umbrella, and a proper pride restraining tears, to open another chapter in the mysterious book of his Destiny. You have witnessed the austere social aims of his parents, and that enterprising schoolmaster Woodrow and the lights and shades in the eyes of Ann Pornick, at work upon him, influencing and moulding him, each influence in its own way, towards his manhood. And now he is a lean and callow youngster of fifteen, with large hands and feet and long limbs and shifty blue eyes, of indistinct speech and retreating manners. Another phase in the process of whittling down begins, another part of the subtle and elaborate machinery which the wisdom of our rulers, the general enlightenment and patriotism of our people, and that spirit of individual enterprise which is our noblest possession have combined to establish for the discipline and development of the youth of our lower middle class, is displayed. The amiable Mr. Shalford advances to bear his share in the work of making Mr. Kipps an Imperial citizen, a ruler of India and Africa, a father of the great age that is yet to be.

Mr. Shalford was a small irascible ignorant man with hairy hands and neatly trimmed beard, who by means of bankruptcy under the old dispensation and a judicious use of matrimony had at last acquired a position of eminence in the local trade. He entertained a delusion that he was an exemplary compound of energy and ability. He considered himself the Napoleon of haberdashers. It was his boast that he had left school at fourteen and started the world with nothing. The very ordinary book-keeping and business method of his shop, he spoke of as "my System" as though it were a thing unparalleled in the world's history.

His hospitality was to take people over his premises, from workroom to stable, bragging very fast about his System. He was the only draper in Tunbridge Wells, he said, who used overhead change carriers; he would start elaborate calculations to show how many minutes in one year were saved thereby, and would lose himself among the figures. "Seven times eight seven nine—was it? Or seven eight nine? Well, well—but it comes to pounds and pounds saved in the year, I assure you. System, you see!" He would exhibit his three delivery vans all striped green and yellow—"uniform, you see —System." All over the premises were pinned absurd little cards, "This door locked after 7.30. By order Edwin Shalford," and suchlike inscriptions. Every new assistant received a green and yellow book of rules, "By order Edwin Shalford," full of cunning expedients for extorting sixpenny fines.

He always wrote "By order," though it conveyed no earthly meaning to him. He was one of those people who collect technicalities upon them as the Reduvius collects dirt. He was incapable of English. When he wanted to say he had a sixpenny-ha'penny longcloth to sell, he put it thus to startled customers: "Can do you one, six half if y'like"—he always omitted pronouns and articles and so forth when he could; it seemed to him the very essence of the business-like. His only preposition was "as" or the compound "as per." He abbreviated every word he could; he would have considered himself the laughing-stock of Wood Street if he had chanced to spell *socks* in any way but "sox." He never stipulated for two months' credit, but bought in November "as Jan." It was not only words he abbreviated in his London communications. In paying his wholesales his System admitted of a constant error in the discount of a penny or twopence, and it "facilitated business" he alleged, to ignore odd pence in the cheques he wrote. His ledger clerk was so struck by the beauty of the System that he started a private one on his own account with the stamp box, but that never came to Shalford's knowledge.

This admirable British merchant would glow with a particular pride of intellect when writing his London orders.

"Ah! do yew think *yew* will ever be able to write London orders?" he would say with slow inordinate pride to Kipps waiting impatiently long after closing time, to take these triumphs of commercial enterprise to post.

Kipps shook his head, anxious for Mr. Shalford to get on.

"Now, here, for instance, I've written '1 piece 1 in. cott blk elas 1 7/8 or'; what do I mean by that *or*, eh? do yew know?"

Kipps promptly hadn't the faintest idea.

"And then, '2 ea silk net as per patts herewith'; *ea*—eh?"

"Dunno, Sir."

It was not Shalford's way to explain things. "Dear, dear! Well, my boy, if yew're not a bit sharper, *yew*'ll never write London orders, that's pretty plain. Just stick stamps on all these letters, and mind yew stick 'em right way up, and try and profit a little more by the opportunities your parents have provided yew."

And Kipps, tired, hungry and belated, set about stamping with vigour and despatch.

* * *

The indentures that bound Kipps to Mr. Shalford were antique and complex; they insisted on the latter gentleman's parental privileges, they forbad Kipps to dice and game, they made him over body and soul to Mr. Shalford for five long years, the crucial years of his life. In return there were vague stipulations about teaching the whole art and mystery of the trade to him, but as there was no penalty attached to negligence, Mr. Shalford, being a business man, considered this a mere rhetorical flourish and set himself assiduously to get as much out of Kipps and to put as little into him as he could in the five years of their intercourse.

What he put into Kipps was chiefly bread and margarine, infusions of chicory and tea-dust, colonial meat by contract at three-pence a pound, potatoes by the sack, and watered beer.

If however Kipps chose to buy any supplementary material for growth, Mr. Shalford had the generosity to place his kitchen resources at his disposal free—if the fire chanced to be going. In addition Kipps was taught the list of fines, and how to tie up parcels, to know where goods were kept in Mr. Shalford's systematised shop, to hold his hands extended upon the counter, and to repeat such phrases as "What can I have the pleasure—?" "No trouble, I 'ssure you," and the like; to block, fold and measure materials of all sorts, to lift his hat from his head when he passed Mr. Shalford abroad, and to

* * *

But he was not of course taught the "cost" mark of the goods he sold, nor anything of the method of buying such goods. Nor was his attention directed to the unfamiliar social habits and fashions to which his trade ministered. The use of half the goods he saw sold and was presently to assist in selling, he did not understand.

* * *

He was also allowed to share a bedroom with eight other young men, and to sleep in a bed which, except in very severe weather, could be made with the help of his overcoat and underlinen, quite sufficiently warm for any reasonable soul.

In return for these benefits he worked so that he commonly went to bed exhausted and footsore. His round began at half past six in the morning, when he

* * *

who, whether he worked well or ill, nagged persistently by reason of a chronic indigestion, until the window was done.

There came a blessed interval when Mr. Kipps was sent abroad "matching."

* * *

After this the shop was settling down to the business of serving customers.

* * *

to hold up curtains until his arms ached, clear away "stuff"

* * *

plumbed an abyss of boredom, or stood a mere carcass with his mind far away, fighting the enemies of the empire or steering a dream ship perilously into unknown seas. To be recalled sharply to our higher civilisation by ——'s "Nar then, Kipps. *Look* alive!"

At half past seven o'clock

* * *

Sometimes people would stay long after the shop was closed, and then it was forbidden to

* * *

Mr. Kipps would watch these later customers from the shadow of a pile of goods, and death and disfigurement was the least he wished for them. Rarely much later than nine, a supper of bread and cheese and watered beer awaited him upstairs, and, that consumed, the rest of the day was entirely at his disposal for reading, recreation, and the improvement of his mind. The front door was locked at half past ten, and the gas in the dormitory extinguished at eleven.

On Sundays

* * *

At times there came breaks in this routine, sale times darkened by extra toil and work past midnight but brightened by a sprat supper and some shillings in the way of premiums. And every year—not now and then but every year—Mr. Shalford, with parenthetic admiration of his own generosity and glancing comparisons with the austerer days when he was apprenticed, conceded him no less than ten days holidays—ten whole days every year. Many a poor soul at Portland might well envy the fortunate Kipps. And how those days were grudged and counted as they snatched themselves away from him one after another!

Once a year came stock-taking, and at intervals gusts of "marking off" goods newly arrived. Then the splendours of Mr. Shalford's being shone with oppressive brilliancy.

* * *

vied with one another in obsequious alacrity

* * *

A vague SELF-disgust that shaped itself as an intense hate of Shalford and all his fellow creatures

* * *

At first, you see, Mr. Kipps did not accept the new way of life with perfect resignation

* * *

His distaste was increased by the inflamed ankles and sore feet that form a normal incident in the business of making a draper

* * *

One of the senior apprentices named Minton, one of those restless objectionable characters who come to a bad end, fanned this discontent.

"When you get too old to work they chuck you away," said Minton. "Lor! you find old drapers everywhere—tramps, beggars, dock labourers, bus conductors—quod. Anywhere but in a crib.

* * *

The idea that fermented perpetually in the mind of Minton, but which he never raised courage to realise, was to "hit the little beggar slap in the eye"—the little beggar being Mr. Shalford—"and see how his blessed System met that."

There were times when little Kipps would lie awake, all others in the dormitory asleep and snoring, and think tearfully of this outlook. Dimly he perceived the thing that had happened to him, how the great stupid machine of retail trade had caught his life into its wheels, a vast irresistible force which he had neither strength of will nor knowledge to escape. Night after night he would resolve to enlist, to run away to sea, to set fire to the warehouse or drown himself, and morning after morning he rose up and hurried downstairs in fear of a sixpenny fine. He would compare his dismal round of servile drudgery with those windy sunlit days at Littlestone, those windows of happiness shining ever brighter as they receded. The little figure of Ann seemed in all these windows now.

She too had happened on evil things. When Kipps went home for the Christmas after he was bound, he hurried out and whistled in the garden. Old Kipps appeared promptly. "It's no good your whistling there, my boy," said Old Kipps in a loud clear tone designed to be audible over the wall. "She's gone as help to Ashford, my boy, *help*. Slavey is what we used to call 'em, but times are changed. Wonder they didn't say lady-help while they was about it. It 'ud be like 'em."

The only pleasure left for the brief remainder of Kipps' holiday after that was to think he was not in the shop. And when he went back there were one or two very dismal nights indeed. He even went so far as to write home some vague intimation of his feelings about business and his prospects, quoting Minton, but Mrs. Kipps answered him, "Did he want the Pornicks to say he wasn't good enough to be a draper?"

This dreadful possibility was of course conclusive in the matter.

After a time the sorrows of Kipps grew less acute, and the brief tragedy of his life was over. He subdued himself to his position. For one thing, his soles and ankles became indurated to the perpetual standing. For another, came a weekly whiff of freedom every Thursday. Mr. Shalford after a brave stand for what he called "Innyvishal lib'ty" and the "Idea of my System," a stand which he made chiefly on patriotic grounds, was at last under pressure of certain of his customers compelled to fall in line with the rest of the local Early Closing Association, and Mr. Kipps could emerge in daylight and go where he listed for long long hours. Moreover, Minton the melancholy left.

Then came other distractions, the natural distractions of adolescence, to take his mind off the inevitable. His costume, for example, began to interest him more, he began to realise himself as a visible object, to find an interest in the costume room mirrors.

In this he was helped by counsel and example. Pierce, his immediate senior, was by way of being what was called a Masher, and preached his cult. During slack times grave discussions about collars, ties, the cut of trouser legs, and the proper shape of a boot toe, were held in the Manchester department. In due course Kipps went to a tailor and his short jacket was replaced by a morning coat with tails. Stirred by this he purchased at his own expense three stand-up collars to replace his former turn-down ones. They were nearly three inches high, higher than those Pierce wore, and they made his neck quite sore and left a red mark under his ears . . .

There were yet other ameliorations. An apprentice, junior to himself, appeared, one to whom he could apply the wealth of opprobrium he had collected during the past year, and to whom he could pass on many petty annoyances that had hitherto stayed and rankled. And in a temporary difference with Pierce, he discovered a long unsuspected physical superiority which greatly enhanced the consideration with which Pierce treated him.

Most potent help of all in the business of forgetting his cosmic disaster, so soon as he was in tail coats, the young ladies of the establishment began to discover that he was no longer a "mere boy." Hitherto they had tossed heads at him and kept him in his place. Now they discovered that he was a "nice boy." It is painful to record that his fidelity to Ann failed at their first onset. One of the young ladies in the costume room first showed by her manner that he was a visible object and capable of exciting interest. She talked to him, she encouraged him to talk to her, she lent him a book she possessed, and darned a sock and said she would be his elder sister. She allowed him to escort her to church. This excited the other young lady in the costumes, her natural rival, and she set herself with great charm and subtlety to the capture of the ripening heart of Kipps. She went for a walk with him and afterwards the ladies exchanged words. In this way was the *toga virilis* bestowed on Kipps and he became recognised as a suitable object for that Platonic passion that devastates even the very highest class establishments.

He took to these new interests with a natural zest. He became initiated into the mysteries of "flirting" and "spooning." Very soon he was engaged. Before a year was out he had been engaged six times. The engagements in drapery establishments do not necessarily involve a subsequent marriage; in fact, they are essentially temporary connexions. These young ladies do not like not to be engaged, it is so unnatural, and Mr. Kipps was as easy to get engaged to as one could wish. There are many conveniences in being engaged—from the young lady's point of view. You get an escort for church and walks and so forth. It is not quite the thing to walk abroad with a "feller" who is neither one's fiancé nor an adopted brother; it is considered either a little *fast* or savouring of the "walking out" habits of the servant girl. Now, such is the nature of human charity, the shop young lady has just the same horror of doing anything that savours of the servant girl as the lady journalist, let us say, has of anything savouring of the shop girl, or the really nice young lady has of anything savouring of any sort of girl who has gone down into the economic battle field to earn herself a living.

So, with an increasing interest and pleasure the years of Mr. Kipps' apprenticeship slipped by. In a little while he cleaned windows no longer, he was serving customers (of the less important sort) and taking goods out on approval, and at last he was senior apprentice, and his moustache was visible, and there were five apprentices whom he might snub and cuff.

The last year of his time was signalised by his joining an art class and so making the acquaintance of Chitterlow, as we have already told. He joined the class in a spasm of self-improvement; by some accident he had read an article on Technical Education in a halfpenny paper. At first he attended the class in Freehand, that being the subject taught on early closing night, and he had already witnessed the elopement and made some progress in the extraordinary routine of reproducing freehand "copies," when the dates of the classes were changed. Thereby he was precipitated into the wood-carving class, which was conducted at that time by a young lady named Walsingham. She was only a year or so older than Kipps, she had a pale intellectual face and black hair, which she wore in an original and striking way over her forehead. She had, he learnt, matriculated at London University, an astounding feat to his imagination, and the masterly way in which she demonstrated how to prod and worry honest pieces of white wood into useless and unedifying patterns in relief, extorted his utmost admiration.

Habit and indeed every consideration demanded that he should fall in love with her, but of course he no more presumed to approach her with any tentative to flirt or spoon than he would have approached an angel. Her pallid intellectual face beneath those sombre clouds of hair put her in a class apart; towards her the thought of "attentions" paled and vanished; towards her there was nothing he could think of as possible but an abject and silent adoration. Once only did he get a chance to do her a service. She could not open one of the school windows, and so he stepped forward.

He could not open it either.

Afterwards in the bitterness of his soul he thought he would never go near the class again. But when the night came he was overpowered by the memory of her and he had to go.

This passion was indeed so strong that for a space it suspended the rest of his sentimental interests altogether. It was the strongest passion he had ever felt since those remote half-childish evenings at Littlestone. He meditated about her when he was blocking cretonne, her image was before his eyes at tea time and blotted out the more immediate faces and made him silent and preoccupied. He became conspicuously less popular on the "fancy" side, the "millinery" was chilly with him, and the "costumes" cutting. But he did not care. Every THURSDAY he jabbed and gouged at his wood, jabbing and gouging intersecting circles and diamond traceries and that laboured inane which our mad world calls ornament, and watched her furtively when she turned away. The circles in consequence were jabbed crooked, and his panels, losing their symmetry, became comparatively pleasing to the eye—and once he jabbed his finger. He did not care and he never knew that she thought of him privately as the stupid young man with the red ears.

(And even so, Dear Lady, it may be some humble soul has also worshipped you.)[1]

At last the five years were up and Mr. Kipps had to leave Tunbridge Wells and go forth into the world, a draper finished and complete. His parting from Mr. Shalford was an affectation of respect; he parted with Miss Walsingham with much profound emotion.

"I very likely shan't come again," he said with a gasp at his own temerity in addressing her.

"Won't you?" said Miss Walsingham.

"No," said Kipps, "I'm leaving the neighb'rood."

"I'm sorry you won't be able to finish the course," said Miss Walsingham, staring without obvious admiration at his blood-stained exercise.

It seemed a cold thing to say at the time and he felt chilled. But afterwards as he turned it over he found a sort of comfort in it. She had said she was sorry!

He had a year at Redhill, a stormy six weeks with a religious fanatic at Camberwell, and then he came as a "junior" in the Manchester department to the Folkestone Drapery Emporium and General Exchange. So it came about that he witnessed Mr. Waddy's painful exhibition of temper on the Leas.

And at the very time when Mr. Waddy was on the cliff of the Leas resolving to leave all his property to Charities, it was decreed by Destiny that Mr. Kipps should be marching along the lower Sandgate Road far below, with a brown paper parcel under one arm and a yard measure in his hand, on his way to show certain figured sateens to an invalid lady at Radnor Cliff.

The day was warm and bright, the oblique paths up the cliff were inviting, and Mr. Kipps deflected from his duty for the sake of a wider view of the sea. He knew from the local guide that France was clearly visible from Folkestone, and day after day he had failed to see it, search as he would. And as he ascended there came a shouting and a creaking whirr of wheels! He turned a corner, perplexed, and beheld Mr. Waddy rushing down upon him and already near.

For the moment Kipps forgot his training as a draper. He grasped the situation in an instant and flung himself forward to the rescue. The front edge of the bath chair struck his shin sharply, his extended hands smote Mr. Waddy about the diaphragm, his parcel went under the wheel and burst, and in the twinkling of an eye things had become static.

Neither spoke. The impact of Kipps had struck the breath out of Mr. Waddy. They stared for a time into each other's eyes. Then Kipps backed awkwardly into an upright position, and was instantly aware of his scattered goods in the dirt. He had stooped and clutched the parcel before he was aware of the extensive injury to his shin. The pain came with the suddenness of a sting.

"Well I'm xxx!" gasped Mr. Waddy—the delivered.

A moment before the grim jaws of Death had yawned for him, and then a violent punch in the stomach and—Life!—life —in the shape of this ridiculous little man waving a fluttering banner of figured sateen and nursing a broken shin.

Mr. Waddy took a deep inspiration and burst into a gasping laughter. "I'm xxx," cried Mr. Waddy, hitting the arm rest of his bath chair. "Of all (unquotable) things if this isn't the (most unquotable)," and his laughter came louder and stronger. "Of all the (unquotable) things!"

"Ho! what next? What next? Ho ho ho!" And the tears ran out of his eyes.

At this Mr. Kipps gave way to the unfamiliar emotion of wrath. "Who the blooming juice are you laughing at? Look here! You couldn't have turned that corner nohow. See? You may think it funny, y'old fool, charging down a place like this. *I* don't . . . Blooming old Scorcher! Y'ought to be 'shamed of y'self."

He paused and resumed with enhanced bitterness.

"*Look* a this sateen! 'Ow the juice am I to show it to a lady now? That's what comes of your blooming games!"

"If the G.V. turned up, it would look nice for me. Eh?" He forgot his injured shin at this thought, and began to struggle with the disordered fabric.

His wrathful eye, regarding Mr. Waddy over the edge of the material, held that gentleman for a moment, only to release him into still louder laughter.

"Can't ye see what I saved ye from?" piped Kipps in an ecstasy of exasperation, dropping one end of the sateen again to gesticulate with an extended hand. "I'm a jolly good mind —I'm a real jolly good mind to take and shove you over now. You wouldn't come scorching down no more cliffs in *this* world—I lay."

"I lay you wouldn't," he repeated, to extinguish once for all some still lingering spark of levity in that gentleman's eye . . .

And turning a severe back on Mr. Waddy he resumed, with indignant mutterings, a jerky irritated struggle with the sateen.

(Printer, a white line. [Wells's note.])

And far above, the good old man with the childlike eyes was looking, in a state of great agitation, for a vanished bath chair.

"Where—ever . . . ?

"Depend upon it—some byes 'ave took it, drabbit 'em . . .

"I wonder he let 'em."

He perceived the Leas policeman and hurried for his advice.

"You 'aven't seen anybody," he said almost sobbing, "hookin' it orf anywhere wi' my invalid?"

❧ 10 ❧
──────────

The Last Endeavour

BUT though Mr. Waddy laughed he had had a shock, and as soon as his excitement had passed this fact asserted itself. Before nightfall he was in pain, and the next day a perplexed doctor took refuge in ominous obscurity and shook his head impressively. There were sedatives and intimations of deepening trouble. "There ought to be someone to nurse you," said the doctor, and repeated this more explicitly to Mrs. Satsuma in the hall.

"A nurse?" said Mrs. Satsuma.

"A trained nurse would be best. But hasn't he any relations?"

"Well," said Mrs. Satsuma doubtfully, and then frankly; "none on friendly terms, Sir."

"Dear, dear," said the doctor. "Then it must be a trained nurse. I had better wire for one."

"He 'as a niece," said Mrs. Satsuma, taking her courage in both hands. "She is a very nice lady—now staying in Folkestone. Perhaps after all, Sir—"

"She ought to know at any rate. I don't want to alarm you, Mrs. Satsuma, but anyone belonging to him ought to know how things stand now."

"Dear, dear, Sir," said Mrs. Satsuma looking very grave. "And is it like that?" Legacy or no legacy, the thing was drawing to its decision, and her need of a friend for the crisis became urgent. "Then p'raps she'd better come."

"But you said—"

"A little tiff, Sir. You know his quick way?"

"Of course when there are relations it's always better—I'll wire for the nurse as well."

"You think it better his niece should come, Sir?" said Mrs. Satsuma concealing her joy.

"Certainly," said the doctor. "Under the circumstances." And so Muriel came.

In spite of all rebuffs her tenderness for her benefactor was unabated. "If only I can do something to help him," she assured Mrs. Satsuma again and again. "I would *love* just to carry in—anything he wanted."

"He'll have a fit if you do," said Mrs. Satsuma.

"But, dear Mrs. Satsuma, *think*! He is my uncle. If I don't —Dear, I may never have the chance again."

This, which she really felt acutely, presently infected Mrs. Satsuma. "He hasn't seen me for years," urged Muriel, "and then it was on the Leas and I had my stylish things on. Suppose I put on cuffs and collar—very plain. It would be like the *Story of an African Farm*.[1] And," she added coyly, "I know something of make-up now, dear. I have acted once or twice . . . He ought not to lie up there alone until this Woman comes."

He did not. Presently entered a dark young person in a possible uniform and with very black eyebrows, and moved mysteriously about the room.

For a time he seemed to take it for granted that this was the new nurse and presented a humped and trustful back, one peaceful ear and a few aggressive tails of hair to her inspection. But a certain jaunty handling of fragile things ended in disaster and aroused his attention. Down went the plate and smashed diversely. There was a movement on the pillow, and a wrinkled nose and red-rimmed wrathful eye became visible, steadfastly regarding her stooping figure.

She found that scrutiny a little unnerving. She picked up the pieces of the plate and left the room. When she returned, both his eyes had emerged from the bedclothes and their expression was indubitable suspicion.

* * *

She answered in an unearthly tone which she had adopted to disguise her voice.

* * *

"It's *you*, is it?" he said venomously.

He did not have a fit certainly, but his rage and excitement were extraordinary. She would not leave the room until he had struggled halfway out of bed in an attempt to get at the bell.

* * *

He was still raving at Mrs. Satsuma when the proper nurse arrived.

* * *

About two o'clock in the morning he startled the dozing nurse with laughter, unmistakable laughter. She could not believe her senses. She watched him, surprised, but saying nothing. She would not let him know she was awake. "Imagine it—imagine all the tomfoolery of it!" he said. And then; "And why not that?"

When presently her heavy lids fell again he was still muttering to himself.

In the morning HIS face was full of purpose. He was active in a flushed way and his temperature was rising. He insisted on seeing old Grimflack, his solicitor <once again. "The last time I shall trouble him," said Waddy. "This I'm certain is final."

To any unprofessional hearer outside the door it would have seemed doubtful that Mr. Waddy was at all ill. The noises of altercation grew high. It was particularly evident that he would see himself and many things further first before he had trustees. People outside upon the Leas heard his objection to trustees, heard the matured distrust of a lifetime descending in a reverberating avalanche upon this vicious but necessary class.

The nurse was herself called into the room> to witness a signature. Waddy's face was flushed and resolute, and under his signature he drove a huge black dash. Grimflack kept his eyebrows raised and AN expression of protest on his face throughout that ceremony. <His voice trembled and broke,

and his hand was so aquiver when he pointed to the place for
her signature that for a moment she was in doubt. He regarded her over his spectacles with melancholy eyes, as
though he meditated holding her responsible for some stupendous wrong. And presently came the London specialist and
doctor Finacue [?].>

(Printer, a white line. [Wells's note.])

That night, too, Waddy laughed a little. "What a world it
is," she heard him mutter. "What a queer little time it has
been. Well, well."

But he was too weak that night to laugh as he had done
before, and presently he was convulsed by hysterical sobbing.

"God forgive me!" he cried, "for I am in the shadow with
all my sins upon me. What have I done with my life? What
have I done with my life? Nothing. Nothing."

Presently he spoke again. "God knows," he said. "God
must know. It wasn't as though I had meant to waste it all.
The Luck has been against me. The Luck."

"School's over. Out into the world. That cabman at the
docks . . .

"And that squirrel. We both looked at the squirrel and the
wind was blowing up its fur . . .

"It seems like yesterday—yesterday.

"How it goes! How the time goes! An action in a hurry.
Youth—manhood. Who's going to have adventure? Who's
going to marry? Going. Going. *Tap. Gone*! Gone. For
evermore . . .

"Luck. It's all Luck."

He relapsed into silence. Afterwards she could hear him
whispering to himself, and then at last it seemed that he fell
asleep.

The next day, as the doctors had feared, came pain sharp
and keen to call out the wasted fighter in him, and all day
long he fought either silently or with snarling outcries against
that searching trouble. There came fomentations, <a struggle
and the pain became a dull aching, grew remote, grew in
some way impersonal. There was a whisper; "He's sinking."
There followed an apathetic interval.>

* * *

After a time he felt drowsy, then he seemed to recover his
mental clarity. He was aware that he was in pain—and it was

not painful. He felt a flagging of the weary heart and lungs, an oppression against which he struggled physically. His brow was damp. There was pain within him, and a sinking feeling, and these dwindled and dwindled like things that recede. Clearer and clearer grew his mind, strangely free from the organic emotions that were wont to cloud it, his thoughts flowed swift and clear.

Things seemed to him very small, though he could not think why they had become small. The world had become a world in miniature, quaint miniature. His mind seemed to have an enlarged grasp of sequence and relation. His memories assembled, the whole of his past seemed gathering to one instant, presenting itself as one coherent understandable little thing. And not only the past. In this new illumination he saw now the inevitable aftermath of his life, saw the future as certainly as the past, saw that it was indeed but a different aspect of things ordained. He saw all that happens in the rest of this story, saw it as a little thread in the whole broadening stream of consequence that flowed from him, saw it continually mingling with the life fonts of others, until at last it merged in the universal ocean of being.

He was neither glad nor sorry. His rage had fallen from him, all the stress and urgency, all the egotisms of life. Yet, had his rage fallen from him? Rather was it not changed? There was life in him still, energy still. Pity too was still with him, mingled inseparably with the joyous quality of laughter. Yes, he still had the spirit of laughter in him. And something more! Abruptly he was aware of a new quality saturating all things, a light of which humour and charity had been the faint terrestrial promise, an infinite humour, the charity that understands. And with the perception of this light, he knew quite clearly that he must be dead.

Yes, he saw it all now. He smiled at his past self, smiled with the sympathetic remoteness of a grown man looking back on childhood, smiled to think how transient and finite his pain had been, and how natural and petty all his injustice and haste and hate. It was a dream, a necessary dream, symbolical, educational, and now—it was at an end. There lay the battered body white and still—the eggshell of an eagle. He was dead. He was free from that gusty uncertain eddy of error forevermore. The lesson was over, the defaced exercise was taken from him. He perceived that he was so far still dreaming that his eyes were closed.

One of that crowd of memories became dominant. What brought before him so vividly that prone figure of Michelangelo's Adam? Then he perceived that he also was in that attitude, reclining, his elbow raising his body, that his other hand was TOUCHED by a hand unseen, lifted by a hand unseen.

He opened his eyes . . .

(Printer, white line. [Wells's note.])

The nurse had roused herself. She had a persuasion . . .

She came across the room and very softly turned the clothes from his face. It WAS VERY still.

⚜ 11 ⚜

Postmortem

AND while that silent riddle yet lay upstairs, there gathered a hushed council in Mrs. Satsuma's room in the basement. There was Master Harry insubordinate in spirit but crushed in action by the presence of his father; there was Muriel openly anxious now for Master Harry's future; there was Chitterlow hushed and dignified in bearing, a sort of bowed head and raised hat carriage, as became a professional actor in the presence of death. The nurse had gone and they had come to shield Mrs. Satsuma from certain vague terrors of the night, and Master Harry and Mrs. Chitterlow were to sleep in the house until the funeral. But Chitterlow declined to share this accommodation. Some queer exotic strain in his blood had asserted itself beneath a thin disguise of refinement. "No," he said resolutely; "not while He is in the house."

They sat about the round table and, to Master Harry's infinite disgust, talked with much affected feeling about the deceased. Chitterlow expressed sentiments of extraordinary tolerance and dealt with this question as he dealt with all questions, with reference to himself. "Even I," he said,"
* * *

"He had a good heart," insisted Mrs. Satsuma, "a generous heart."

Master Harry's emotions broke forth through the bounds of discipline. His little heart swelled. "He was a o' *Beast*," he said with emphasis.

This shocking opinion *de mortuis* created a diversion and for a time Master Harry had the centre of the stage. Mrs. Satsuma expressed her horror of his impiety. Mr. Chitterlow arose, knocked over a chair and "clouted" him, and his mother made some poignant remarks. She had thought her Harry was a little gentleman, she said.

* * *

At this frightful reflection Master Harry, who had stood his "clouting" with Spartan firmness, gave way to loud and uncontrollable sorrow, and hitting having been tried to assuage him in vain, he was for the sake of decorum consoled by a bound collection of Sullivan's "British Working Man," a favourite volume of the late Mr. Waddy's. With this he retired sniffing ruefully into a corner. He became interested. So soon as his elders had resumed the conversation, he produced an aniline pencil and proceeded to adorn the figures with pipes of a diagrammatic description, all the available chimneys with epicyclic smoke, and his mouth with an elegant violet mourning.

The conversation approached the topic of legacies with slow decorum. "After the funeral, I s'pose," said Mrs. Satsuma, "the will will be read."

"I suppose he has made a will," said Chitterlow in the offhanded tone of a man who makes a remark out of the morning's paper.

"Mr. Grimflack was here—two days before," said Mrs. Satsuma as calmly, but her eyes betrayed her.

The three thought.

"He's in the back room, isn't he dear?" said Muriel.

Mrs. Satsuma nodded over the table.

"He used to have a bureau—"

"It's in the front room," said Mrs. Satsuma looking up at the ceiling.

"I suppose—" said Muriel.

"It could do no 'arm to look," said Mrs. Satsuma.

Pause.

"I don't understand these things," said Mrs. Satsuma. "I have—in a sort of way—tried to see—"

"Harry would understand," said Muriel.

"Isn't his desk locked?" asked Chitterlow.

"I've got his keys, poor dear," sighed Mrs. Satsuma.

"I suppose you're anxious?" said Chitterlow. "Of course I think all this sort of thing ought to be left to the lawyers. Personally I'm not curious. That isn't my disposition. I know my work and I know what's not my work. So long as I can finish my play I don't care *that*"—he made a gesture of snapping fingers—"not that, for the old man's money. Still— of course, there's a feeling. It might help, I admit. Of course, if you *want* me to look—"

"You would like him to, dear, wouldn't you?" said Muriel sweetly.

Mrs. Satsuma said "One would like to know," and so the keys were given to Chitterlow and he went upstairs. When presently Muriel went up to him he was carefully replacing the papers in Mr. Waddy's bureau. "*I* can't find anything," he said without looking up.

"It must be somewhere," said Muriel. "I suppose—". Her roving eye came to rest on the folding doors to the back room in which Waddy lay.

"Don't go in there," said Chitterlow. Muriel looked at him, and Mrs. Satsuma appeared in the doorway.

"I believe," said Chitterlow slowly, "that he's died intestate."

Mrs. Satsuma instantly sat down in the chair nearest the doorway.

"Aren't there any other papers?" asked Muriel.

Mrs. Satsuma shook her head slowly.

"Nowhere?" said Muriel.

"Nowhere," repeated Mrs. Satsuma.

"He died intestate," said Chitterlow proclaiming a fact. He had such confidence in himself that he was instantly convinced of a thing if once he heard himself say it.

"P'RAPS," SAID MRS. SATSUMA, "THE LAWYERS TAKE CARE—"

"What's *that*?" said Muriel pointing to a disorder of papers on the upper shelf of the bookcase.

"Recipes," said Mrs. Satsuma.

"*Recipes*!"

"Yes— Recipes of bills."

"Oh! *receipts*," said Muriel approaching the case. She opened the glass door and reached down the wire file, dense with papers.

"There's a lot," said Chitterlow standing up.

"Yes," she said, "it's bills."

"Isn't there *any* where else?" asked Muriel.

"Not where *he—*" began Mrs. Satsuma.

There came a smash of fire-irons, THE BREAKING OF GLASS, and a frightful howl from downstairs.

* * *

"Fancy all these bills," said Chitterlow—"*paid*!"

He approached the bookcase in a spirit of vague curiosity. Very probably he would never see anything of the sort in his life again.

He wondered at the multitude of things the man had received credit for; things possibly that he, Chitterlow, had never even attempted to buy. The first bill he examined was a wine merchant's and dry exciting reading. The second was for a bedside table, and the third for a lot of books. The next was a tantalizing record of cigars. "Write off for whatever you want," muttered Chitterlow. "And you get it!" He spent some time in gloating over the realities of wealth. He reached down another of the files. It differed from the others in the greater uniformity of its white sheets. He was surprised to see that the uppermost document was not written on a bill-head. Then he read: "This is the last will and testament of me William Bosworth Waddy."

His face lit with surprise. His movements became quick and precise. He detached the white sheet from the file and scanned it eagerly—with a lengthening face. He turned it over and scrutinized the vacant back. His face expressed bitter disappointment. "Spiteful old Brute," he said at last.

Then, struck by a thought, he put it carelessly on the bookcase ledge and turned hastily to the file again. The next document was also a will! OF AN EARLIER DATE.

He ran a trembling hand down the edges of the densely packed documents on the file, pausing here and there.

They were all wills!

He relieved his astonishment in a mild ejaculation.

He glanced at the folding doors, then—file in hand—went with stealthy strides towards the bureau. He placed the file upon the writing slope and stood hesitating with one eye on the door of the room. Then he stole across the room, turned the key, and returned to the bureau. Finally he went to the folding doors, and they were already secure. He seated himself and prepared to do business methodically at the bureau.

An afterthought prevailed with him, and he rose up, returned to the door of the room and unlocked it again.

He glanced at the will he had first examined. It appeared to be the most recent. He read aloud. "In trust for my alleged relation Master Harry Chitterlow seven hundred pounds." "The whole to be expended on board and lodging—except when he is with his parents—on education and on clothing for the said Harry Chitterlow." "A good preparatory school where corporal punishment is in actual and frequent use." "Express my regret that his father is now too old for similar benefits . . ."

"Nice old boy," said Chitterlow. "*Nice* old boy. And all the rest to charities! Every penny!" He put it down carefully at his right hand and turned to the second bequest.

This was a few weeks earlier in date; it must have been drawn up between the reading of *Little Lord Fauntleroy* and the visit of Master Harry. There was a spiteful allusion to Chitterlow that tried the reader's magnanimity, but the attitude towards Muriel and Master Harry was decidedly more amiable. On the whole it presented Mr. Waddy in an unusually idealistic mood.

* * *

Through all the series the references to himself were numerous and painful, but he had his duty to his wife and child to consider.

* * *

And while he was doing these things, exterior tumults and the passing of an uproar to the room above AND A SMART SMACKING SOUND suggested that upon Master Harry the supreme penalty of bed in the daytime was being (with difficulty) inflicted. To such tumults however Chitterlow's mind was accustomed.

About halfway through the file he discontinued reading

and began to ransack his pockets. The expression of his face went from anxiety to dismay and jerked back abruptly to satisfaction. He produced three frayed but efficient wax vestas from his waistcoat pocket and placed them carefully on the pen tray. He nodded to them in a confidential manner. Then, after a glance at the folding doors, he resumed his examination of the file

* * *

After a long time Muriel came upstairs again.

"We can't find anything," she said.

He was seated with his back to her, his head resting on his hand. He did not turn. "Any what?" he asked in an indifferent tone.

"Any—will."

"It's here," he said calmly and, still without looking, held a paper over his shoulder.

She advanced and took it and read with dilated eyes.

Chitterlow leant back in his chair and fixed his gaze on the central pigeon-hole of the bureau. "That is the latest," he said "in existence. There are a number of earlier ones on this file. In them all there are lots of nasty little snacks and allusions—He never understood me, right up to the end."

Muriel looked at him. Her face quivered with excitement. "But *this*—" she said and stopped.

"The money's a help, of course. I never wanted it, of course. I never asked for it. It's yours. Still—"

Mrs. Satsuma appeared in the doorway.

Muriel turned. She held out the will and her eyes were shining with tears. "Dear," she said, "you were right. He was cross and insulting, but—"

Mrs. Satsuma gasped. "Me?"

"Yes," said Muriel as though she gave it. "Fifty pounds a year."

Mrs. Satsuma's face was expressionless with emotion.

"And dearest," gasped Muriel; "my little gentleman! My little gentleman will be a little gentleman still." She was weeping. She became speechless and held out her arms.

For a space the two ladies forgot Chitterlow in their congratulatory excitement, and then Mrs. Satsuma became aware of him standing at the further window. His expression betokened a gloomy sternness, his pose was strongly sugges-

tive of Napoleon on the deck of the "Bellerophon," one foot
forward and a hand thrust into his coat. She disentangled
herself from Muriel and gaped at this magnificence. Her eyes
were interrogative.

"Ssh!" whispered Muriel. "He's hurt. Something in the
will. He's spoken of unkindly."

"Oh!" said Mrs. Satsuma. Chitterlow did not appear to
hear and the good lady was anxious to change the subject.
Something in the empty fireplace caught her eye.

"My!" she said. "What's this? What a girl it is!"

She went and peered.

"How—ever?" she said. She turned a curious face to Muriel. "It's burnt paper! *Who* can 'ave—?"

Simultaneously the two ladies were struck with the same
thought. Muriel glanced swiftly at Chitterlow and then at
Mrs. Satsuma, Mrs. Satsuma's wide eyes went between Chitterlow and Muriel to and fro. Chitterlow appeared not to notice
these things. The pause lasted as long perhaps as one might
count twelve.

When Mrs. Satsuma spoke again her voice was so low as
to be almost indistinct.

"It's that girl," she said. "I better clear it away before she
comes in."

She stood erect, stared once more at Chitterlow and disappeared in search of hearth pan and brush.

Chitterlow turned. "He never understood me," he said.
"Never."

He went to the bureau and took up the file. "We had
better, I think, replace the will on the file—now that your
curiosity is satisfied." He held out his hand. Muriel looked at
him hard as she gave him the will. He walked across the room
to the bookcase with a certain relief apparent in his manner.
Certain disagreeable doubts in Mrs. Chitterlow's mind were
suddenly dismissed; and indeed what *is* the good of brooding
on disagreeable things?

She walked to the window. The morning had been over-
cast but now the sun was breaking through. A great shadow
rushed athwart the Leas and passed, and all that level space
was suddenly warm and brilliant, and beyond upon the sea
vague vast patches of sombre grey fled before the light.

But Chitterlow's gloom remained until the midday meal.

They began lunch with a certain constraint that vanished with the soles, and gave place to a subdued exhilaration. Mrs. Satsuma remarked that there was need for bearing up, and that Mr. Waddy had left certain fag ends of whiskey behind him. She returned with a box of cigars also, and Mr. Waddy had always been very particular about his cigars.

"You may just as well have them," said Mrs. Satsuma generously. "They're as good as yours, so to speak."

The three sat among the débris of the meal at last, and even Chitterlow's demeanour approached cheerfulness.

The whiskey was very fine old whiskey and he had shown its quality by taking two outsize doses neat. Muriel's intimacy with Mrs. Satsuma, in spite of the social gulf that was widening between them, was even conspicuously unaffected. Muriel was determined that no condescension should appear in her manner, that she would say nothing to remind the old lady of her own essential ladyhood. Chitterlow remarked that Waddy evidently knew a thing or two about cigars, and laughed and broke his ash into a plate. He also praised the whiskey. It was "very fine" whiskey and he took some more.

It awakened a stream of agreeable reminiscences. There was a place in Fleet Street known only to such "boys" as himself that had a very particular whiskey. He alluded also to the whiskey of the Honourable Thomas Norgate. That had been good certainly but this he thought was better. When he reverted to the legacy he found he could not speak quite freely.

He set out to explain himself to Mrs. Satsuma. He said that he was a very peculiar man and that it was necessary to understand his attitude. He added in a lengthy parenthesis that everybody did not understand him, that he was bound to say that Mr. Waddy did not understand him, and yet he wished to make it perfectly clear, and especially to Mrs. Satsuma since he valued her friendship greatly, that in spite of all that had happened he bore Mr. Waddy no ill-will; he had said always and he said now that Mr. Waddy was a very fine old boy, a very fine old boy indeed. HE HAD A PREJUDICE AGAINST RED HAIR NO DOUBT, BUT THAT STILL LEFT HIM A VERY FINE OLD BOY. He paused and reflected. Mr. Waddy's whiskey, he added embarking upon a short humorous parenthesis of the second order, was also very fine old whiskey, and he then became aware, it seemed, that he had wandered from his original intention, whatever that may have been, and he helped himself to a fresh dose of whiskey while he prepared a fresh point of departure.

He was, he said, not in the least elated by his good fortune, and added in parenthesis that it was not his good fortune so much as Muriel's, or rather the boy's. Pursuing this parenthesis he pointed out that his views differed from Muriel's about the destiny of their son. She wanted him to be a gentleman. Now people wanted various things, some wanted some things and some others; she, Mrs. Satsuma, might want things that he, Chitterlow, did not want and vice versa. Dismissing this question of the diversity of human desires in an admittedly incomplete state, he proceeded to what he in particular wanted. He held that an artist was greater than a gentleman, a thing that Bernard Shaw had very admirably shown. In this matter he agreed with Bernard Shaw, although in other matters they did not agree. Bernard Shaw was no doubt a very fine dramatic critic, so too was William Archer. They had never written a play, at least a play worth speaking about, that is William Archer had not, and he, Chitterlow, had. He proceeded to discuss the state of dramatic criticisms generally and the present prospects of playwrights. Their possible gains exceeded any possible legacies, he maintained. He proceeded to a parenthetical autobiography showing how his peculiar qualities had distinguished him and tracing their origin. He made dark allusions to the Honourable Thomas Norgate. And then breaking through his subject rather than bringing it to an end he repeated that he was not elated and that money matters had never been a source of anxiety to him. He held that fortune favoured the brave. He commenced and forgot to go on with an illustrative story in parenthesis. Ignoring himself he insisted that Muriel was extremely brave. After a brief inconclusive parenthesis on RED HAIR AND bravery that seemed to concern some obscure fight in the past, he revived the theme of Muriel and proceeded to a glowing testimonial to her purity, courage, virtue and charm, with which testimonial his oration happily and not untimely concluded. Mrs. Satsuma, who had been a little puzzled by portions of this discourse, became an appreciative auditor of this masterly peroration.

Mr. Chitterlow then filled his pockets with cigars and went for a walk, the afternoon being bright and fine. He walked out upon the Leas and up to the Sandgate lift and back. At first he smouldered with eloquence and entertained thoughts of accosting one or two solitary persons and giving them a more complete analysis of his character than he had hitherto attempted; but soon the fresh south western cleared his head from the fumes of Mr. Waddy's cellar, and he began to think with greater clarity than he had done since he destroyed the two latest wills in Mr. Waddy's room.

He faced now a fact he had hitherto deliberately ignored, the practical fact that a legacy to Muriel was really money for him to spend. As this thought matured in his mind his walk became more elastic. He began to draw pictures, delightful pictures, of himself spending money. No bothers now about credit—at the slightest hint of trouble he could pay. He would have a complete suit of mourning from top to toe, kid boots, black bordered handkerchief and a deep crape band leaving about an inch of his hat—not more. They would have the best mourning money could buy. And as for a funeral. The old boy had come to the right shop for a funeral, anyhow. He, Chitterlow, acting for Muriel, would tell them boldly to spare no expense.

And afterwards! Fancy going to a wine merchant's to order wine! No fuss about prices, my boy, but good it *must* be. The wine merchant would soon understand him. No flat. A chap who was up to things. He knew what was expected of a gentleman.

It is ever a dangerous thing to think of buying. The topic carried Chitterlow away from the edge of the Leas almost without his noticing it, obliquely across the grass and into the Sandgate Road. It directed him with unerring accuracy past the Town Hall into the midst of the shops. His passion for buying rose with every window he passed. At last a row of black ties in a draper's window arrested him as the inevitable necessity. There seemed to be nothing more in life unless he bought a dozen (no less) of those ties.

He entered the shop.

Now, common men when they enter draper's shops dodge the shopwalker, sneak towards the nearest counter, and whisper their mean requirements to the least aggressive looking assistant that they can in their confusion discover. But actors, born or professional, are not as other men. When they enter they "fill" the doorway, and go right "up centre" of the shop. They open out towards the majority of people in the shop, who for the rest of the time constitute an audience within the meaning of the actor's mind. So Chitterlow designed to enter. And having riveted attention he would buy a dozen ties—a whole dozen. But suddenly came the unexpected and he had to improvise. He saw before him a face curiously familiar and with recognition in its eyes. The thought carried him back to Tunbridge Wells, to a study of character undertaken with a view to use in the still unfinished play, to the mean but acceptable personality of Kipps.

He held out his hand high in the fashionable way. "Hullo, dear Boy!" he cried. *"You*! Here!"

The only flaw in the wild bliss of Kipps was that half the staff of the shop were downstairs at tea. No matter—the others would describe the affair.

"*Ra* ther," he countered with spirited familiarity. "Whad'r *you* doin' here?"

* * *

"Put it down to me, dear Boy—and say nothing."

Mr. Chitterlow curved into the middle of the shop, waved a farewell ("So long"), and passing rapidly through six graceful attitudes, made an *exit* by the shop door.

Kipps watched him vanish past the window, gazed doubtfully at the pile of mourning goods before him, took his duplicate book from the fixtures, made a sprawling account, and raised his voice in a hesitating "Sayn."

✤ 12 ✤

The Anxieties of Mr. Kipps

M R. Kipps was gnawed by anxiety.

It was just that slack time after the midday meal and before customers come in, when anxiety is particularly prone to gnaw. It gnawed, if one may indulge in a conceit, with three fangs. There was first, that perpetual anxiety of the shop assistant, the insecurity of his situation. There had recently been rows.

They were not simply everyday nagging, they were the sort of rows that had in Kipps' previous experience preceded a "swap." Certain minor transactions had earned the expressed disapproval of the shopwalker. He had been told in set terms that he was not smart enough in his window dressing, he had been advised that he was considered slack in service, and one day he had been reproved before a customer for not knowing the stock. These things had robbed him of self-confidence. When he had returned from the adventure upon the Leas, he had funked describing it. He knew he had no business on that ascending path. He had tried to invent some plausible falsehood, but it was one of his professional disadvantages that he was a remarkably poor liar. So he had smuggled another piece of sateen in the place of the damaged one, and after terrible

99

qualms submitted it to the shopwalker to check back. And now the wheel marked sateen was hidden temporarily in the fixture behind. If that came to light—! Unless something was done it was bound to come to light; then Mr. Kipps considered that his destiny was clearly to be spelt U.P. But how to get rid of it? He might of course buy the piece under the pretence that he wanted to make a present to his mother, but that would be a matter of pounds, and even then the dirty state of the goods might appear and necessitate nasty explanations. The old gentleman had indeed promised him that he would make good the damage, had taken his name and address. But that was a full week ago. Of course it might be possible to cut off all the damaged portion secretly and make away with it. Yet men have been "quodded" for less. There was a chap who got into trouble once, through the *Exchange and Mart*, Kipps recalled, for "sneaking" stuff. He figured himself meeting the eye of the "Guv'nor" with fifteen yards of sateen under his waistcoat . . .

He couldn't do it.

This topic became intolerable. But fleeing it, he blundered promptly into another scarcely less pleasing one, he was bitten by the second fang, to recur to our earlier image. And the second fang was the question of Chitterlow's credit. The shopwalker had insisted that Mr. Kipps should be held responsible for that. With unusual insight Mr. Kipps esteemed that money as lost. That would make a big hole in his "sugar" for the holidays, indeed it was a question whether it would "run" to holidays after that deduction. He would have to go home to New Romney. That seemed an inconceivably dull and stupid way of spending those precious days.

Usually Mr. Kipps could find refuge from such troubles in meditations of an amorous and sentimental sort, but just at present this department of his life was in a painfully complicated tangle. He had "made rather an ass of himself" over a certain girl in the entering desk. Presuming on an incidental engagement, he had, in an exuberant moment, written her a letter of anticipation, expressing the warmth of his joy when at last she should be his "dear little wife." (As a matter of fact she was a large fair girl, taller and much broader than Mr. Kipps, with superficial blue eyes and a strident laugh.) It was not the sort of letter Gabriele D'Annunzio would consider erotic, but nevertheless, though it might not satisfy these exalted standards, there was no disputing that it was still a very silly letter. In it he dealt in a sketchy manner with one or two etymological difficulties, and at the end he had dropped into verse. The essential indiscretion of the letter had arisen through the compulsion of rhyme.

At the time of composition he had regarded this letter as a "lark." But when his next approaches towards the extensive exterior of its recipient were met by a distant manner and the remark that she had "hardly expected" it of him, his opinion changed. Had he fallen from his gentlemanly ideal? Had his letter been indeed no refined "lark" at all, but something "coarse" and "vulgar" and an "insult" to a young lady? And what steps had she taken or might she not take in order to show him up? He strongly suspected her of showing this letter to the girl in the ribbons department, who had also become distant in her manner. Matters were not mended by a discussion at the tea table and much feminine tittering over how to spell two of those etymological difficulties! Mr. Kipps had got *very* red. It was a painful, anxious position of affairs; on the one hand was the Scylla of ungentlemanliness, and on the other the Charybdis of being "larfed" at. And the way of escape was so narrow as to seem hopeless.

What made this business in some unaccountable way more complex and irksome was the fact that he had met Ann Pornick in Folkestone. Suddenly he had been reminded of emotions that had now lain undisturbed in his mind for years, and they jarred in the most extraordinary way with his memory of that letter. After she had been replaced and forgotten and given over as lost for evermore, Ann had come once more into his world.

His meeting with her made apparent even to himself how much his circumstances had moulded him since those naïve imaginative days. He was vaguely aware of a contrast, as if something, he knew not what, had gone from him. He met her

* * *

She was a housemaid!

* * *

About her he was a man divided against himself.

* * *

"I shall be able to see her again," said Kipps the native.

"Won't do to be seen about with a slavey," said Kipps the Draper, son of Old Kipps. From this point of view it became of the utmost importance what Miss _____, of the glove department, might think if she saw him speaking to anyone so remotely below his social level.

If in some complex extraordinary way he could contrive to see her

* * *

She had told him her father was dead and her family scattered. Mrs. Pornick had married a "gentleman-tailor" (first cousin to a "gentleman-farmer") to whom she had gone as cook-housekeeper. She had cut herself off from her family at his request.

* * *

ANN'S image had certainly got itself somewhat effaced. She had not the noble superiority of Miss Walsingham the liveliness of

* * *

And yet—and yet

* * *

And suddenly dispersing all these perplexities came a new perplexity. Round the corner of the fixtures appeared West, the clerk, with a letter extended. Kipps took this. West walked past him to stare out of the window over the back boards and make inaudible remarks of a warmly complimentary colour to the young lady who was scrutinising its contents. Kipps examined the envelope. "Ullo!" he said. The handwriting was strange, the postmark Folkestone.

"What—ever can *this* be?" said Kipps.

Resolved to plumb the mystery of this letter to the bottom, he went so far finally as to open it. The note he unfolded impressed him as being a hybrid between note paper and a bill. "Grimflack, Weston & Grimflack" asserted themselves and gave particulars of their telephone number, telegraphic address, and London agents.

West heard a sort of crooning ejaculation. He turned.

"Jest look at this, West," said Kipps patting the letter and then proffering it. "What's a chap to do with a thing like this?"

Pause, during which Kipps surveyed the enigma of West's face.

"Something very much to your advantage," read West. "Why it means that you're jolly well in luck, Kipps, that's what it means.

"THAT'S HOW THEY SPRING LEGACIES ON YOU," SAID WEST.

⚜ 13 ⚜

Mr. Kipps Hears
Astonishing Things[1]

THE premises of Grimflack, Weston and Grimflack, he discovered, were <not nearly so impressing as he had expected, a mediocre respectability, brass plate and wire blinds. But they were impressive enough to make him take a couple of turns before he could enter the office.>

He took a deep breath IN THE DOORWAY AND DISCOVERED two youthful clerks regardING him curiously. HE SELECTED THE YOUNGEST AND HIS MANNER BECAME EXTREMELY PROPITIATORY. "I 'ad a—Letter," said Mr. Kipps, "saying, or at least *arsting* me—to come round 'ere." HE fumbled for the letter.

"What name Sir?" said the youngest of the clerks very respectfully.

"Grimflack, Weston and Grimflack."

"But *your* name SIR?"

"Arthur Kipps."

The youngest clerk glanced at his fellow and the respect in his manner deepened. He invited Kipps towards a ground glass door, pointed out how to steer round a sort of counter to reach it, opened it before him and announced to some person within "Mr. Kipps Sir."

Kipps became aware, IN A SETTING OF DUSTY ROOM, of a
large inclined oblong of unwashed parchment and above it
like a November sunset a bright pink shining pate. A series of
lean fingers clutched the sides of this OBLONG in the centre of
which APPEARED a lesser rectangle still more unwashed than
the rest, A RECTANGLE OF precious writing embellished with
old English words. As the door had opened a tremor had
passed over this DOCUMENT and at the sound of the clerk's
voice announcing "Mr. Kipps," the skin crunchingly col-
lapsed, folded in upon the central rectangle and revealed a
thin clean-shaven face with long yellow teeth and brown eyes
that regarded Kipps over gilt glasses.

"Mr. Kipps," said this person. "Ah!"

For a moment he seemed to be so greatly embarrassed by
the document in his hand AS TO BE INATTENTIVE TO OTHER
MATTERS. The very young clerk placed a chair conveniently
for Kipps and HOVERED HELPFULLY FOR A MOMENT; the
old gentleman MOVING HIMSELF FROM THE DOCUMENT said
"Thank you Williams, thank you," and by means of his eye as
it were, expelled Williams from the room and closed the door
after him.

Mr. Kipps maintained an appearance of sangfroid by a
considerable effort. He placed his hat methodically on the
desk immediately in front of the gentleman, his umbrella in
the tall waste-paper basket, seated himself and, leaning
slightly forward, placed his hands on his knees. Some temporary dislocation of his breathing caused a momentary inflation
of his cheeks.

Mr. Grimflack was an elderly wrinkled little man with
fine gold-rimmed glasses and a general baldness relieved by
tufts of thistle-down greyness. He watched all these things
nervously. "That's right," he said at last. "Pray be seated, Mr.
Kipps." He fumbled with some papers before him, placed a
pile under a heavy paper-weight, and rubbed his chin with
four flattened fingers. "And you are Mr. Kipps?" he said
abruptly. He regarded him through his glasses and then very
carefully verified his impression with the naked eye over their
rims.

"I am that," said Mr. Kipps.

The waste paper which from the outset had evidently
accepted the umbrella of Mr. Kipps with resentment, now

recovered from the astonishment of this outrage and flung the intrusive body violently upon the floor. Mr. Kipps disappeared for a moment from Mr. Grimflack's vision. He reappeared with a scarlet face attempting to balance the implement against the edge of Mr. Grimflack's desk. It went down again and Mr. Kipps then placed it resolutely across the papers on Mr. Grimflack's desk beside his hat, and resumed his position of attention, gasping. Mr. Grimflack who had followed all these movements with nervous jerks, eyed the umbrella as if it fascinated for some seconds, and then resumed the conversation by an effort.

"You are the Mr. Kipps who is employed at the Folkestone Drapery Emporium?"

"Granted," said Mr. Kipps.

"And on the Thursday before last you stopped a runaway bath chair on the Leas."

"I did. It was a old gentleman—"

Kipps stopped suddenly. Perhaps he was wanted as witness to the old gentleman's behaviour!

"Ah!" said Mr. Grimflack and appeared to be trying to remember some premeditated action. Then he recalled what it was. He stood up with an extraordinary attempt at amiability. He proffered a lean hand. "Then, my dear Sir, allow me to congratulate you," he said. His glasses slipped from his nose and he made a faint ejaculation happily covered by the clash of the glasses against his waistcoat buttons.

Mr. Kipps, after a momentary hesitation, stood up spasmodically, grasped the extended hand resolutely—it felt like a purse of bones—and asked in a muffled tone how Mr. Grimflack did. He also said he was glad to see Mr. Grimflack, and then he let go and awaited a fresh cue.

Mr. Grimflack reseated himself in a *quasi* automatic manner, and Mr. Kipps promptly did the same. They heard the successive concussions of the chairs—lump, lump—in the outer office.

"Let me explain your good fortune," said Mr. Grimflack, evidently recovering the thread of his premeditated remarks.

He replaced his glasses, lifted the paper-weight and put it down again, and coughed.

"This old gentleman," he said; "Mr. Waddy, that is to say —has since died."

"Died!" said Mr. Kipps, and across his mind the word "*Legacy*" screamed. But he felt it becoming to be painfully shocked. "Died! Good gracious me!"

"Yes. There is no doubt the accident rendered his state—played a considerable share in determining his indisposition. Though he had been weakening for some time."

There came a second thought into the mind of Mr. Kipps —*Inquest*!

"Fancy!" he said, pretending to ignore his personal share in the matter. "Well, I *am* sorry. Him dead! And he seemed that vigorous too—"

"He was—in many ways—vigorous to the last," said Mr. Grimflack, and was lost for a moment in reminiscence.

"You must understand," he resumed, "that Mr. Waddy—"

"Waddy!" said Kipps. "I've heard that name. Somewhere. But never mind. You go on, Sir."

"Mr. Waddy was possessed of very considerable property."

Mr. Kipps made a sound, "Arwosee!" to express ingenuous surprise.

"And he had no near relations or anyone who could legitimately claim to succeed him. Consequently the disposition of his property was a matter of very considerable anxiety to him.

"Behind manners—" Mr. Grimflack hesitated for a moment and coughed, "—manners that were sometimes a little lacking in consideration for the prejudices of those about him, and a certain quickness, a hastiness almost, of temper that at times misled him, Mr. Waddy concealed a very noble and generous disposition. He has said to me frequently, among other remarks, that the disposition of his property was the worst trouble that ever came to him. He was conscientious, he wished to do good with it, only his circumstances—his circumstances prevented him. And he—fluctuated. Indeed his life was a painful indecision. Painful. He was continually making wills. Now he would leave it as a fund for the prosecution of patent medicine vendors, now for the purpose of smoke prevention, and now for the suppression of ritualism. There were so many things he wished to have utterly put down that he never came to any permanent decision. Now he would distribute it in certain proportions among people who seemed to have a claim to it, and now in other proportions. The current will he invariably left in my charge; the rest he did not destroy, but kept on an ordinary bill file in his own apartments."

"Ah!" said Mr. Kipps.

"His last will was executed five days ago."

"After the accident?" said Mr. Kipps breathlessly.

"After the accident. And by this will—"

Mr. Kipps felt the oddest feeling inside, and his hands tightened on his knees. The effort to maintain an expression of innocent interest was considerable.

"By this will, and subject to certain not very difficult conditions, he leaves the whole of his property, which after the settlement of all claims and outgoing charges, amounts to about five and twenty thousand pounds—"

Mr. Kipps' face manifested a temporary cholera.

"—to. The conditions———"

"Stop a minute," said Mr. Kipps, with an agitated grey face, a waving hand and a tone of quiet remonstrance. "Will you just say that over again, please. Just say it once again."

"What over again?"

"What you've just said."

"He leaves the whole of his property, which amounts finally to about five and twenty thousand pounds, to you."

"*Me*—that is?" Mr. Kipps had the air of eager intelligence.

"Yes—*you*. Mr. Kipps—employed at the Folkestone Drapery Emporium, and who———"

"Steady on a bit," said Mr. Kipps. "Five and twenty. YES. Thousand. Pounds!"

He extended his legs stiffly and stared at Mr. Grimflack's oilcloth. "Five and twenty. Thousand. Pounds."

He felt deflated—helpless. Beyond a clear knowledge that he was not saying or doing the right thing to say and do, his mind was a blank.

He looked at Mr. Grimflack with a sudden suspicion.

"This isn't any joke?" he asked. "You're sure of what you're telling me?"

"The will is here," said Mr. Grimflack and raised the paper-weight.

Kipps took the document and examined it earnestly upside

down—his mind paralysed—then he turned it right way up and attempted to read. But the letters kept running about.

"But whad he go and do this for?"

"He leaves it to you," said Mr. Grimflack in a tone of severe disapproval, "because he says you are the only person to do him a disinterested service in the last twenty years. He said *that*. He made me write that down. He says that you had no time to think, but he chooses to overlook that. On account of his position. And so—the property is yours."

Mr. Kipps drew a deep breath and inflated his cheeks. He replaced the will on the desk.

"The fact of it is," he said weakly, "that I can't take it in just at present. That's how it takes me, if you understand me—jest for the moment." HE PUT HIS ELBOW ON THE DESK AND SHADED HIS EYES.

"I can quite understand that it is a surprise," Mr. Grimflack remarked.

"It's a lot of money," said Kipps. "Sounds a lot of money, anyway How much might—whatever you said it was—come to in a year? Puttin' it like that."

Mr. Grimflack referred to a piece of paper. "Mr. Waddy's income for last year was twelve hundred and sixty-three pounds fifteen shillings."

"Twelve 'undred and sixty-three pounds fifteen shillings," repeated Kipps, awestruck. "Why, I never had anywhere—mor'n thirty—in my life."

He looked at Mr. Grimflack's little pink nose squeezed and wrinkled between the gold glasses. He began to realise certain consequences of this fantastic event. CHEERFULNESS DAWNED, INCREASED, GREW TO AN IMMEDIATE PROMISE OF THE LIGHT OF JOY. "I say," he remarked WITH A CRACK IN HIS VOICE, "but this is about the end of drapering for me, Sir, eh?"

Mr. Grimflack smiled. "Unless you have a very strong taste for it," he said.

"Why! I suppose I need hardly stay out my month."

"You'll only lose your current wages if you never go back," said Mr. Grimflack.

Kipps gasped.

"Whatever shall I do with my time?"

"Yes," said Mr. Grimflack, "that's a natural question."

He made a little grimace and his glasses dropped off. He took them in his hand and began to tap the edge of his desk. SOME PART OF THE PREMEDITATED INTERVIEW DRIFTED INTO SIGHT AGAIN.

"I hope, Mr. Kipps, you will pardon me if I make a few remarks—a few words of advice. For a time at any rate I'm your legal adviser—your solicitor—and I am the executor of the will." He tapped and thought a short interval. "Practically — I may tell you I was averse to this will in its present form. As you will hear—it is complicated. I tried to dissuade Mr. Waddy— To leave a sum of this sort unconditionally—practically unconditionally so far as methods of spending go—to a young man who has led a—a life of comparative restriction—"

"Yes," said Kipps. You cannot follow explanations very well when something with a voice like a trumpet is going round and round your head shouting "Twelve Hundred a Year! Twelve Hundred a Year."

"Who is not used to wealth— You see I do not mince matters."

"No," said Kipps.

"May very possibly end in his ruin. To such a young man there will be countless temptations—"

"And what did he say?"

"Nothing I can repeat. It was to the effect that Fortune had mocked him, and all he did was to pass the Luck on. . . . I don't think he was animated by any benevolent motive in leaving you this money. Frankly I do not. And that brings me —naturally—to the conditions under which it has been left."

Mr. Grimflack paused. His face assumed an expression of extraordinary distaste, little bright areas appeared in his nose and cheeks and ears. "The will," he said, "was a hasty will." He took the document in his hand, regarded it through his glasses with a disparaging eye. He cleared his throat and assumed an expression of personal disengagement. "However —here are the conditions of the will—very elaborate and unusual conditions I must admit—er—practically dictated by Mr. Waddy. In effect, you must undertake not to give or make over in any way any portion of this money to a man named Chitterlow. You must—er—become a party to a properly attested agreement to that effect."

"Chitterlow!" cried Kipps, astonished. "Why!—I know a chap——"

"An actor?"

"That's him," said Kipps with extended finger. "Why! I known him for years. GOT RED 'AIR."

"In that case these provisions may not be so unnecessary as I was inclined to think."

* * *

"He's been left money too. Told me only three days ago. From his—what you might call—uncle-in-law."

"In that matter," said Grimflack, "Mr. Waddy was—what anyone who did not know the facts of the case might call—his uncle-in-law. But—so far as I can gather—Mr. Chitterlow was a little premature

* * *

"You are not to *give* any portion of this money to this Mr. Chitterlow or to his wife or his son, nor are you to give it to anyone in order that they may administer it for their benefit, with certain exceptions. You may pay for the board of their son and for his education, but only at a boarding school where you have satisfied yourself that physical chastisement is an ordinary feature in the curriculum, and you may pay Chitterlow for any work he has done—except play writing—which Mr. Waddy in his will declares not to be work at all—but you may only pay after it is done, and at a reasonable rate. But beyond that you must not go. You undertake not to do so, and if you do, this agreement whose signature is an essential condition to the execution of this will in your favour, becomes by that act what practically amounts to a deed of gift of all your property to the Charity Organisation Society. I say practically— It might be revoked. The will was dictated to me by Mr. Waddy—I was warned by the doctor not to excite him and he was already excited. Opposition would have excited him more. It would no doubt leave scope for litigation—considerable litigation I am afraid— However IT IS NOT FOR ME — That, briefly, Mr. Kipps, is the effect of this complicated, unwise, and very extraordinary will of which I am the executor. I drew it up under protest. For a dying man. Under any other circumstances . . . *Ahem!* . . . It is for you to contest its limitations—the bequest to you is indisputably valid. That at least is the great thing."

"Yes," said Mr. Kipps, "that's the *great* thing."

"Precisely." And Mr. Grimflack paused.

* * *

"It's 'ard on Chitterlow," said Kipps. "But I don't see 'ow it's 'ard on me."

⚜ 14 ⚜

The Golden Dawn[1]

A T last the interview was over, Mr. Grimflack had handed
him what he called "a little advance" and with that
tangible FIRST FRUIT of the dream thrust deep into his inner
pocket, Kipps got HIS PUZZLED MIND out of the room. The
very young clerk darted forward and opened the door and Mr.
Kipps emerged into the sunlight and traffic of the Upper
Sandgate Road, blowing out his cheeks with a sense of infinite
relief. After the first exultant leap of surprise he had sat with
a sense of positive oppression, of almost unendurable restraint,
under the deliberate sentences, the explanations, the warnings
and parenthetical lucidities of Grimflack's discourse. ALL
THAT TIME THE TRUMPET VOICE HAD BEEN URGING HIM TO
DANCE. To behave with decorum, to feign a sober alertness to
many dangers, had been a matter of intense effort. At moments he had wanted to shout, and more particularly when
Grimflack had explained that he need not serve out his
month. It was that negative fact that occupied his mind now
to the exclusion of all other things, he had AS YET no imagin-
ings of the positive import of twelve hundred pounds a year.
TWELVE HUNDRED A YEAR WAS TWELVE HUNDRED A YEAR
AND THAT WAS ALL! He need not go back to shop now, nor

to shop tomorrow, nor the next day, nor the day after, never
—before him there spread out suddenly a glittering vista of
days. <The Emporium was over forever. Forever! Twelve
hundred a year!

He felt absolutely incapable of going back to the Emporium for a space. He must get this mass of relief in focus
first.

He walked along the road to see just exactly what it
meant. Twelve hundred a year!> There would be no more
getting up to wake the apprentices in the morning, no more
dusting before he washed, no more snatched breakfasts—there
came then his first positive forecast of his good fortune, eggs
and kidneys for breakfast every blessed morning if he liked—
no more long mornings with rows and nagging, no more
customers to serve, no more swaps and snubs. HOLIDAYS!
HOLIDAYS! All the year was to be one long Holiday now, the
Sundays OF HIS FUTURE, THE EARLY CLOSING AFTERNOONS
had spread out and touched one another. But it was better
than that; if the freedom of the great vista of days was
Sabbatical, their interest was to be altogether greater than
Sunday ever possessed. All those lovely weekdays, when shops
are open and the brighter sort of people walk about and
carriages are frequent, were at last entirely open to his inspection! TWELVE HUNDRED A YEAR!

Even now he was free, *now*! It was not next week or next
month, but now. He perceived how entirely wise Grimflack
had been, how suddenly, how utterly impossible, shop had
become. Fancy having to finish out the day! The long hours—
till eight! And perhaps late customers even then! IT CAME TO
HIM WITH AN EFFECT OF UTTERLY NOVEL DISCOVERY, AS A
THING ASTONISHINGLY FORGOTTEN, HOW INTENSELY HE
HAD ALWAYS HATED HIS DAILY LIFE . . .

He became aware of a little old lady standing BEFORE
HIM. She wanted to ask the way to the Lift. She had to repeat
her question twice before Kipps could get it focussed. ROOT
TOOT, ROOT TOOT—TWELVE HUNDRED A YEAR!

"DRINK," SAID THE LITTLE OLD LADY TO HERSELF, AS
SHE WENT UPON HER WAY.

He DRIFTED ROUND THE CORNER towards the Leas. Always when he had been stealing moments of freedom during
the errands of his apprenticeship, and on early closing nights

when his PURSUIT OF THE HIGHER LIFE CHISEL IN HAND AT
THE ART CLASS had not demanded his presence, he had been
accustomed to go upon the Leas. ON THE LEAS IT WAS THAT
HE WORE ALL HIS NEW CLOTHES FIRST AND SMOKED HIS
CIGARETTES. Pleasant people were always walking there, and
children playing and the Lift full of visitors going up and
down, and below was boating and bathing and perhaps a SHIP
WORKING out of harbour or an ironclad or liner in the offing,
always in abundance a daily life of interest and brightness, a
life—Life!—something entirely different from the System in
which his being HAD BEEN caught FOR SO LONG. The Leas
had always been—if not a window, at least a peephole out of
that. And now WITH A DISPOSITION TO INDIRECTNESS THAT
HAD GROWN UPON HIM THROUGHOUT ALL HIS YEARS as a
draper, he gravitated inevitably thither, to look out upon life
again but no longer as one who LIVES outside the game.

He might come here every day if he chose AND STOP AS
LONG AS HE LIKED!

The thought of coming to sit and TO promenade turned
his mind to the thought of clothes. He had always wanted to
possess a coloured cloth jacket suit with one of those PANAMA
STRAW hats with black bands that are so refined and popular.
Of course now—! Why a suit like that could be got for three
pounds say and the hat for five shillings! What was that to
twelve hundred a year? His vision opened out. He might get
patent boots with cloth uppers. He might get all sorts of
boots. All sorts of clothes! ALL SORTS OF THINGS! FANCY A
ROW OF BOOTS—ON TREES! LIKE THOSE HE SOMETIMES SAW
WHEN HE WENT OUT ON APPROVAL[?]! Hats! STICKS! He
tried to ascertain definitely how much clothing one could
afford on twelve hundred a year! SUPPOSING OF COURSE ONE
SPENT IT CHIEFLY ON CLOTHES—ONE MIGHT SPEND IT ON
ANYTHING!

Of course he would have to pay for his board and
lodging!

He became arithmetical.

He felt he must find a seat somewhere and sit down before
he could think all that at once. It was such a thundering lot of
money. <Good Lord! What a lot of money it was! It drew
out like a concertina as he regarded it.> It was—how much a
day to spend? Four pound—nearly four pound A DAY! *Pounds*,

YOU KNOW! Three pound anyhow. A suit a day practically. It was—how many times Carshot's "screw"—Carshot who got forty pounds a year? It was no good walking about and trying to do sums like that. HE MUST SIT DOWN SOMEWHERE.

Then he remembered that he had a house about, THE HOUSE WITH THE BLUE GREEN BALCONY. WHAT DID HE CALL IT? He forgot the necessity of sitting down to compute. "Lord!" he whispered "A HOME!" and forgot his fellow creatures. HIS GAIT OF SLOW AMAZEMENT GAVE WAY TO ONE OF QUICK PURPOSE. He turned westward and presently . . . *his* house. There it was, quite safe, a tall white house stucco fronted, bright white and with balconies of DULL BLUE AND GREEN—VERY DISTINCTIVE. He walked towards it staring. HE HAD GONE THERE ONCE LONG AGO WITH GOODS ON APPROVAL—HE WAS NEARLY CERTAIN. He stopped in the middle of the path and stared. HIS! Presently with the current of promenaders deflectING right and left of him he REDIS-COVERED his fellow creatures. He glanced at people about him and then back to the house. He wanted to stop someone and say, "I say you know—that's *my* 'ouse! That tall 'ouse—there."

He noticed several people were looking to see what he was staring at. He went on and walked past it, looking at it. He faltered and turned about. He was taken with curiosity and flittered across the grass towards it—TO SEE IF IT HAD A LETTER BOX OR WHAT IT WAS UNDER THE KNOCKER. THAT WAS IT, A LETTER BOX, RIGHT ENOUGH. He became abashed at his resolution in approaching it, SPECULATED what anyone looking from the window, THE BLIND OF WHICH WAS NOT DOWN, might think of him, and he turned back towards the path along the cliff edge. He sat down on a seat a little along the Leas and put his arm over the back and regarded his new possession. HE WHISTLED AN AIR VERY SOFTLY TO HIMSELF, PUT HIS HEAD ON ONE SIDE. Never had there been a house quite so wonderful to look at. THE TRUMPETING DIED AWAY.[2]

A very stout old gentleman with a very red face and very protuberant eyes sat down beside Kipps, removed a Panama hat OF THE NEWEST DESPERADO CUT, and mopped his brow and blew. Then he began mopping the inside of his hat. KIPPS

WATCHED HIM FOR A SPACE WONDERING HOW MUCH HE MIGHT HAVE A YEAR, AND WHERE HE BOUGHT HIS HAT. THEN HIS HOUSE REASSERTED ITSELF.

An impulse overwhelmed Kipps. "I say," he said, LEANING FORWARD TO THE OLD GENTLEMAN.

The very stout old gentleman started and stared at him.

"*What* did you say?" he asked fiercely.

"You wouldn't think," said Kipps, INDICATING WITH HIS FOREFINGER, "that that 'ous there belongs to me."

The old gentleman twisted his neck round to look at the house Kipps' gesture had indicated. Then he came back to Kipps, looked at HIS MEAN LITTLE GARMENTS with apoplectic intensity, and blew at him by way of reply.

"It does," said Kipps, a little less confidently.

"Don't be a Fool," said the old gentleman, and put his hat on and wiped out the corners of his eyes. "It's hot enough," PANTED the old gentleman indignantly, "without FOOLS." Kipps looked from the old gentleman to the house, and back to the old gentleman. The old gentleman looked at Kipps, and snorted and looked out to sea, and again, snorting very contemptuously, at Kipps.

"Mean to say it doesn't belong to me?" said Kipps.

The old gentleman just glanced over his shoulder at the house in dispute, and then fell to pretending Kipps didn't exist. "IT'S BEEN LEF' ME THIS VERY MORNING," SAID KIPPS.

"Aw!" said the old gentleman, like one who is sorely tried. He seemed to expect the passers-by presently to remove Kipps.

"IT *'as*," said Kipps. He made no further remark to the OLD GENTLEMAN for a space, but looked with a little less certitude at the house.

Presently he got up, and retraced his steps, ever and again looking back at the house. A curious doubt grew upon him and turned him back to the Upper Sandgate Road. He went as far as Grimflack's office. It was there, quite convincingly. He went on down a quiet side street, unbuttoned his coat, took out three bank notes in an envelope, looked at them and replaced them, then he fished up five new sovereigns from his trouser pocket and examined these.

"That's all right, anyhow," said Kipps.

He was suddenly struck with the bitter taste of a belated repartee.

"Thunderin' old Ass! I wish I'd shown 'im these.

"Don't be a Fool indeed! WHY! I don't suppose 'e's ever 'ad a 'undred pounds of 'is own in 'is life."

<He wandered for a time preoccupied with this incident. He became quite huffy and repeated in the tone of a man who touches the quick of a thing [?]. "Not a 'undred pounds of 'is own all 'is life. Quite beyond 'im!"> He came round by Grace Hill to shop windows. HE STOPPED. HE HAD ALWAYS BEEN ACCUSTOMED TO STOP AND EXAMINE THEIR CON-TENTS. IT BECAME overpoweringly evident to him that he was a person who could buy. An incontinence of purchase swept him away. He went into Melchisdec's and bought a banjo.

He emerged from Melchisdec's, the banjo in one hand and his umbrella in the other and with a certain indecision as to whither he was to go next.

It became apparent to him that he was a young man At Large, altogether too much At Large, that seeing that he had left the Emporium—where his box and property were—he had no sojourning place in the world. <Clearly he must go home to New Romney and this was Tuesday! The Romney bus would be starting about noon. But then he ought to go back to the Emporium to get his "things." Of course he would have to take away all his things. Would the box hold them? If not, should he buy another box. It seemed to him it would be rather nice to buy another box.> He was STILL involved in the unwonted exercise of PLANNING HIS OWN actions IN-STEAD OF MISINTERPRETING THE ORDERS OF SOME ONE ELSE when his thoughts were whirled for a while into quite another channel by a distant glimpse of Chitterlow marching buoyantly along a cross street. It was evident from the man's step even that he didn't yet know how things were. CHITTERLOW

* * *

He passed out of sight like an eclipse. Kipps was immediately glad this had not been an actual encounter, and it came to him for the first time vividly that this astonishing transfiguration of the universe had been accomplished at the expense of Chitterlow. The glorious serenity of the future was suddenly clouded by the possibility of a Jacob and Esau encounter, and the contemplation of that cloud carried him to THE establishment.

* * *

< He found himself outside the little side window full of Manchester goods that he had not dressed that morning. He stopped short ten paces from the door. Now what exactly was he going to do?

Chiefly he knew that he was going to astonish them.

It seemed to him that he should walk in strumming his banjo. There would be Carshot behind the counter and the new apprentices. He would go up and down the department a bit and puzzle them. Then suddenly he would hold out that handful of sovereigns to them and say, "See what I just been given!" It might even be a bit of a lark to give them each a sovereign! . . . Yes. That would be funny! He laughed as this idea struck him and made a movement for the door to carry out his scheme forthwith.

As he opened it, he saw the apprentice before him pretending to do some useful work, saw the apprentice's expression change to astonishment at the banjo. Kipps let the door swing behind him, coughed and drew his fingers over the strings. "What Ho!!" he remarked. "What price this?" The apprentice's face assumed an expression of horror. His eyes directed the eyes of Kipps up the department. "Customers!" gasped the apprentice.

Now Kipps had quite forgotten the possibility of customers. He was checked. Carshot, also horrified, stood with a partially unfolded lace curtain in his hand, and the eyebrows of the junior apprentice and a momentary glimpse of his nose and eyes appeared at the top of a lace curtain that he was holding up for the better inspection of the three customers in question. They were quite the most appalling customers that it is possible to conceive. They were large—a different and altogether larger species of humanity as it seemed to Kipps—and vividly dressed. The chief of them was a very enormous and dignified old lady with bleached hair and a brilliant bonnet, and as her mind slowly took cognisance of Kipps, with a very deliberate movement> she shook out HER glasses FROM THEIR long tortoiseshell handle and regarded him with calm hostility. The tall girls who stood beside her—they HAD refused to bend into chairs—REGARDED HIM WITH THE SAME WELL-BRED FRIGIDITY OF INTEREST. THEY seemed to look down on Kipps, physically, mentally, morally and socially. <He had intended to come upon and astonish Carshot, and behold he had blundered on the Most High Gods!> The eyebrows of the junior apprentice—he had ducked behind the curtain A LITTLE so that Kipps could no longer see his eyes—were the eyebrows of one who is forever utterly dismayed. <The curtain quivered with his apprehensions. Kipps felt himself drowning in disapproval. He felt he must have the immediate support of some other human being or perish there and then. He sought the eye of the second apprentice. He affected to ignore all the world. "See the banjo" he said.

The second apprentice looked at it out of the corner of his eye.>

* * *

Kipps made a feeble gesture as though he would hide his banjo behind his umbrella, glanced once again very swiftly at the lady with the GLASSES AGAIN, THEN TURNED ABOUT AND fled incontinently ROUND THE FIXTURES into the main shop.

And that too by some singular fatality appeared to be full of customers, strange, hostile, faintly curious <persons turning at the appearance of Kipps and staring like Aquarium fish, or not even turning but continuing their purchases. Where was the fun of that début? Some of the girl assistants were too busy to notice him, others were clearly embarrassed by this weird apparition. Buggins was showing someone into the millinery. Kipps took in all these things as he fled down the length of the main shop. He had made a ridiculous fool of himself. It seemed to him that he must fall in a faint before he reached the door to the house. He escaped into the house, falling on the mat. He fled swiftly and silently up the staircase fearing to meet even a servant while that banjo still burnt his hand. He slammed the door of the dormitory behind him, threw down> his banjo on the bed, SAT DOWN BESIDE IT and blew. . . .

THERE WAS NOTHING FOR IT, FOR A MAN WHO HAD MADE SUCH A FOOL OF HIMSELF AS HE HAD DONE, BUT COMPLETE AND FINAL FLIGHT.

It occurred to him that it would soon be time for the New

Romney bus to start. If he lost that he might have to stop the night in the Emporium. <He set to work with great vigour collecting his things and packing his box and portmanteau. As he did so the acute shame of his discomfiture passed. He would get out of this place forthwith. It was a hateful place. Anyhow if he had looked a fool, he was starting on a holiday that would last forever. He had the laugh of them there.

He finished his tumultuous packing. He stood up and anxiety about catching the bus gripped him. He decided he would leave his box and get off with his portmanteau. His eye fell on the banjo. After all, it was a lovely thing! He couldn't leave it. It was conspicuous of course but if he left it behind the apprentices might "muck it about." He hung over it for a space, then gripped portmanteau and umbrella in one hand, and banjo in the other and started for the bus. He met no one on the house stair. He let himself out by the side door and walked up the street, panting.

The New Romney bus, in the summer months, is a very noble edifice. It is red and white, with New Romney in letters of gold; you get into it from below and the windows make a pleasant buzzing in your ears. Like man and the nobler animals its inside is the less important part of it. It has a roof that will carry baggage, there is room for umbrellas beside the driver, and below and above the driver's seat is another seat and above that another, so that the outriders of the New Romney bus sit in tiers like Renascence angels. There are great lamps on either side of the New Romney bus and underneath between the wheels swings a great hold for luggage nearly to the ground. Except for the Southeastern Railway, which goes to Abbledore junction and thence to Ashford junction and so into the main stream of traffic, this is New Romney's only link with the world. And Kipps clambered up into the seat above and behind the driver, and sat there holding his banjo and feeling like a God. And when the bus started the rumble of its wheels went to the words, "Twelve Hundred a Year. Twelve Hundred a Year."

There sat beside him a young servant who was sucking peppermint and a little boy with a sniff and beside the driver were

* * *

Kipps sat among these people with a rapt look upon his face, perpetually turning over the wonderful news that his parents were presently to hear.

* * *

The sun was sinking

* * *

Their shadows grew long below them and their faces were transfigured in gold as they rumbled along towards the splendid west. The sun set before they had passed Dymchurch, and as they came lumbering into New Romney past the windmill, the dark had already come.

Kipps kept turning over in his mind how he could most surprisingly break the great news to the old people. He was still undecided when he alighted at his father's door. The driver handed down the banjo and the portmanteau and Kipps, having paid him, turned into the shop in a tumult of vague excitement and> ran the portmanteau smartly into Old Kipps whom the uproar had brought TO THE DOOR OF THE shop in an aggressive mood and with his mouth full of supper.

<" 'Ullo, Father, I didn't see you," said Kipps.

"Blunderin' ninny," said Old Kipps. "What's brought *you* here? Ain't early closing is it? What's all the shouting about. Eh?">

"Got some news for you, Father," said Kipps dropping the portmanteau.

"Ain't lost your situation, 'ave you? What's that you got there? I'm blowed if it ain't a banjo. Goolord! Spendin' your money on banjos! Don't put down your portmanty there—any how. Right in the way of everybody. I'm blowed if ever I saw such a boy as you've got lately. Here! Molly!"

"Somethin's happened," said Kipps slightly dashed. "It's all right, Father. I'll tell you in a minute." Old Kipps took the banjo as his son picked up the portmanteau again.

The living room door opened quickly, showing a table equipped for supper with elaborate simplicity, and Mrs. Kipps appeared.

"If it ain't YOUNG Artie," she said. "Why! Whatever's brought *you* 'ome?"

" 'Ullo, Mother!" said Artie. "I'm coming in. I got somethin' to tell you. I've 'ad a bit of Luck."

He staggered with the portmanteau round the corner of the counter, set a bundle of children's tin pails into clattering oscillation, and entered the little room. He deposited his luggage in the corner beside the tall clock, and turned to his parents again. His mother regarded him doubtfully, the yellow light from the little lamp on the table escaped above the shade and lit her forehead and the tip of her nose. Old Kipps stood in the shop door with the banjo in his hand, breathing noisily. "The fact is, Mother, I've 'ad a bit of Luck."

"You ain't been backin' GORDLESS 'orses, Artie?" she asked.

"No fear."

"It's a draw he's been in," said Old Kipps. "Jest look here, Molly. He's won this 'ere trashy banjer and thrown up his situation on the strength of it—that's what he's done. Goin' about singing."

"You ain't thrown up your place, Artie, 'ave you?"

It suddenly occurred to Kipps that throwing up his place *was* a bit rash. "I been left money," he said. "I been left forty fousand pounds."

"And you thrown up your place?" said Old Kipps.

"I 'ave," said Kipps.

"And bort this banjer, put on your BEST noo clo'es, and come on 'ere?"

"Well," said Mrs. Kipps. "I never did." (Printer, space these words. [Wells's note.])

"I shouldn't ha' thought that even *you* could ha' been sich a fool as that," said Old Kipps.

Pause.

"It's *all* right," said Kipps a little disconcerted by their distrustful solemnity. "It's all right—reely! Twenny-six fousan' pounds. And a 'ouse—"

Old Kipps pursed his lips and shook his head.

"A 'ouse on the Leas. I could have gone there. Only I didn't. I didn't care to. I didn't know what to say. I wanted to come and tell you."

"How d'yer know the 'ouse—?"

"They told me."

"Well," said Old Kipps, and nodded his head portentously towards his son, with the corners of his mouth pulled down in a portentous, discouraging way. "Well, you *are* a young Gaby."

"I didn't *think* it of you, Artie!" said Mrs. Kipps.

"Wadjer mean?" asked Kipps faintly, looking from one to the other with a withered face.

Kipps looked from one sceptical, reproving face to the other, and round him at the familiar, shabby little room, with his familiar cheap portmanteau on the mended chair, and that banjo amidst the supper things like some irrevocable deed. Could he be rich indeed? Could it be that these things had really happened? Or had some insane fancy whirled him hither?

Still—perhaps a hundred pounds—

"But," he said. "It's all right, reely, Father. You don't think—? I 'ad a letter."

"Got up," said Old Kipps.

"But I answered it and went to a norfis."

Old Kipps felt staggered for a moment but he shook his head sagely from side to side.

"But I saw a nold gent—perfect gentleman. And 'e told me all about it. Mose respect'ble he looked."

"It's a shame of 'im," said Mrs. Kipps. "A young chap one might—"

But Mr. Kipps had a sudden idea. He clapped his hand into his trouser pocket. "Look 'ere!" he said and produced three bright sovereigns and some silver; "and 'ere." He thrust his hand into his breast pocket, drew forth the bundle of bank notes, and after an instant's hesitation handed his father one. The parental expressions changed. "Eh?" said Kipps and watched their faces intently. Mrs. Kipps put the coin between her teeth and regarded her son with unfavourable eyes. Then she turned her attention to the notes.

Old Kipps produced his spectacles from his breast pocket and put them on. There was a stillness broken only by a crisp crackling and the stertorous breathing of Old Kipps. <He held it up to the light, squinted at it

* * *

Never was a note so tested.> At last HE handed the note to his wife and as she scrutinised the document he regarded her through his spectacles, and then took impressions of her visage both under and over them.

"James," said Mrs. Kipps at last in an awe-stricken voice. "After all— *It's true!*"

Then both turned their gaze to Kipps.

"Whoever—?" began Mrs. Kipps.

"It was a nold gentleman. I saved his life—like—on the Leas. 'Is bath chair was running orf with 'im. So I stopped it like."

* * *

"Don't you 'ave nothing to do with this Grimflack.

* * *

"You 'dminster it yourself, my boy.

* * *

"Brast it," HE EXCLAIMED SUDDENLY. "What's that?"

That was the jingle of the shop bell. Old Mr. Kipps rose ANGRILY and went out to the shop. Soon they heard his voice in a brisk altercation. He was explaining that the shop was closed, only he'd forgotten to fasten the door and put up the shutters. The intruder appeared to be impudently proposing to take advantage of this accident to make a purchase. This impertinence Mr. Kipps repelled with considerable acrimony, pointing out to the unseasonable customer still obstinately adhering to his improper intentions, that if he were to serve him he might keep his shop open day and night for every little whipper-snapper in the place. He came back into the living room, ruffled but triumphant.

* * *

"Lor!" said Mrs. Kipps, "you ain't ever been *tellin'* people, Artie?"

* * *

" 'Ow much djer give for it?" said Old Kipps.

Kipps hesitated.

Old Kipps reverted to the instrument. "Well," he said, "that's two pounds gone of it, anyway." He held it up to the light, and scanned its contours with a deprecatory eye. "I s'pose they told you these _____ was silver," he said. "I thought so. That's their ways. German silver they are, really. This was made in Germany. You can tell from the shape. It's rubbishin' stuff. Polished like and showy but no good to play. O' course you must go buying in one of those Folkestone shops 'stead of lettin' me get you a good un while you was at it. Well, well." He put the instrument down on the side table.

<"And now," said Old Kipps, "you got to think jest what you'll do with the money.
* * *

"I'd be careful with this Grimflack, my boy.">

❧ 15 ❧

Esau and Jacob

THE passing of five days found Kipps in mourning of unparalleled profundity and back in Folkestone again. He
had returned to Folkestone only at Mr. Grimflack's earnest
request and because he found himself unable to tell that
gentleman of two dreadful reasons he had for dreading the
place. He had witnessed Mr. Waddy's cremation (as directed
in the will) and now he was in occupation of the house on the
Leas—it had been taken furnished for a year—and in the care
of Mrs. Satsuma.

His three days at New Romney had failed towards the end
of the perfect glory of his home-coming. There had been
paragraphs "on" the papers, with his name in full and headed
"Remarkable Windfall," paragraphs which had filled him
with simple glory but which Old Kipps regarded as occultly
dangerous. There had been glorious walking to and fro
through New Romney and down to the sea and back, and
round New Romney again and so on, with a fine sense of the
universal astonishment, until Old Kipps pointed out the silli-
ness of this "perpetual ninny-trot round." On Sunday he had
gone with his parents to church—Old Kipps came also to
protrude a new gold watch chain, and Kipps was publicly

questioned and congratulated by important personages. There was a distinct allusion in the sermon; and into the offertory that day a half sovereign fell, and its tinkling descent was followed by a quite audible "Yaaps, you Gaby," of Old Kipps —too late to stop this astounding folly. It became evident to our *nouveau riche* that his parents distrusted his wisdom greatly and considered him in grave need of general discouragement; the constant stream of admonition not to do this, that, or the other foolish thing, as it occurred to them, became at last, in spite of their evident concern for his good, even irksome. Then the meeting with Sid Pornick—who was still in the place assisting in the bicycle shop—was unexpectedly disagreeable.

Sid's attempt at genial unenvious congratulation did not last a minute. "It's a bloomin' strike of Luck," he said, "that's what it is," with the smile fading from his face. "Of course," and he blew out his cheeks, "better you 'ave it than me, o' chap. *I* couldn't keep it, if I did 'ave it."

" 'Ow's that?" said Kipps, a little hipped by Sid's patent chagrin.

"I'm a Socialist, you see," said Sid. "I don't 'old with Wealth. What *is* Wealth? Labour robbed out of the poor. At most it's on'y yours in Trust. Leastways, that's 'ow *I* should take it."

* * *

But these were minor vexations to the trouble that gathered in Folkestone, visible of an evening far away on the eastward border of the Marsh. There came the first intimation of this in the letter from Grimflak urging his return in order to mourn and bury his benefactor. "A young lady giving the name of Daisy Dorcas called here yesterday enquiring for your present address. I did not feel authorised to give her this, but I suggested she might call again when I had received instructions from you. She promised to give me a note for direction to you, but so far it is not to hand."

It WAS to hand the next day. And in pleasant phrases it took up the indiscreet matrimonial anticipations of Mr. Kipps. She had already resigned her position in the desk of the Emporium, she said, and was making a list of her *trousseau* . . .

When he had finished it, his forehead was thickly bedewed. "O Lord!" said Mr. Kipps. "O Lord ha' mercy! She ain't at all the sort of girl . . . She's not . . . 'Ere I say! What the *Dooce* am I to do?"

(Printer Clarendon Caps. [Wells's note.])

That was one of the two things that bothered his soul, and made his return to Folkestone a deed of dread. The other, scarcely less heavy, was his fear of meeting Chitterlow. It was unreasonable, of course, but he felt as though he had in some incredibly vile way ousted Chitterlow from his "rights"; and he was convinced that even now Chitterlow must be pervading Folkestone seeking his life. Consequently, on his return from the cremation at Woking he went to his house on the Leas in a closed cab, and stirred not abroad at all, until at last an urgent note from Grimflak dragged him forth.

He scanned the Leas up and down before he plunged down the steps, he walked with rapid circumspection. And suddenly his heart stood still. He saw her. She and a short stout lady, recognisably her mother, were advancing towards him, with the serene resolute faces of people whose course lies clear before them. He was at a corner, and for the instant their faces had no recognition. His BLACKS! He turned the corner sharply and broke into a smart trot.

He had a half exultant moment as he whipped into the Sandgate Road, exultation at his own promptness and good fortune, a thought of all the unpleasantness he had so quietly escaped. He dodged sharply into the Sandgate Road, glanced back and changed his trot into a walk. He was safe!

Then he became aware of a tall, RED-SURMOUNTED figure standing outside Parson's library, a tall figure LIKE A FLAMING CENSER OF WRATH, that at once advanced across the road with gestures of recognition . . . *Chitterlow*!

"Hello!" cried Jacob Kipps faintly.

ESAU Chitterlow smiled—a smile that mingled irony. He lifted a large FRECKLED white hand to shake. He gave an actor manager's bow. "*Good* afternoon, Mr. Kipps," he said with elaborate politeness.

Kipps took the proffered hand in a limp shake. "I been looking for you," he decided to say. It was quite true. He *had* been looking for Chitterlow. Unfortunately he had not seen him soon enough.

"Ellow me to congratulate you," said Chitterlow, still

flavouring himself with irony. "On my Uncle's will." *His* uncle, now!

The sensations of Kipps, the conscious supplanter, were horrible. He did not know what to say, and his mental distraction was increased by the thought that MISS DORCAS MIGHT have seen him after all and be even now in hot pursuit.

"I been wanting to have a talk with you, o' chap," he said; "d'you mind walking a little this way?"

He indicated the direction of the town.

"If you want to talk about anything," said Chitterlow, "there's seats on the Leas."

Kipps looked in that direction for an excuse. Even now she might be within twenty yards of the corner. "I got to go that way," he said, laying a hand on Chitterlow's arm and indicating the Town Hall by a movement of his head. "I—I got business in the harbour soon. If you don't mind."

"Just the same to me," said Chitterlow turning with him. "Less private—that's all."

"I been wanting to see you tremendous," said Kipps setting the pace briskly. "O' course— Nat'shally I been thinking of you ever since I heard about that will."

Pause. They crossed the street in silence.

"I won't hide from you, Kipps, that it's been a bitter disappointment to us," said Chitterlow, emerging abruptly from meditation. "Of course I'm a peculiar character and so far as I'm concerned I shouldn't care *that*"—he snapped defiant fingers in the face of a matronly person who chanced to be passing—"for the old man's money. I shouldn't care *that*. I should say to all his money—*Bif*! But then, I'm not alone in the world. There's Muriel. That's where this business knocks me, you know. So far as I'm concerned I don't want money. If I have money I spend it, I can't keep it, it's no good to me. A playwright's money comes in lumps and goes in lumps. Must do—it's their nature. TEMPERAMENT. THE ARTIST'S TEMPERAMENT. I've had money before and shall have it again. Chaps like he was haven't any idea the money there is in plays. Or they would treat me differently. Yet it's pretty plain there *is* money in plays . . ."

They were going down the hill now where the pavement is narrow and foot passengers abound. A lady with a small herd of daughters drove miscellaneously at them and parted them. Chitterlow was forced off the pavement, and Kipps jammed for awhile amidst the people outside a toyshop window. When at last they reunited, Chitterlow gripped Kipps by the arm to prevent any repetition of this annoyance. He brought his face very close to Kipps and performed the gesticulations necessary to speech with his disengaged arm.

The interruption had not been without its benefit in bringing Chitterlow back from the extensive topic of the drama to the more immediate issue of the legacy. He stated that although, by reason of his inherent magnanimity, he was not disappointed on his own account, Muriel was. She had come to look to her Uncle, he said, and she had had every reason given her to look to her Uncle. Practically there had been promises
* * *

There had been, he admitted, coolnesses between himself and Mr. Waddy, due to that gentleman's lack of intelligent understanding of playwriting and to his own high spirit. But
* * *

MR. WADDY HAD REPEATEDLY pressed them all to stay with him. In saying this Chitterlow was not lying; he had a singularly flexible imagination and it was so that the facts appeared to him at that time. He instanced other proofs of Waddy's favour. Under the circumstances Muriel's disappointment was, he held, an understandable thing; he would not have respected her if she had not been disappointed. This led him to a general discussion of why he respected and why he did not respect Muriel. He embarked upon a general discussion of her in relation to himself. She had, he said, the finest (completely untrained) contralto voice in England . . .

These things carried them down the Folkestone High Street—the narrowest, steepest, and one of the most interesting High Streets in the world—and out into the roadway below. Thence Chitterlow proposed they should go on to the Pier, but Mr. Kipps recalling the Dorcases, decided that the East Cliff and possibly even the Warren were more adapted to so intimate a conversation as engaged them, and so they progressed, arm in arm, Chitterlow's face close to Kipps' ear, and both swaying with his sweeping gestures as they ascended the East Cliff.

Neither recalled anything of the business Mr. Kipps had professed to await him in the harbour.

As they went on their way over the East Cliff, Chitterlow emerged suddenly from a lengthy discourse quite close to the subject under discussion. He said he did not envy the good fortune of Kipps—that if anything he had said had seemed to tend in that direction he had said the thing he did not mean to say. If there was any man for whom he had a profound respect it was Kipps. He corrected himself and said the word should be friendship. He counted Kipps his friend. He hoped that Kipps considered him a friend.

Kipps understood himself to say that this was so.

Their characters, pursued Chitterlow, certainly contrasted in several points.

* * *

At these remarks Kipps had been profoundly moved. His heart swelled within him. No one had ever praised him before. A noble desire to be worthy of these enconiums possessed him.

"I don't mean to go back on any o' my friends," said Kipps. "I *do* mean not to do that."

"You're not that sort," said Chitterlow with fervour.

"And that's why I been looking for you," said Kipps. "I tell you, Chitterlow—from the very first—I been anxious to see you about this."

* * *

So they talked through the long afternoon, clambering from terrace to terrace of altitudinous generosity and esteem. They passed over the East Cliff and plunged into the sinuous variegated Warren that is Folkestone's particular boast.

(Picturesque description of the Warren. [Wells's note.])

* * *

And through it all they went, supplanter and supplanted, whipping their emotions into an imposing froth. Kipps marched stiffly through it all. Chitterlow, relieved from the faint restraints of the town, waved violent arms AND TOSSED A HOT COIFFURE towards the sunny world. Now they were arm in arm, now Chitterlow led the way along some narrow ridge, lifting his splendid voice with shouts of fraternity, now he danced on a pitch of greensward flinging dramatic "bangs!" and "Bifs!" into the circumambient INANE. They were blood brothers in an hour. Chitterlow found at last such a joy in his

generous appreciation of the luck of Kipps, that he would not
have altered Waddy's will for the world, and Kipps' one idea
was to emerge presently from the torrent of words that
FLOWED OVER him and offer collusive participations. They
were back upon the East Cliff sitting on a seat and watching
the Calais boat returning when that chance finally came.

"O' course," said Kipps, "what I done is partly in your
interest. If it 'd been a choice between you and me, I'm not
such a man as to stand between a nold man and 'is proper
hairs."

Chitterlow seemed puzzled. Kipps perceived he did not
know the conditions of the will. He proceeded to explain—dis-
playing ostentatiously a delicate regard for Chitterlow's feelings as he did so.
* * *

It quite surprised Kipps in a little while to perceive how
firmly this new footing had established itself. Chitterlow honoured him by throwing no doubt upon these generous intentions. He explained this at some length, and devoted the best
part of half an hour to a disquisition upon Waddy's opposition
to his playwriting. Partly he thought Waddy was tainted by
Puritanism, WHICH CHITTERLOW INVARIABLY SPOKE OF AS
IF IT WERE SOME HORRIBLE MENTAL DISEASE, partly
* * *

He proceeded to elaborate suggestions for evading the
conditions of Waddy's will. He insisted upon making it perfectly clear that he would not have done this for everybody,
but for Kipps he was willing to do many things that for
anyone else he could not do on account of his peculiar pride
and spirit. But in Kipps he rejoiced to find a peculiar and
beautiful flavour of honour, and he owed it to Kipps as much
as to himself to aid in every way to develop this honour. He
then went on to point out
* * *

In many ways they might be of great use to each other.
* * *

In conclusion Chitterlow said that he would not readily
forget all that Kipps had told him that afternoon. It had
increased his respect for Kipps enormously—indeed it had
increased his respect for all mankind. He parted with a warm

handclasp and Kipps went on his way with shining eyes, AND FORGETTING FOR THE MOMENT ALL HIS ANXIETY ABOUT DAISY.

But as the hours passed and Chitterlow's inductive magnetism evaporated, his meditations became of a more pensive and even of a less generous tinge. He reflected that
* * *
And his anxiety about Daisy steadily resumed its sway.

✢ 16 ✢

Chitterlow Raises the Siege

M^{URIEL}
* * *
   Kipps besieged by Daisy and her resolute mother. The ladies occupy the hall and drawing room and Kipps is upstairs. Assisted by Chitterlow he effects his escape and flees (with Chitterlow as Mentor) to Ostend. . . .

♣ 17 ♣

Mr. Kipps at Ostend

KIPPS and Chitterlow at Ostend—sketch of Ostend.
Chitterlow tenders useful advice about the accent of
Mr. Kipps—early exercises in aspiration.

"I ah—have."

"Pfhew were—foowhere."

The man in the next room heard him at it the next
morning.

Mr. Kipps gambles overnight and has a headache in the
morning. Ill temper. Threatening letter from Daisy. Chitterlow will go to England and "put a stopper on this." Manifestly the thing to do.

Kipps left at Ostend.

Alone. Very miserable and pined for home and Ann
Pornick. Was wealth after all a delusion and a snare? He
went and looked at shops but he could not buy anything
because he was afraid he would look a fool about the
change.

Sums on paper. He had spent more than a hundred
pounds already. One Hundred Pounds!

Mr. Kipps suspects the Hotel people of especial over-
charges to him.

"C-est possible acheter un the dans Folkestone avec—you
know—srimps—pour ninepence, un franc, that is, et vous me
charger—"

Spasms of meanness and flight to a cheap boarding
house.

There he encounters MR. CHESTER COOTE

❧ 18 ❧

Mr. Chester Coote

ONE face struck Kipps as familiar, and the recognition seemed to some extent returned.

The person in question eyed Kipps ever and again with a sort of watered interrogation out of large greyish eyes. He was dressed in a quiet grey suit that Mr. Kipps esteemed gentlemanly, and his hands were white where they were not a little blue, largish at the joints, with a curious look about them as though they were not prehensile. Mr. Kipps noticed him handling his knife and fork, which he did with precision. This person's articulation of his words (he was talking English to a faded lady in black next him) was always deliberate and beautifully clear, his voice might have seemed to many people perhaps a trifle too—how shall I express it?—ovine, but Kipps found no fault with it. He had a pallid complexion, an irregular mouth, and straight fairish hair. And ever and again came the vague watery eye back to the face of Mr. Kipps.

When he was nervous—he was evidently transiently nervous now—its clear flatness quivered, if you can understand that clumsy way of putting it. The dinner finished, he rose with the others and preceded Mr. Kipps out of the room. His movements did not flow from position to position as they do with common people, but had a quality of convulsiveness, as though there was some occasional slight obstruction in his bearings which it required an accumulation of energy to overcome. His knuckly left white hand was clenched, Mr. Kipps observed. Directly they were out of the dining room he turned to Mr. Kipps with a smile that showed his gums and, speaking in a voluminous voice with an affected accent that presently disappeared, said: "Ah fancy ah recognase youah face."

Mr. Kipps reflected the smile. "I 'ave—ah, *have*—the same fancy." He bowed.

"Do you by any chance"—the gentleman in grey suddenly raised his hand and smoothed his back hair; it was, Kipps speedily perceived, an habitual gesture with him, almost as if he suspected a sprouting chignon. "Do you by any chance gnaw Folkestone?"

"I, ah—I mean— I *ham*—a Folkestone inhabitant."

"Then we must, we must be accustomed to passing in the street perhaps. I am in the, ah, offace of Grimflack and Weston, solicitahs."

"That must be it," said Kipps brightly. "Very likely that's it. Directly I set eyes on you I thought, I know that face."

"It's curious how one meets people," said the young man in grey.

"Ain't—I mean—yes. Yes, it is so." In his confusion he got out his cigarette case.

"Have you been heah long?"

"Well," reflected Mr. Kipps. "No, not long—not very long. D'you mind if I smoke?"

"Not at all. I don't smoke myself—it gives me no pleasure, but of course if *you* enjoy it— Let me provide you with a match . . . Let me show you the smoking room. He led the way to a . . .

* * *

Their talk grew more and more confidential as the night wore on. Mr. Kipps was secretly much uplifted to be on such easy, such familiar terms with a young man in the position of a solicitor's clerk. He did not venture to broach subjects, but he followed up each lead of Chester Coote assiduously. Two preoccupations detached themselves from the diverse topics that passed between our young men, emerged and manifested themselves as dominant. The one was a sincere and earnest desire on the part of Chester Coote, amounting indeed to an obvious self-forgetfulness, to be an Influence for Good upon those about him, and the other was—Girls. The former was the lesser but it was earlier apparent.

He spoke of a Coffee Tavern in which he was interested in Folkestone; he presented himself working bravely and on terms of intimacy with the local clergy in the work of inducing "rough fellows," fishermen, sailors and the like, to play backgammon, to give up swearing, and to drink instead of alcohol Ginger Whiskey and Pain's Herb Beer—sterilised compounds with just the sensations of the evil thing and none of its after effects—EXCEPT THAT IT UTTERLY DESTROYED THE LIVER.

He mentioned too his solicitude about a young fellow he knew, handsome, gifted, and liable to many temptations. This young fellow he said was a sceptic.

"Lor!" said Kipps, "not a Natheist?"

"I

* * *

Mr. Coote went on to talk of temptations, he hinted at strength to be derived from higher sources, he pointed his remarks towards Kipps. It dawned on Kipps that this flabby under-exercised creature was endeavouring to Influence him for Good —he felt nothing but gratitude and a certain pride. It had not occurred to him before that he stood in any great need of being influenced for good. But from Coote's implications that idea followed inevitably. His pride increased as Mr. Chester Coote spoke more directly of wealth and power coming suddenly into the hands of such a "spirited young fellow" as himself. He was suddenly moved to speech of a grave and intimate character.

KIPPS took up the thread of the discourse. The spirit of confession, that precious balm of the human soul, had possession of him.

* * *

HE HAD CERTAINLY LEARNED MUCH FROM CHITTERLOW AND HE GAVE IT OUT TO COOTE WITH BOTH HANDS,

* * *

He alluded to the gambling of the previous night; by a deft looseness of phrase he spread it over several years.

* * *

He hinted at worse things and Chester Coote becoming suddenly eager, he took refuge in the honour of a gentleman.

* * *

"That was all very well when money was limited," said Kipps, "but I must go steady now."

"YOU *must*," SAID COOTE, MUCH CONCERNED. "MY DEAR FELLOW, I

* * *

Chester Coote spoke of steadying influences. He too, he said, with a quaver in his bleating bass, had had a wild past. But for him there had come the sweetest and best influence in the world, a Certain Young Lady.

* * *

He smiled consciously when he mentioned the Young Lady, and displayed a number of broken and yellow teeth, his eyes shone a little, and a faint flush illuminated the tip of his nose. The mere pronoun "she" seemed to have its seduction for him. He spoke of poetry. Did Kipps write poetry? *He*, Coote, did.

* * *

There were those who found points of resemblance to Rossetti.

He talked of other Young Ladies. He embarked upon anecdotes and character studies. He was careful to name no names, he conscientiously suppressed most of the essential facts, but Kipps found these vague shadows of stories sympathetic and moving. An irresistible desire to reciprocate moved him. He ran over the list of his engagements, in search of some Pure Love he might profess. Ann he hesitated over, but he rejected her on account of her social position and the immaturity of their years. He decided the one pure ennobling love of his life was for Miss Walsingham. He said as much. As he said it he believed it. Of course he mentioned no names —HE KNEW WHAT WAS EXPECTED OF A GENTLEMAN. He told the thing as a simple modest story of silent unsuspected love.

"I would 'ave done anything for her," said Kipps, "—anything."

* * *

"It was a nart school, she was a nart teacher. She taught wood carving. That's 'ow I came to know—"

He stopped in mid sentence. Coote had suddenly gripped his hand. "My dear fellow!" said Coote. "*Not* at Tunbridge Wells!"

It was a dramatic moment. Both young men stopped dead. "Why—yes!" said Kipps astonished. "You don' mean to say—"

* * *

Coote was tremulously agitated. The essential busybody in him flared crimson in cheeks and ears and nose; his eyes even showed a sort of drowned twinkle.

* * *

"She is the brother—sister I mean—of that young fellow I was speaking of just now.

* * *

"Fancy you knowing her. Of course

* * *

"I could introduce you.

* * *

"Now look here! Here is something we could do. I would not do this for anybody but our talk tonight has been strangely interesting. I feel you are a type of character I would do much to assist. Come with me to Tunbridge Wells. Give up this life of aimless pleasure you are leading, and let me introduce you to *Her*. My sister knows her mother—quite well.

* * *

After they parted for the night, Coote was so excited that he had to take a turn outside the hotel. Here was Something to Do that appealed to every fibre of his nature. On the one hand this spirited uneducated rich young fellow, needing a Pure Love sorely to save him from the exuberance of his own spirit, and on the other a Girl, the sister of his colleague. Sexuality touched by sentiment, sentiment drowning in sexuality, it appealed to him with overpowering—intoxicating force. He saw already a complicated web of diplomacies, of swift tact, and—intimacies—that he should weave about this charming, romantic, serious and touching situation. He could write about it all to that Certain Young Lady—radiant fatherly things. He was singularly free from gross egotisms.

The countless shadows the electric lights gave him went up and down, up and down, before their *pension*. They crowded about him, crossed in front of him, elongated, retracted, like a host of attendant spirits. He was dimly aware of that companionship though he did not perceive its nature. He had a vague feeling of fellowship—of support—of something going with him; he conceived of it as that Higher, that Abstract Cooteishness in which all well-meaning, Egotistical, Unintelligent souls meet together. His blissful self-satisfaction lit his features at last to a vitreous lustre. He spoke a few words of sympathy and kindly advice to an anaemic woman of unknown nationality outside the door of the Pension, and while she was still answering him, WHICH INDEED SHE DID WITH QUITE NEEDLESS LENGTH AND VIVIDNESS, he went in and to bed.

✢ 19 ✢

_____

At Tunbridge Wells

IN five days the altruistic energies of Mr. Coote had accomplished much. With a tremendous display of fumbling facility he had conducted Mr. Kipps back to England.

* * *

He had told a great number of people in confidence

* * *

His re-introduction of our creature of good fortune to his former instructress was a miracle of gentlemanly tact.

* * *

The outcome of a lengthy discussion with his sister.

* * *

Miss Walsingham

* * *

General picture of Tunbridge Wells and the Walsingham circle.

* * *

Début of Miss Walsingham's brother—George Goethe Walsingham.

* * *

was coming on Saturday to stay until Monday morning. It was evident that he was the chief object in life of both his mother and sister. Mr. Kipps sank into comparative insignificance—even before he arrived. His coming shadow insisted on recognition.

* * *

"Goethe will think

* * *

"Goethe will alter

* * *

Kipps had an impression he must be very large—he filled so much of the canvass, but when he appeared at last he had the effect of being distinctly small. But that soon passed off.

He had a delicately chiselled aquiline nose and a small prominent chin, his dark hair fell across a high white forehead, and his eyes were dark and piercing. When he turned up his coat collar, and quite frequently that chanced to happen, the resemblance to the more romantic renderings of Napoleon the Great was remarkable. He rarely laughed, but his smile was deep, and it was speedily manifest that he was in the habit of pinching the ample ear of his junior—Chester Coote.

* * *

Kipps did not get on with him very well. He had a feeling in the presence of this imposing young man that it would have puzzled him to name. Partly it was terror, partly hostility, and there was an equally strong desire to avoid, propitiate, and see somebody else take this creature down. Kipps tried to express the compound by telling himself he "didn't quite make Walsingham out yet."

Towards Kipps he bore himself with a carefully mitigated contempt. About the head of our young man he flung occult flat-bursting sayings, that were identified by Coote as epigrams —whatever epigrams might be. Other things he said were labelled "cynical"—and at that his satisfaction became evident in his face. Kipps would have given his ears to know what cynical was, so that he might cut in with a stroke or so.

* * *

Suggestion of extraordinary subterranean activity of Coote.

He is presented flushed, tremulous, active, dropping a hint here, arranging a *tête-à-tête* there and so on.

⚜ 20 ⚜

Mr. Kipps—and Fate

KIPPS quite believes NOW that he cherishes a hopeless love for Miss Walsingham.

They have a long talk together.

Immense satisfaction of Mr. Kipps in getting on so well.

Proposes by reflex action—not intending to do so—drifts into it.

Astonishment at being accepted.

Private thoughts of Mr. Kipps on his way home.

"I'm a lucky dog. I *am* a lucky dog . . ." His face scarcely harmonised.

"Lord!" said Mr. Kipps. "And shan't I just have to behave!"

* * *

Did he after all love her so greatly? It came to him that he also cared for Ann Pornick—a great deal. He dismissed this topic abruptly.

The thing was done!

He recalled Daisy Dorcas. He wondered what she would do when she heard of the affair.

He had a sleepless night.

<He *was* a chap, a regular chap for getting affairs in a tangle.

Vague Ideas of "offing somewhere" passed across his mind>

✢ 21 ✢

Chitterlow Redux

"WHATEVER made you come to this place?" asked Chitterlow like a man with a grievance.

He had just descended from the train.

* * *

"I didn't like Ostend," said Kipps. "I 'ad to go somewhere. See? But how about—*that*? Eh?"

Chitterlow seized Kipps by the arm. "I've done 'em—to rights, old chap. You needn't worry your head any more about *her*. She's off. SETTLED HER UP FOR FIFTY DOWN AND GLAD TO GET IT. But—Tunbridge Wells! You might have thought. Why! You *know* I've been here before. You must know that . . ."

* * *

"If you don't mind, old chap, I'd rather *not* go through the High Street.

* * *

"How's it settled?" asked Kipps.

Now it was the incomparable Chitterlow's peculiarity that he could no more describe events as they had happened than he could fly, for whatsoever thread he began upon that thread incontinently vanished down a parenthesis, like a lizard down a crack.

146

* * *

But slowly the story loomed up through the parenthetic mist.

* * *

A vignette of Chitterlow DEMANDING to see what evidence she had, and being handed the letter; of Chitterlow then boldly holding this letter in the gas flame, with Mrs. Dorcas's wrist in the other hand, until nothing but charred paper remained. Of Chitterlow discharging the best line he ever thought of in his life. "And what other evidence is there now, ma'am?"

* * *

Altogether a very triumphant Chitterlow.

* * *

"I went round to see old Grimflack about it—told him all the business—he told me to do it in fact. He's a very firm old boy.<Any letter you've written is your copyright."

* * *

"Good Line" said Chitterlow. "Good Line">

* * *

There follows the account of a party of some sort, at which there will be present the art school master and his wife, important local social personages, young Walsingham, Kipps —and Chitterlow. The Walsinghams are too poor to entertain, but this festival is given by a prosperous married sister who is delighted with the approaching marriage with Kipps—"*such* a catch!" Kipps is nervous and rather too much in the centre of the picture for his taste. High-toned conversation on books, poetry, gardening and art. Kipps and Miss Walsingham keep a nervous eye on each other. Chitterlow after a momentary embarrassment greets the art master effusively, re-introduces Kipps to him and arranges a commission for a picture on the spot. Chitterlow at first elaborately polite, and then developing a deepening animosity to Walsingham. Croquet disturbs Chitterlow's temper, and whiskey and soda being produced by Walsingham, Chitterlow gets talkative and excited. DESCRIPTION OF THE GAME OF CROQUET. Insists on a personal argument with Walsingham. Strikes "a particularly pungent vein of reminiscence." Brags, gesticulates, challenges. Betrays hostility to all the Walsinghams. Analyses the position. The party ends in confusion, bad temper and general disorganisation.

22

Atropos

A N interval of eight weeks. Mr. Kipps, vastly improved in dress and pose, seated on a seat on the Leas meditating upon Fate. He is not happy. He is trying to understand how things have come to pass.

Résumé of the intervening occurrences.

Miss Walsingham (in tears?) at the thought of the neighbours' comments, made him send off Chitterlow forthwith after the occurrences in the last chapter.

The scene with Chitterlow was painful in its earlier stages and finally expensive. By an ingenious subterfuge it was arranged that Kipps should finance a touring company, by which Chitterlow should be employed as actor-manager. But Chitterlow having been induced to leave the neighbourhood by these expedients and go to THE POTTERIES—Miss Walsingham and her brother set their faces firmly against this. "Trifling with the spirit of Mr. Waddy's wishes."

THE EXPLANATION HAD BEEN THE HARDEST HE EVER ATTEMPTED

A VIGOROUS TELEGRAMMING.

Since when a veil of impenetrable silence has covered Chitterlow.

Kipps felt like a murderer.

Young Walsingham has left Grimflack's office and set up for himself—with the business of Kipps to begin with. This has led to a painful interview with Grimflack anent the transfer.

Kipps has passed Ann Pornick in the street and pretended not to see her.

Miss Walsingham is energetic in the improvement of Kipps' mind.

Kipps and the Higher Life

Miss Walsingham is not well developed in these notes AND A WORD OR TWO MAY BE GIVEN TO EXPLAIN HER; putting it crudely, she is an over-educated aesthetic prig. Her temper is not good. Her regard for Kipps very dubious. She wishes to help her brother. (She also wants to get married and stop teaching.) With a gross disregard of his feelings she sets about shaping Kipps into a sort of Fabian aesthete. Kipps is brought into almost violent contact with Beato Angelico, Botticelli, Wagner, Browning, Italy, Munich, the Keltic renascence, and the essential vulgarity of being English. His well-meant efforts to fall in line with the Sad and Beautiful Higher Life have of course the effect of satire on Miss Walsingham's sensibilities and angered her. She suspects him of poking fun. Kipps at first abject and docile, then eager but unintelligent, at last almost sulky.

Comments from New Romney are frequent. Kipps has not been home since his first visit. He contemplates the introduction of Mrs. and Miss Walsingham to his father and mother with grave doubts.

From a profound meditation upon these things he is aroused by his fiancée.

"I am going to give you a good talking to," said Miss Walsingham, and her face bore out that promise.

❧ 23 ❧

_____

Vanished!

* * *

Excitement in Folkestone and Tunbridge Wells—paragraphs. Suspicion of the reader is directed to Chitterlow.

Has he fled? OR BEEN MADE AWAY WITH? OR SIMPLY GOT LOST?

Miss Walsingham shows feeling and "gives it" to her mother, who throughout the whole affair has been quite anaemic and passive.

Mr. Walsingham's position. "You nagged at him," said Mr. Walsingham. "You nagged at him as though you were married already.

* * *

Entry of Mr. Coote upon a scene of wrath.

Mr. Coote still diplomatic.

"I've found him," he said.

* * *

"He must come back at once."

"The fact is, he can't!"

* * *

"He's married already."

"But who?"

"I can't tell you—it's too horrible."

* * *

"A servant!"

"*What?*" cried Miss Walsingham. "How dare you tell me that?"

Chapter ends with a general pecking of the benevolent Mr. Coote.

❧ 24 ❧

The Marriage of Mr. Kipps

MR. Coote's intelligence was correct; Mr. Kipps had married. And since the circumstances of his wooing were unexpected and singular they shall be set down here at length. You will recall a certain "talking to" that Mr. Kipps received. At the time it produced a profound melancholy. But when he reached the privacy of his apartments his melancholia gave place to another and less wonted feeling; he was angry. He said he would not stand it, and finding nothing happened, he repeated this statement. Then he became active, tramping the length of the room, muttering, talking, WORKING himself up to deeds. He associated Miss Walsingham's name, a name he was pledged to cherish and revere, with terms of rage and revolt. He said that if he stood it much longer he would be damned. Still no harm befell him.

Presently he had got to the pitch of throwing a casual boot at the wash-handstand. He perceived he was free to break every scrap of furniture in the room if he thought fit. His sense of freedom increased. And as if it were an immediate consequence of that, came an idea, a resolve, a radiant and splendid way out of all the grey, desolate and terrible life of culture set with thorny names, and intricate pictures and wastes of perfected boredom, into which Mr. Chester Coote and his unfortunate idealisation of Miss Walsingham, and the Fates had led him.

Suddenly Mrs. Satsuma heard him descending the stairs—he missed a step and fell part of the way—saw him emerge from the front door and rush hastily forth upon the Leas.

* * *

The door opened, revealing a pleasantly FURNISHED hall, lit by rose-tinted lights, and in the centre of the picture, neat and pretty in black and white, stood Ann. At the sight of Kipps her colour vanished.

"Ann," said Kipps. "I want to speak to you."

"This ain't the door to speak to me at," said Ann.

"But Ann! it's something special _____."

"I got to take dinner in ten minutes," said Ann. "Besides. That's my door, down there. Basement."

"But Ann, *I'm*——"

"Basement after nine—them's my hours. If you're calling here, what name please? But you mustn't go talking to *me*."

"But Ann, I want to ask you——"

Someone appeared in the hall behind Ann. "Not here," said Ann. "Don't know anyone of that name," and incontinently slammed the door in his face.

"What was that, Ann?" said the lady in the hall.

"Ge'm a little intoxicated, Ma'am—asking for the wrong name, Ma'am."

"What did he want?" asked the lady doubtfully.

"No name that *we* know, Ma'am," said Ann, hustling along the hall in her briskest manner.

* * *

"What?" said Ann. "Be engaged?"

"No," said Kipps, "not engaged. I *am* engaged. I got to be married. You got to marry me."

He was resolved to have matters clear and settled forthwith.

* * *

Ann at last consents to elope with him.

* * *

"Tomorrow," he said.

"Tomorrow," she answered.

They clasped hands.

"I wouldn't do this for anyone, mind you," said Ann

* * *

Kipps opened the letter nervously. He hesitated before reading. "I wonder what he's got to say," he remarked. "I didn't tell you all, Ann. I made 'im a sort of promise . . ."

He looked at her with speculation in his eyes. Then with sudden determination he began to read the letter.

As he read his expression changed. He puffed out his cheeks and blew.

Thus the letter ran, in a bold hand that slashed all the minor words to mere dots and strokes.

"*Dear old Chap,*

Thanks for everything—even the disappointment. I quite understand your difficulties, knew at once, when I saw your solicitor that a change had come o'er the spirit of our dream. You'll want all your money—for him. No ill will, and as it happens, we've struck oil. The company will start after all—and pay. You shall see us.

> *Ever yours*
> *Harry Chitterlow (the fair old original H. C.)*

N.B. No ill will—I understand.
N.N.B.† A crowded house last night and we knocked 'em."

And folded into a small compass was a playbill that proclaimed a repertory.

Footnote † Possibly an invention of Chitterlow's on the model of P.P.S.

⚜ 25 ⚜

The Honeymoon

QUAINT incidents.
    Ann has never been to London—"Why not go?"
 Visit to the Crystal Palace and that sort of thing.
 Odd and original plans for the future.
 Ann wants to have a household without servants. She knows a thing or two about them.
 "I'd jest as soon do the work without 'aving to stand impertinence," said Ann.

✢ 26 ✢

Mr. Kipps Faces the Music

THE drawing room of a Folkestone boarding house (reserved by special arrangement).

The three Walsinghams awaiting the coming of Kipps.

She is bitter at the part she has played, and struggling between a refined horror of coarse extortion and the grimmest resolution to get all she can out of Kipps. Their determination to plunder is limited by their extreme respect for public opinion. What will be said in Tunbridge Wells?

Since Walsingham has already "touched" Kipps' capital in certain speculations, he is anxious not to make a rupture.

"Of course you can say that you found out that he was engaged to the girl," suggested Mrs. Walsingham.

"You can SAY anything about that," said Walsingham.

"You are simply entitled to some compensation—if only for the loss of the art school work," said Walsingham.

"But think how it will look!" cried Alice.

There follows an interview between Mrs. Walsingham, Mr. Walsingham, and Kipps.

Mr. Kipps was out of breath, and holding his intelligence together by an effort, but still there was a certain air of settled resolution on his face that contrasted with the anchorless drift of motive that had once expressed itself there.

* * *

"Think of her feelings," said Mrs. Walsingham.

* * *

The treaty fell under ———— heads.

Firstly, seeing that the virgin heart of Miss Alice Walsingham had been wantonly, needlessly and unprofitably ravaged by the Passion of Love excited by the vision and seductive behaviour of Mr. Arthur Kipps, and that she had in these transports given up her remunerative employment as an art teacher—an employment yielding as had been calculated by her brother, a gross income of one hundred and fifty pounds a year, and seeing that she had in the artless display and glory of her Passion rendered Tunbridge Wells no longer a comfortable home for herself, it was provided that the said Kipps should take on a lease for twenty-one years the house he had occupied upon the Leas at Folkestone, paying rent, taxes, all outgoings for that period, that he should purchase the furniture therein contained, and that he should then invest her with the same so that she might there harbour and comfort her mother and brother, and further distract and solace her ravished and desolate mind by using the said house as a High Class Boarding House for Persons of Position KEPT BY LADIES.

And secondly it was provided that the legal business of the said Arthur Kipps and the management and control of his property should remain as heretofore in the hands of Mr. George Goethe Walsingham.

* * *

Thirdly, it was stipulated that the parties to this agreement and all others concerned therein on either side, should in the interest of the said Alice Walsingham, her pride, high culture and refinement, conspire to tell and maintain a lying version of the circumstances of the breach of the engagement between the said parties to the effect that

* * *

And *Finally*, in consideration of these articles it was agreed that Miss Walsingham would forgive—though she could never forget the passionate excitations, heart-breaking coquetries, and desolating charm of the said Arthur Kipps. And—though this was a clause Mr. Kipps had not bargained for—she would even steel herself to meet him and his wife and accord them a social recognition beyond their merits, it being alleged that the continued benefit of Mr. Walsingham's professional services necessitated this stipulation, and that it was necessary to sustain the credibility of the story provided for in clause three.

* * *

And this convention being at last arrived at, Mr. Walsingham rose up and offered Kipps his hand.

But Mrs. Walsingham remained cold, congested and distant in manner to the end.

* * *

Mr. Kipps . . . returned to the modest and unassuming boarding house where Ann awaited him.

⚜ 27 ⚜

_____

Projects

SO Kipps got through one great situation but there was still
more music to be faced.

✴ ✴ ✴

"And how's your fancy lady?" said Old Kipps, whose
latest news dated from the Walsingham epoch.

"What fancy lady?"

"Miss Nose-in-the-Air. What's too good to see us."

Kipps saw an opportunity. "Why—I told her, if my father's not good enough for you—I'm not. See? So it's off!" He
tried to give the thing a natural air, but he was short of
breath.

Old Kipps looked at him keenly. "She's throwed you over,
my boy," he said. "Let that be a lesson to you."

✴ ✴ ✴

"A common slavey," said Old Kipps. "Jest a common
slavey."

✴ ✴ ✴

"One of them Pornick lot," said Old Kipps, and after an
awful pause and in a tone of saintly sorrow, "well, they'll have
the laugh of us _now_, my boy."

✴ ✴ ✴

Kipps away from Ann is forced into a foolish attitude. He promises social triumphs.

* * *

"You'll see me hobnobbing with 'im yet," said Mr. Kipps.

"You don't understand young Ann—she's not like the rest of 'em. I tell you she's a Natural Lady. Mother here couldn't be more of a lady than her."

* * *

It was uphill work, and he was led to some spacious promises.

There was something like a proposal to buy Old Kipps a "bit of an estate"—if possible with private fishing from which interlopers could be "warned," or a disputed right of way.

In his desire to carry things off in a proud and promising style he may also have led his father to believe that the house he had taken at Hythe was of a more spacious and aristocratic description than the facts warranted. It was only by an hour of strenuous discussion (never before had Kipps so "stood up to the old people") that he could win an ambiguous grunt of forgiveness and a suggestion that one of them would come over and see Ann the first bus day after the young couple got into their new house at Hythe—"We shouldn't like her to come here, Artie, not where everybody knows what she's been," explained Mrs. Kipps with tactful movements of her head. "And we can't come on Sunday because of the trains being that awkward at Appledore and Ashford—hours and hours—and we can't both come of a weekday because of the shop."

✤ 28 ✤

_____

Varne Prospect

THE next day our young people moved into their new house.

* * *

Sketch of their furniture.

It is incomplete but no more shopmen for *them*. They are going to fill up at sales.

* * *

"Look 'ere, Artie," said Ann and she held out a number of white oblongs.

"What's that?" asked Kipps and examined them.

* * *

"It's a visitin' card," said Kipps with a certain pride of knowledge. "You get 'em arf a crown the 'undred."

"I know," said Ann. "I dessay you do. But *I* got 'em different, Artie . . . I forgot about Callers, leastways I didn't think they'd come after us. And as Gwendolen looked a bit headachy and it was such a fine afternoon, and I wanted to 'namel over that floor she's done so bad without 'er knowing, I says to her 'You go out Gwendolen, and get a breaf of air,' and out she goes . . . Well, jest as I was hard at it 'namelling, I hear a rap and down I go. It was a lady, Artie, a lady I'd never set eyes on before and two nice growed up gels, all dressed up. And the lady says right out and proper, 'S Mrs. Kipps in?' And me all painty, with a apron and no cap on—neither missus nor servant like. There, Artie, I could 'a sunk through the floor with shame, I really could. I could 'ardly get my voice. I couldn't think of nothing to say but just 'Not at 'ome' and out of 'abit like I 'eld the tray. And they give me the cards and went and 'ow I shall

❧ 29 ❧

Mrs. Chudleigh Mornington

THE "lady (by birth) familiar with questions of etiquette and social procedure" sat in a becoming attitude on Mrs. Kipps' sofa and surveyed our young couple. Her name was Mrs. Chudleigh Mornington. She was a small energetic looking little woman, indisputably stylish, with a distinguished rustle, a gold pince-nez and a not unpleasing smile. Her voice was becomingly modulated, and there was a certain quickness of speech that suggested a phase of teaching in her past. Kipps, with an extremely red face, was explaining things, occasionally glancing at Ann for confirmatory assurances, and Mrs. Chudleigh Mornington kept punctuating his halting suggestions with elegant and encouraging movements of the head. "You see," he said, "we recently come into money. We was respectable people like before that but not very well off. Was we Ann?"

" 'Ousemaid, Mum," said Ann, and received a charming smile.

"And, well—fact is—I was in business. And consequently it's a bit 'ard, you understand, to know jest what to do, like. F'r instance—there's cards. And furniture. And—well, several things like that. We aren't quite up to it."

"Precisely," said Mrs. Chudleigh Mornington. "And you want Help."

"Yes," admitted Kipps. "We do."

Mrs. Chudleigh Mornington considered, with her eyes ON
* * *

"May I ask how old you are?" she said suddenly to Ann.

"Two and twenty."

"And you?"

"Twenty three."

"Happy young people! How do you manage to be so young! And you are—well off?"

"It's about two thousand a year," said Mr. Kipps modestly. "Leastways, it was. But there's a 'ouse I 'ave to pay the rent of —well, it's *about* two thousand. It's partly dividends, that's why I can't give it a nexact figure."
* * *

Practically Mrs. Chudleigh Mornington was to take possession of the house and Ann.
* * *

Almost her first act was to dismiss the _____ Gwendolen.
* * *

The Tyranny of Mrs. Chudleigh Mornington begins.

Miseries of living up to one's position. Mrs. Chudleigh Mornington is a caricature of the "correct thing," a sort of incarnation of the etiquette and social gossip article of a lady's paper. She has a great force of will. I design her to be a sort of parallel to Mrs. Grundy—a Mrs. Grundy "up to date." What Mrs. Grundy is in morals, Mrs. Chudleigh Mornington is to be in social relationships. She is COMMON Social Ambition in the flesh.
* * *

And Mrs. Chudleigh Mornington was decisive about the house. She inspected the plans and pronounced them quite unsuitable—quite.
* * *

She decided the trouble of the name promptly.

Melrose Cottage ⎫
Melrose Villa   ⎬ Architect's suggestions
Radnor Villa   ⎪ in ascending order.
Varne Villa   ⎭

Something 'omey ⎫
The Nook   ⎬ Kipps in reaction.
The Nest   ⎭

30

The Rule of
Mrs. Chudleigh Mornington

THE rule of Mrs. Chudleigh Mornington grows into an oppressive tyranny. Her method of teaching—Mrs. Kipps spends hours learning tables of Precedence, they hold exercise meetings on the Art of Conversing, Kipps is made utterly miserable about his accent. They "can't do anything right."

Their days are as strictly ordered as if they were in a convict prison.

Kipps envies a small shopkeeper. "I *could* manage a little shop, Ann."

Distress of our young people.

Culminates in an appalling dinner—their first dinner party.

This dinner party must be the bulk of the chapter.

Walsinghams present and perhaps Coote.

After the party is over Ann is reduced to tears.

"Slavey in a lodgin' 'ouse," said Ann, "is ease and comfort compared to such goings on."

"Let's go orf somewhere," said Kipps.

"No," said Ann. "No more orfing for me—not for them Walsinghams to larf at me again."

* * *

"People like that," said Mrs. Chudleigh Mornington, "one doesn't ask to a Proper dinner. But he will do very well to begin upon."

"Oh lor!" said Ann. "Is there dinners and dinners?"

"There's everythings and everythings, my dear," said Mrs. Chudleigh Mornington.

* * *

"Before everything else, you *must* mind your aitches. Nothing—absolutely nothing—is so important as that."

Kipps had a momentary gleam of analysis. "I wonder why a little thing like that *is* so important."

"Because it sounds so horrible."

"But foowy does it sound so ar—horrible? It doesn't sound horrible to—ar—me."

"It does to any properly trained ear."

"But foowy do they train their ears—?"

"Because it *is* horrible. My dear Mr. Kipps you really must not ask so many questions—"

"No, I s'pose not. Still, it's rummy to me that it's all right if you phew—I mean talk Scotch, and all wrong if you tork—I mean tolk—Kentish. It do seem rum."

"Does."

"Thanks—yes—it does seem rum."

"It's not a bit of good arguing," said Mrs. Chudleigh Mornington. "Things *are* so."

"That's true," said Kipps, "though one can't help remarking that it's rum. All the same."

* * *

The Kippses going to Parson's library to get the proper book. They never asked for any particular book but always for *the* book. They never read it though. It is not necessary as Mrs. Chudleigh Mornington tells them what to say ABOUT IT. Description of Kipps reading.

A little dinner. The Kipps couple brilliantly coached for the occasion, entertain, outshine socially, and dismiss—the Walsinghams.

As we get on people are introduced. There must be a pushful parson and his incredible wife, a literary nonentity, one or two of the clever little women who are quite smart on a small allowance, and Mrs. Chudleigh Mornington's own titled lady.

* * *

"You must go to London," said Mrs. Chudleigh Morning-ton remorselessly. "No one stops in Folkestone during the winter—no one."

"But we DON'T *want* TO GO TO LONDON."

"Life," said Mrs. Chudleigh Mornington, "has its duties as well as its pleasures."

* * *

In Chapters 17 to 30 young Walsingham will appear occasionally in ways that will be invented as the story is written—in order to keep him before the reader.

✤ 31 ✤

The Anaemic Binyon

A ND while these things were happening to Kipps, Chitterlow

* * *

The *Deus ex machina* alluded to in that last letter by the
figurative expression "oil," who had stepped in to secure
Kipps from the worst of his betrayal of Chitterlow, was a
person named Binyon. He emerged as a financial force after
three crucial days, or the career of Chitterlow as actor manager (under subterfuge) would have become strictly meteoric.
The natural vigour of Chitterlow's nature, his unparalleled
gift for believing whatever it was pleasant for him to believe,
had made the hesitating half-promises of Kipps a final settlement of his enterprise. He had returned in a state of dazzling
elation to Folkestone, and from six o'clock in the evening
until three o'clock the next morning their humble apartment
was a tempestuous tumult of organisation. Muriel was almost
equally excited, and, having put Master Harry to bed, found
out words in the dictionary, addressed envelopes, copied notes,
and filled his pipe with an enthusiasm that had slumbered for
years. At half past three o'clock the echoing footsteps of
Chitterlow pervaded the moonlit streets. He was going down

to the Harbour post office to catch the night post, a vast sheaf of letters in his fist. That there was no night post was surely Folkestone's fault rather than his.

The letters that presently radiated throughout the world
* * *

a masterly series of advertisements, with brilliant precautions against discovery by Walsingham, to secure the manager and dummy who was to hoodwink
* * *

letters to an extraordinary variety of "dear boys" couched in an amazing slang
* * *

subtle inspirations towards paragraphs, addressed to various friends Chitterlow claimed, men who had boasted of influence with the press
* * *

From that night Chitterlow's activity knew no stay. So potent a force is Faith, such Faith as Chitterlow had in Kipps, that it enabled him to move mountains, to get credit here and credit there
* * *

until it gathered at last in scattered apartments in a back street in Hanley
* * *

The Company
* * *

An odd assembly,
* * *

And amidst them all, taken notice of by no one, not even taken notice of by himself, effaced altogether by their clamorous brilliancy, was Binyon, the nominal manager, the alleged capitalist, the mask and subterfuge of Chitterlow and Kipps.

One word summarises the appearance of Binyon—anaemic. In detail he presented
* * *

His voice was so low and indistinct that to listen to him for any length of time gave one a sort of cramp like stooping.
* * *

The remarks one dredged up out of the inaudible were
* * *

Master Harry took his share

* * *

Chitterlow biffed and banged them all into a melodramatic enthusiasm.

* * *

And so with a cheerful splash the Great Combination was launched upon its eventful career, CREATED BY THE MERE PROMISE OF THE WEALTH OF MR. WADDY.

✢ 32 ✢

_____

Collaboration

THIS chapter presents incidentally the Combination on Tour, with a vignetted incident or so, while dealing essentially with the collaboration of Binyon and Chitterlow upon the play.

* * *

Binyon, apart from these little idiosyncracies, was no fool. As he deciphered his way through that convulsive writing, his resolve to jest vanished, his opinion of Chitterlow rose. He was surprised—and maybe the reader who also has as yet seen Chitterlow only from the outside, may share his surprise—to find that the great play was not Bosh. It was the most amazing jumble of good stuff

* * *

An imagination FOR dramatic situations and emotional aspects, of an astonishingly powerful sort, combined with the discrimination of a rather dull jackdaw,

* * *

Admirably conceived scenes spoilt and ruined by some interpolated jest that would have shamed a Patent Medicine Almanac.

* * *

Binyon's first impulse was to steal as much as would make an efficient play.

* * *

They spent a night upon it. In the small hours, the following terms were practically conceded: Firstly, that Binyon absolutely and unreservedly withdrew an ill-advised initial proposition that Chitterlow could not write, single-handed, a better play than any at present existing on earth, and that the permission accorded him (Binyon) to collaborate on the play under discussion was a generous gift, a more than sufficient recognition of the financial circumstances under which the Great Combination had been launched, and no admission of even the most partial defect in Chitterlow's outfit as a man of Genius. Secondly, that under the aforesaid conditions Binyon's share in the collaboration was to be essentially subordinate, alterations and amendments were to be suggested by him in a respectful and diplomatic manner, he was to be not so much a playwright as a playwright's labourer, writing all the dialogue under instructions from Chitterlow (e.g. "make it witty here"), and that in all cases of difference between them, the matter should be referred to and the final decision rest with Chitterlow as chairman of the collaboration. Thirdly, that Chitterlow did of his own free grace, and not grudgingly (this he explained at great length) consent that the name of Binyon should appear as joint author of the play, that the play should be produced and published as By Chitterlow and Binyon, just as if Binyon had in reality contributed some sort of value to the play and, disregarding the impossibility of doing this where Chitterlow was concerned, it being further conceded

* * *

And all these things being CLEARLY UNDERSTOOD BY BOTH PARTIES, Binyon took the manuscript home to his lodgings about the hour of dawn, while Chitterlow still active and voluble went upstairs to tell Muriel of his essential greatness and all that he had said and done and all that Binyon had admitted. He ended with computations of the material benefits Binyon would derive from that night's work. Chitterlow on the very lowest data, put them roughly between one and five thousand pounds. They agreed very generously that Binyon was a "very firm old boy" and deserved his good fortune, and after Chitterlow had given a very brief sketch of how he proposed to spend his five thousand pounds, he douched his head with cold water and returned to rest, sleeping the sleep of the just until half past eleven on the following day.

* * *

Now it had long been Binyon's ambition to write a play. But the fastidious sensitiveness of his nature

* * *

Whenever he hit upon anything, it always seemed so absurd, so artificial and needless that he should do this particular thing in preference to any other particular thing.

* * *

A sort of paralysis.

* * *

So for eight years he HAD GONE to and fro upon the earth, his plot remained an arid waste, and Chitterlow too HAD GONE his ways, breeding an inordinate, stupendous jungle of weeds.

* * *

Incidents in the collaboration.

Binyon secretly makes a play from a germ in Chitterlow's matter. This is version A. He does not show it to Chitterlow. "He will never stand this." He sets it on one side and does a much more Chitterlowesque version. This he presents diffidently.

Chitterlow misses his "best things."

Uproar. Chitterlow will do it himself. From the first he mistrusted this collaboration.

Binyon leaves the company, taking with him Version A.

❧ 33 ❧

The Play
Gets Launched at Last

CHITTERLOW considers his honour at stake. Rewrites the play dumping back everything Binyon had eliminated and cutting out all Binyon had introduced, and so produces it.

Stormy reception.

Chitterlow makes a defiant speech.

He said he was a very peculiar person.

Tactless behaviour of Master Harry—insulting the audience.

Violence—riot. Chairs broken, scenery injured.

Financial wreck of the Great Combination.

Chitterlow facing the storm.

⚜ 34 ⚜

The Revolt of the Kippses

CHITTERLOW appeals to Kipps.

Walsingham objects to Kipps assisting Chitterlow, and tries to intimidate him. (Although the restrictions upon gifts to Chitterlow in the will of Mr. Waddy are of no legal value whatever.)

The "Hastings lot" happen on misfortune and appeal. Possibly "aunt" is dying and wants to see Kipps before she dies.

Mrs. Chudleigh Mornington explains that it will be outrageous for him to go to Hastings in face of an accepted dinner invitation.

"If your aunt was a person socially known."

Revolt.

All this can scarcely be invented in detail at this stage. Suffice it to say that Kipps hands sums of money to the Hastings people and to Chitterlow. To Chitterlow he gives the bulk of his bank balance, about £300. (Muriel, Harry.) Kipps also quarrels with Walsingham and hints at long smouldering suspicions. Chitterlow blows this spark of suspicion into a blaze. Kipps says he is "going to look into things."

⚘ 35 ⚘

_____

Mr. Walsingham
Makes a Fitting End

SOMEONE else was already looking into things. And the aspect of things was not encouraging.

Mr. George Goethe Walsingham sat in the room that was reserved for him, in the house upon the Leas, that dignified white house with a black and gold balcony whose lease and furniture had solaced his sister's sorrow. He sat at a magnificently equipped desk, and the light of the very highest class of study lamp fell upon his Napoleonic brow. He really had been extremely Napoleonic.

* * *

only he seemed to have begun at the wrong end and come upon Waterloo at once.

Things would not bear looking into. Even Mr. Kipps could scarcely fail to note that forty thousand pounds worth of securities had vanished in the unauthorised speculations of a brilliant, daring, but singularly unfortunate career.

* * *

There were moments in that long meditation when Walsingham even came within distant sight of the suspicion that there is something a little silly about the Napoleonic Idea.

* * *

There was no remedy, in all directions lay disaster. Well, at any rate, he was master of his fate still—to a certain extent. He repeated Werther's phrase.

* * *

He bent to the bottommost drawer and turned the key.

* * *

He drew forth a little revolver, as dainty as a toy. He looked at it, examined the cartridges and placed it on the desk before him.

"Freedom," he said.

* * *

He paced the room with his hands folded behind him. He wondered if they heard his footsteps, firm and measured to the end. (As a matter of fact the boarder below was swearing softly.) Should he write or say something to his sister, something that should be unimportant at the time but afterwards memorable on account of its context.

* * *

No, he would be an enigma to the last—the silence of the Sphinx—the Sphinx had always exercised a considerable influence on his imagination.

* * *

His mind surveyed all the events in his brief career.

* * *

He walked to the desk and took up the revolver—examined it closely.

* * *

He put the barrel into his mouth, stood so for a moment, and withdrew it. He remarked that he was perfectly cool. Now, let him think just exactly how it would go.

* * *

Suppose the bones of the palate turned it aside.

* * *

He recalled a case of a man who had lain for four and twenty hours in agony.

* * *

It would never do to bungle it.

* * *

Might it not be better after all to hold the pistol sideways, so, at his temple? But then pulling the trigger might cock up the barrel.

* * *

He found himself regretting he had not bought a larger pistol.

* * *

He was foolish to have entertained these doubts.

* * *

He put the pistol down and began pacing the room. He was sure now the pistol was too small to kill, that it would bore a hole through him and leave him agonised.

* * *

He could already feel the pain.

Was he funking it? Certainly not! He was a man of the Napoleonic type grasping and controlling his fate.

* * *

He went back to the desk and took up the pistol. Were the cartridges all right? Suppose one misbehaved, and he just smashed or bruised the roof of his mouth.

(Printer, a white line. [Wells's note.])

Miss Walsingham

* * *

She heard a shot and the sound of a body falling.

* * *

"I wish you'd not be perpetually spying on me," came his voice.

* * *

And his adoring sister went upstairs.

* * *

A dark figure stole out of the house.

* * *

It was Walsingham, and in his hand he bore a valise and over his arm a rug.

the night boat for Boulogne.

* * *

And in a horrible heaving darkness, wet through with spray, clutching and staggering and in a state of the wildest internal tumult, this last victim of the Napoleonic legend passes out of our story, passes on towards the unknown next ITEM in the predestinate series of mischiefs and miseries that his birth and the folly of his breeding inevitably assure.

⚜ 36 ⚜

_____

Ruined

STATEMENT of accounts.

Mrs. Chudleigh Mornington proposes to take Hughenden and run it as a boarding house.

* * *

Amazing irruption of Chitterlow.

Astounding generosity.

He will return the money Kipps lent him!

No—he _has_ money.

The play is accepted in London—Binyon's version. Chitterlow has forgotten their quarrel. "Good old Binyon!"

Tumultuous emotions.

* * *

"Why! we might 'ave that little shop," said Kipps with tears in his eyes.

"We 'aven't got any position now—that's been the expense."

* * *

They both resolve to do their best to comfort "poor father."

"They'll feel it," said Kipps, "a'most more than us. They've always took such pride in me getting on and all."

L'Envoy

S O far as Mr. Kipps' book-keeping can be said to throw any light on the matter, the shop pays. AND INDEED HIS RUIN WAS NOT SO COMPLETE AS HAD BEEN IMAGINED. A COMFORTABLE RESERVE
* * *

Here follows a minute description of the HYTHE High Street and the position of the little shop. All the neighbours will be described and named, only—the shop will not be there. For, as a matter of fact, the existing shop TO BE mentioned as being to the left of it and the silver shop to the right are next door neighbours.

Allusions to certain small but sensible charities of Kipps.

The concluding scene in the kitchen behind the little shop, presents Ann tubbing her eldest son, Arthur Waddy Kipps, and Kipps sitting and watching her
* * *

"Not if it's girls," said Ann. "Surely not if it's girls."

"Ann," said Mr. Kipps. "I'm not clearly sure if it isn't Waddina for girls, or something of that sort. That I dunno. But something of that sort it's got to be, girls or no girls,

180

Waddina or Waddess or Waddy. You has your way in most things, but on that point I'm firm. See?"

"No, I don't Artie. But p'raps I shall when the time comes. . . . However—it ain't girls at present, Artie, so there ain't no call to be cross. No, zer ain't no call to be korse. See? Dough dey called ums Waddy all de same, dey did, and said dey was to be edj'cated. Dey called ums Waddy all de same."

The End

A Note on the Text

By Harris Wilson

As I have indicated, my main purpose in this edition is to bring to print in as finished form as possible, in terms of the material in my possession, a reading text of an extensive unpublished fragment of an early Wells novel in progress. I should emphasize that this edition is in no way intended to be a variorum or generic textual study; other novel manuscripts in the Wells Archive would be much more suitable for such a project. Probably because of Wells's decision to abandon *The Wealth of Mr. Waddy* in 1899, much of the draft manuscript material has disappeared, and that which does remain is for the most part in a chaotic and fragmentary state.

In the textual appendix I have given a gross description of the existing layers of holograph and typescript drafts, including the typescript upon which I have based the reading text, for each chapter. *The Wealth of Mr. Waddy* is a transcription of the typescripts and holograph manuscripts selected for this reading text. There are no silent emendations, except that punctuation has been regularized in the text to make it uniform and that the headings of Chapters 2 and 3 have been set to conform with the other chapter headings. When incorporating transitional material between *Mr. Waddy* and *Kipps*, I have eliminated passages irrelevant to either version without comment. All other emendations are listed as the final item in the textual appendix. In those rare instances in which I am not certain of a particular word in Wells's handwriting, I have followed that word with a question mark in brackets.

The surviving drafts do, of course, present an interesting illustration of Wells's general method of composition. He first sketched broadly the entire plan of the novel, including a tentative list of chapter headings and characters. His typist prepared this material according to Wells's directions and he began detailed composition. This draft was typed and in turn revised; the process was repeated until Wells was satisfied.

Wells's method of composition is not, of course, unique. Most writers follow something of the same process of draft and revision. It is important to note, however, that Wells's revisions are largely quantitative rather than qualitative. He works for the most part with sentences and phrases rather than words. This propensity quite probably offers a partial explanation for Wells's inability to write a first-rate play. Also, the progress from first draft to finished copy is largely accretionary. Wells does not hesitate to discard pages or whole chapters on occasion, but the typical Wells draft manuscript is a relatively unmolested central text with insertions in the form of balloons crowding the margins.

Another characteristic of Wells's composition is his practice of writing in "chunks." He would write several pages of holograph manuscript in solid detail and then, apparently because of a momentary failure of inspiration, instruct his typist to leave blank a space from one line to an entire page. On a subsequent revision, sometimes after a lapse of weeks or months, depending on other material on hand, he would fill in these spaces or occasionally simply eliminate them. The reader will find ample illustration of this practice throughout this text.

TEXTUAL APPENDIX

The reader should understand that an entry for any given chapter, such as "five drafts," does not necessarily mean that consistent progress can be traced to a culminating copy. Only in comparatively rare instances, because of the state of surviving materials, is this process possible. By and large, as I have said, my reading text is based on the Pinker typescript with subsequent

revisions. I have indicated in the Notes those chapters in which I
have been forced to depart from that procedure.

Description of Manuscript Materials

Chapter 1. Seven drafts (4, 13, 11, 5, 1, 21, 5 pp. respectively),
1 draft holograph; 1 part typescript, part holograph; 1 carbon,
4 typescript. All moderately to carefully revised. Included also
are five fragmentary versions of present Chapters 1, 2, 3, which
Wells originally intended to be Chapter 1 of the novel. Pinker
typescript (7 pp.), moderately revised.

Chapter 2. Nine drafts (1, 2, 3, 1, 4, 11, 8, 2 pp. respectively),
all fragments, 3 drafts included in drafts of intended Chapter 1.
Mostly moderately to carefully revised typescript with an occasional holograph page. Pinker typescript (12 pp.), heavily revised; two pages of holograph manuscript.

Chapter 3. Seven drafts (5, 5, 2, 12, 6, 5, 8 pp. respectively), 3
drafts included in drafts of intended Chapters 1 and 2, 1 holograph, 2 carbon, 4 typescript. Moderately to carefully revised.
Pinker typescript (23 pp.), heavily revised; seven pages of
holograph manuscript.

Chapter 4. Four drafts (5, 4, 3, 3 pp. respectively), 2 typescript
drafts, 2 carbon. Lightly to carefully revised Pinker typescript
(11 pp.), moderately to heavily revised; two pages of holograph manuscript.

Chapter 5. Eight drafts (2, 7, 7, 2, 2, 4, 5, 7 pp. respectively),
1 holograph draft, 4 carbon, 3 typescript. Lightly to carefully
revised. Pinker typescript (19 pp.), moderately to heavily revised about three pages of holograph manuscript, much of it
interspersed as individual paragraphs.

Chapter 6. Eight drafts (1, 1, 4, 8, 6, 8, 3, 2 pp. respectively), 4
carbon, 3 holograph, 1 typescript. Lightly to carefully revised.
Pinker typescript (28 pp.), moderately to heavily revised,
about twelve pages of holograph manuscript, much of it interspersed as individual paragraphs.

Chapter 7. Three drafts (4, 12, 5 pp. respectively), 2 drafts one-
half holograph, one-half carbon. Last draft carbon, carefully
revised. Pinker manuscript (20 pp.), moderately revised.

Chapter 8. One draft (4 pp. holograph manuscript unrevised).
Pinker manuscript (7 pp.), unrevised.

Chapter 9. Three drafts (12, 4, 4 pp. respectively), 1 draft 10
pp. holograph, 2 carbon; final 2 drafts carbon. Lightly to heav-

ily revised. Chapters 7, 8 and 9, Pinker typescript (23 pp.), very lightly revised. Much of these chapters, as noted in the text, is a close duplication of Chapters I, II, and III of *Kipps*.

Chapter 10. Ten drafts (7, 2, 4, 1, 6, 3, 3, 4, 5, 1 pp. respectively), 8 drafts almost completely holograph with occasional typescript or carbon pages, 2 typescript. All carefully revised. Pinker typescript (15 pp.), last four pages heavily revised.

Chapter 11. Three drafts (14, 7, 1 pp. respectively), first draft entirely holograph, 2 and 3 carbon. All moderately revised. Pinker typescript (21 pp.), very lightly revised.

Chapter 12. Two drafts (4, 1 pp. respectively), one entirely holograph, the other carbon, both very fragmentary. Pinker typescript (9 pp.), very lightly revised.

Chapter 13. Eight drafts (9, 5, 12, 9, 6, 8, 1, 2 pp. respectively), 3 in holograph manuscript, 5 in carefully revised typescript. One typescript is in a different typeface from the Pinker typescript, probably indicating that Wells has begun the transition from *Mr. Waddy* to *Kipps*, although none of the material in the draft appears in *Kipps* as finally published. First two pages an apparent transitional draft between *Mr. Waddy* and *Kipps*. The remaining 14 pages, Pinker manuscript, very lightly revised.

Chapter 14. Ten drafts (4, 3, 2, 1, 2, 13, 3, 1, 4, 2 pp. respectively), 6 in holograph manuscript, 14 in carefully to lightly revised typescript. Included in these drafts are 1 typescript and 2 holograph versions of a personal encounter between Mr. Waddy and Kipps at the drapery shop, an episode that never occurs in *Mr. Waddy* or *Kipps*. First seven pages an apparent transitional draft between *Mr. Waddy* and *Kipps*. Episodes in Emporium, and Kipps's omnibus ride to New Romney (7 pp.), largely holograph manuscript. Kipps's meeting with his father and mother, Pinker typescript (8 pp.), lightly revised.

Chapter 15. Three drafts (8, 7, 6 pp. respectively), 1 in holograph manuscript, 2 in typescript, lightly to moderately revised. Pinker typescript (17 pp.), very lightly revised.

Chapter 16. One holograph page containing only the chapter number and the word "Muriel" followed by the phrase, "Three lines blank." Pinker typescript (1 p.), no revisions.

Chapter 17. One page draft, typescript very fragmentary. Pinker typescript (2 pp.), no revisions.

Chapter 18. Ten drafts (2, 2, 4, 2, 4, 4, 1, 1, 1, 3 pp. respectively), 3 in holograph manuscript, 7 in lightly to carefully revised typescript. Pinker typescript (12 pp.), very lightly revised.

Chapter 19. Three pages of very fragmentary holograph manuscript. Pinker typescript (6 pp.), no revisions.

Chapter 20. Typescript included in text. Pinker typescript (2 pp.).

Chapter 21. Typescript included in text. Pinker typescript (4 pp.), lightly revised.

Chapter 22. Typescript included in text. Pinker typescript (3 pp.), very lightly revised.

Chapter 23. One draft (3 pp.), very fragmentary manuscript. Pinker typescript (3 pp.), no revisions.

Chapter 24. Typescript included in text. Pinker typescript (6 pp.), very lightly revised.

Chapter 25. One page draft, typescript, very fragmentary. Pinker typescript (1 p.), no revisions.

Chapter 26. One draft (3 pp.), about three-fourths holograph manuscript, the rest carbon. Pinker typescript (6 pp.), very lightly revised.

Chapter 27. One draft (4, 2 pp. respectively), about one-half holograph manuscript. Pinker typescript (4 pp.), no revisions.

Chapter 28. One fragmentary draft (4 pp.), in holograph manuscript. Pinker typescript (6 pp.), no revisions.

Chapter 29. Two drafts (4, 7 pp. respectively), 1 holograph, 1 typescript, both very fragmentary. Pinker typescript (4 pp.), no revisions.

Chapter 30. One holograph page. Pinker typescript (7 pp.), no revisions.

Chapter 31. One holograph page containing only the chapter number and title, a fragmentary sentence "And while these things were happening to Mr. Kipps, Chitterlow." Pinker typescript (7 pp.), very lightly revised.

Chapter 32. One draft typescript outline (2 pp.), very fragmentary and lightly revised. Pinker typescript (7 pp.), very lightly revised.

Chapter 33. Typescript included in text. Pinker typescript (1 p.), no revisions.

Chapter 34. One page draft of holograph manuscript. Pinker typescript (1 p.), no revisions.

Chapter 35. One draft (8 pp.), of fragmentary holograph manuscript. Pinker typescript (3 pp.), no revisions.

Chapter 36. Typescript included in text. Pinker typescript (3 pp.), no revisions.

L'Envoy. Typescript included in text. Pinker typescript (4 pp.), moderately revised.

Emendations in the Copy-Text

The first items in this list are in the typescript on which my text is based; my emendations follow the brackets. In the holograph material which is set in small caps there are several instances of underlined words. Since there is no italicized type for small caps the words are shown here first as small caps, then, following the bracket, as italicized. Phrases drawn from earlier drafts are indicated by asterisks. Wells's common practice in holograph manuscript was to use the ampersand; I have followed his secretary's practice of converting the sign to "and."

1.4–5	BUDDING HANSOMELY [	BUDDING HANDSOMELY;
1.9	along edge [	along the cliff edge
2.21	word.! [	words!
4.7	"The good old man [	The good old man
5.9	NEVER [	*Never*
6.20	good, [	good;
7.14	break [	brake
8.9	from [	with
8.14	admirably [	admirably,
8.19	able bodied [	able-bodied
8.21	self control [	self-control
8.24	leisure [	leisure,
8.27	good [	good,
8.32	modern [	modern,
9.28	FOLLOWED, [	FOLLOWED;
10.30	good sized [	good-sized
10.31	old fashioned [	old-fashioned

11.20	about Mr. Waddy he believed strongly [about Mr. Waddy, as we have noted. He believed strongly
11.38	self complacent [self-complacent
12.31	after dinner [after-dinner
12.38	intercepted charity [inflated charity
13.18	"gentlemen forsooth!" ["Gentlemen forsooth!"
13.21	Cxxxxxxe Rxxk [C——e R——k
14.9	well known [well-known
15.4	good looking [good-looking
15.19	comes." [comes.
15.20	"Always." ["Always.
15.30	Muriel [Muriel,
16.2	self defence [self-defence
22.25	ONE HIS WORST [ONE OF HIS WORST
22.27	Satsuma [Satsuma,
22.31	lady's [ladies'
23.4	IMPOSSIBLE [IMPOSSIBLE,
23.27–28	AUBURN HEADED [AUBURN-HEADED
27.20	RED HAIRED YOUNG MAN [RED-HAIRED YOUNG MAN
27.21	REDDISH BROWN [REDDISH-BROWN
28.37–38	delicate minded [delicate-minded
28.39	debût [début
29.1	SEA GREEN [SEA-GREEN
29.40	storm tossed genius [storm-tossed genius
31.25–26	red haired little man [red-haired little man
31.32	dare devil [daredevil
31.34	end however the effect [end, however, the effect
34.6	LIKE IBSEN [LIKE IBSEN,
34.12	GINGER HEADED BEAST! [GINGER-HEADED BEAST!
36.11	lodging house [lodging-house
39.11	sort [sort,
39.18–19	CAMELS HAIR [CAMEL'S-HAIR
39.41	stand [stand,
40.4	happen [happen,

40.16	hero who . . . twenty in [hero, who . . . twenty, in
40.26	fancied he gathered that [fancied, he gathered, that
40.37	DONOVAN [*Donovan*
44.31	Through all vicissitudes she maintained [But through it all she maintained.*
44.39	Variety [variety
45.31	red haired xx [red-haired xx
46.3	self pity [self-pity
46.3	self condolence [self-condolence
46.9	MAGNA EST VERITAS ET PREVALEBIT [*Magna est veritas et prevalebit*
47.9	Millenium [Millennium
47.26	His upbringing developed [Master Harry's upbringing had developed
47.33	Cometh up as a Flower [*Cometh Up as a Flower*
48.3	dressed. From [dressed, but from
48.4	contumacious but [contumacious, and
48.12	had been from [had been to
48.38–39	re-read it [re-read *Little Lord Fauntleroy*
49.11	gold tipped dreams [gold-tipped dreams
49.19	self respect [self-respect
49.29	irritating it is true that [irritating, it is true, that
49.30	self control [self-control
49.31	draghtboard and men [draughtboard and ⟨*L'Art*
53.4	table, ('*L'Art d'être Grandpère*') [table (*L'Art d'être Grandpère*)
56 ch. title	this Mr. Kipps, his Parentage [This Mr. Kipps, His Parentage
60.18	lessons of envy pride [lessons of envy and pride
62.5	muver. [muver."
62.25	Littlestone on sea [Littlestone-on-Sea
64.4–5	after life [afterlife
64.10	story telling [story-telling
64.20	half holidays [half-holidays

65.14	lower class [lower-class
65.27	for ever [forever
65.32–33	crew—; the [crew— The
70 ch. title	Kipps became [Kipps Became
71.14	Tunbridge Wells he said, [Tunbridge Wells, he said,
73.37	carcase [carcass
74.33	SELF disgust [SELF-disgust
78.4–5	self improvement [self-improvement
78.11	wood carving [wood-carving
78.16–17	as astounding feat [an astounding feat
80.5	see it [see it,
83.37	red rimmed [red-rimmed
84.37	She was herself called into the room [The nurse was herself called into the room⟩ to witness*
85.24	An auction [An action
85.36	aching grew [aching, grew
86.23	agotisms of life [egotisms of life
86.41	for evermore [forevermore
87.4–5	Michael Angelo's [Michelangelo's
91.11	fireirons [fire-irons
92.24	Little Lord Fauntleroy [*Little Lord Fauntleroy*
94.1	Bellerephon ["Bellerephon"
95.11–12	had shown his [had shown its
95.20	"very firm" ["very fine"
98.7	rivetted [riveted
99.15	self confidence [self-confidence
101.4	etomological [etymological
101.11	failed [fallen
101.33	naive [naïve
103.5	means." [means.
104.1	premises of Weston and Grimflack [premises of Grimflack,* Weston and Grimflack

104.14	Weston and Grimflack [Grimflack,* Weston and Grimflack,
105.11	clean shaven [clean-shaven
105.25	tall paper basket [tall waste-paper basket
105.30	gold rimmed [gold-rimmed
105.34	paper weight [paper-weight
106.38	paper weight [paper-weight
107.23	him." [him.
107.25	coughed. [coughed,
108.15	chorea [cholera
108.39	paper weight [paper-weight
109.8	choses [chooses
110.15–18	said Kipps. [said Kipps. You cannot . . . Twelve Hundred a Year."*
110.23	temptations [temptations—"
111.23	playwriting [play writing
113.1	Mr. BEAN [Mr. Grimflack*
113.4	out of the room of the initialled boxes. [out of the room.
113.11	Mr. BEAN'S [Grimflack's*
113.16	BEAN [Grimflack*
114.3	for ever. For ever! [forever. Forever!
114.26	BEAN [Grimflack*
115.14–15	all his Emporium years [ALL HIS YEARS as a draper,
115.41	POUNDS [*Pounds*
116.20	say; [say,
117.30	'As ['as
118.4	these." [these.
118.21	Bazaar [Emporium
118.21	was [were
118.25	Bazaar [Emporium
118.39	trasfiguration [transfiguration
118.41	Chitterlow and [Chitterlow.
120.2	WELL BRED [WELL-BRED
121.23	room for (blank) beside [room for umbrellas beside
122.1	that his uncle and aunt [that his parents*
122.13	at his Uncle's door [at his father's door*
122.20	you." [you,"
122.24	news for you, Uncle [news for you, Father*

122.32	Uncle [Father*
122.33	as his nephew [as his son*
122.39	" 'Ullo, Aunt [" 'Ullo, Mother*
123.4–5	turned to his aunt and uncle [turned to his parents*
123.5	His aunt [His mother*
123.9	the fact is, Aunt ["The fact is, Mother*
123.40	his nephew [his son*
124.14	reely, Uncle [reely, Father*
129.14	lugged him forth [dragged him forth
129.28	RED SURMOUNTED figure [RED-SURMOUNTED figure
130.6	hot pursuit down _____ road. [hot pursuit.
130.22	crossed _____ in silence. [crossed the street in silence.
131.19	REPEATEDLY Pressed [REPEATEDLY pressed
131.34	recalling _____, [recalling the Dorcases
131.39–40	ascended _____. [ascended the East Cliff.
133.13	ostentatious [ostentatiously
133.17	has established [had established
134.1	Kipps went on _____ with [Kipps went on his way* with
135 ch. title	raises [Raises
139.18	"Not ["not
140.7	MUST [*must*
142.9	Coote-ishness [Cooteishness
142.9	well meaning [well-meaning
144.30	by Coote and and as epigrams [by Coote as epigrams
145.10	dog." "I [dog. I
146.15	High Street (?) [High Street.
147.7	with Mrs. _____ wrist [with Mrs. Dorcas's wrist
147.21	Art School [art school
147.27	High toned [High-toned
148.5	Resumé [Résumé
149.21	well meant efforts [well-meant efforts
152.14	befel him [befell him
153.9	rose tinted [rose-tinted
154.26	FOOTNOTE [*Footnote*
155.8	imperience [impertinence
156 ch. title	Kipps faces [Kipps Faces
156.15	Art School [art school

159.19	"Well ["well
167.5	WANT [*want*
167.9	XVII to XXX [17 to 30
174 ch. title	The Play gets launched at last [The Play Gets Launched at Last
176 ch. title	Walsingham makes [Walsingham Makes

Notes

2 *The Habits of Mr. Waddy*

1. A blank space of twenty-one lines follows. Wells's custom in the drafts of his manuscripts was, if he felt a passage needed more development than he was prepared to give it at the moment, to instruct his typist in a note to leave spaces varying from one line to twenty blank. In a subsequent draft he would fill these spaces in or, in many cases, by the notation "run on" instruct the typist simply to eliminate them. I have indicated throughout those spaces left unfilled or unclosed in the manuscripts on which my text is based.

2. Five lines blank.

3. Wells may be referring facetiously to himself here, since he made much ado of buying a new cotton hat during his convalescence from his kidney ailment in August, 1898. (See the panel of "picshuas" in *Experiment in Autobiography*, II, 589.)

3 *Muriel*

1. An early draft of this chapter indicates that Wells had in mind one of the novels of Mrs. Henry Wood. A major character named Muriel, however, does not appear in Mrs. Wood's best-known novels, *East Lynne* (1861), *The Channings* (1862), *Mrs. Halliburton's Troubles* (1862), nor in other novels by Mrs. Wood that I have been able to examine. It is obvious, however, that Wells is thinking of one of the extremely popular "governess" novels written by Mrs. Wood, Charlotte Yonge, Anne Thackeray and many other popular women novelists in the last half of the nineteenth century.

2. Apparently both author and novel are fictitious.

3. By Dinah Mulock, published in 1857, a sentimental rags-to-riches novel.

4. Prince Lucio Rimânez in Marie Corelli's *The Sorrows of*

Satan, 1895. He is Satan incarnate and confers immense wealth on Geoffrey Tempest, the novel's hero. True to type, Rimânez is suave, handsome, and ingratiating.

5. Five lines blank.

4 Mr. Chitterlow

1. The provinces.

2. *Romance of Lady Isabel Burton*, told in part by herself and in part by W. H. Wilkins (1897). The chapter in which Lady Isabel meets for the first time Sir Richard Burton is entitled, "I Meet My Destiny."

5 Cut Adrift

1. One line blank.

2. This curious mixture of playwrights is revealing in terms of Chitterlow's grounding in his craft and his own ambition as a playwright. Henry Arthur Jones and Sydney Grundy were serious and active proponents of realism in English drama in the later nineteenth century. George Robert Sims, Louis N. Parker, and Edward Rose, who is mentioned later, were writers of popular melodrama.

3. In Edna Lyall's *Donovan*, 1882, the principal character, Donovan Farrant, is the black sheep of his family. He becomes an atheist and a cardsharper. He is led back to a state of righteousness on both counts through the influence of his "ideal woman," Gladys Tremain.

6 Little Lord Fauntleroy

1. Arthur Orton was popularly known as the "Tichbourne Claimant." An English immigrant to Australia, he claimed to be Lady Tichbourne's elder son, who had been lost at sea in 1854. Orton was eventually tried and found guilty of perjury. In 1895 he published a confession of his fraud in the press.

2. By Mrs. Oliphant, published in 1873.

3. First published in England in 1886.

4. A naval battle (July 3, 1898) which the United States won decisively in the Spanish-American War. Powerful influences were exerted to draw England into the war on the side of Spain.

5. Two lines blank.

6. *The Wild Irish Girl*, 1806, by Sydney Owenson (Lady Morgan) was a celebrated book in its time and strongly influenced the portrayal of subsequent Irish heroines.

7. *Cometh Up as a Flower*, 1867, is a fictitious autobiography of Nell Lestrange, who, with her sister, Dolly, grows to womanhood under the indifferent care of a widowed and indigent father. The behavior of Nell is audacious, to say the least, by Victorian standards. For instance, after a *mariage de convenance*, she offers herself (but is refused) to Dick McGregor, her true love.

8. Mrs. Henry Wood used crime and supernatural events in her early novels extensively to satisfy her readers' taste for sensation, but like her sister novelists of the time she consistently extolled the simple virtues of middle-class life.

9. Six lines blank.

10. Three lines blank.

11. Six lines blank.

12. Four lines blank.

13. The passage appears in "Les Enfants Gatés":

> Si je vois dans un coin une assiette de fraises
> Réservée au dessert de nous autres, je dis:
> —O chers petits oiseaux goulus du paradis
> C'est à vous! Voyez—vous, en bas, sous la fenêtre,
> Ces enfants pauvres, l'un vient à peine de naitre,
> Ils ont faim. Faites les monter, et partagez.—

Victor Hugo, *L'Art d'Être Grand-Père*, (Paris, 1884), p. 230.

14. Two lines blank.

15. Wells merely sketches the following scene.

16. End of sketched scene.

7 *A Full Account of This Mr. Kipps, His Parentage and Upbringing*

1. Two lines blank.

2. Five lines blank.

3. Four lines blank.

4. Three lines blank.

5. Three lines blank.

6. Two lines blank.

7. The rest of the present chapter and the two following in *The Wealth of Mr. Waddy* are essentially the same, although frequently very sketchily developed, as the corresponding chapters in *Kipps*. From this point on, because of the increasingly fragmentary nature of the surviving manuscript, gaps left by Wells for subsequent completion are indicated by three spaced asterisks

throughout the text. Readers will find, however, that the general narrative movement can easily be followed.

9   How Mr. Kipps Became a Draper and a Fickle Soul
1. End of material duplicated in *Kipps*.

10   The Last Endeavour
1. By Olive Schreiner, published in 1883. Muriel is thinking of the episode near the end of the novel in which Gregory Rose disguises himself as a woman in order to serve as Lyndall's nurse during her fatal illness.

13   Mr. Kipps Hears Astonishing Things
1. The first two pages, according to typeface, an apparent transition between *Mr. Waddy* and *Kipps*.

14   The Golden Dawn
1. The first four pages, according to typeface, an apparent transitional draft between *Mr. Waddy* and *Kipps*.
2. The following scene between Kipps and the stout old gentleman appears essentially unchanged in *Kipps* in Book I, section 3, Chapter 6, "The Unexpected."